"Gentlemen! We've got a lawman with us tonight."

Stamping their boots, the crowd jeered, hissed, and cursed.

Rafe figured he was well and truly shut in the outhouse and tumbling downhill. But he'd been in worse situations and come out alive. He just needed a plan that didn't aggravate the situation.

She held the handcuffs above her head and clicked them together in rhythm. She pointed at her audience, and the saloon filled with deep, raw voices.

She's a wild woman, a renegade, a lady gone bad.

Lady threw back her head and laughed, twirling in a circle as she continued to click the handcuffs.

Rafe wanted to grab her, shake her, and take her to bed. But he couldn't let her get the best of him. "Darlin'," he drawled. "You want me to show you how to use those cuffs?"

She turned to face him. Excitement brightened her agate eyes as she raised one arched eyebrow. "Lawman, you want to play?"

Lady Gone Bad

SABINE STARR

KENSINGTON PUBLISHING CORP.
www.kensingtonbooks.com

BRAVA BOOKS are published by

Kensington Publishing Corp.
119 West 40th Street
New York, NY 10018

All Kensington titles, imprints, and distributed lines are available at special quantity discounts for bulk purchases for sales promotions, premiums, fund-raising, educational, or institutional use.

Special book excerpts or customized printings can also be created to fit specific needs. For details, write or phone the office of the Kensington special sales manager: Kensington Publishing Corp., 119 West 40th Street, New York, NY 10018, attn: Special Sales Department; phone: 1-800-221-2647.

ISBN-13: 978-0-7582-6600-2
ISBN-10: 0-7582-6600-6

First Kensington Trade Paperback Printing: September 2012

10 9 8 7 6 5 4 3 2 1

Printed in the United States of America

In Memory of
Uncle Brent and *Cousin Brenda*
They set this book in motion.

ACKNOWLEDGMENTS

Elaine English for being a great agent and wanting more after a wild ride in a red pickup on a slick road in an Oklahoma rainstorm; *Alicia Condon* for being a savvy editor with terrific taste; *Donna Elisabeth Gimarc* for excellent editorial advice and loyal friendship; *Kathleen Baldwin* and *Gretchen Craig* for insight, input, and fun lunches; *Janet Harris* for the Bend research and being a fine editor, educator, and friend.

Sharlot for her wonderful Choctaw name, and *Genieva, Jeanie, Nancy, Patsy,* and *Wanda* for being friends and listening to my stories all these years; *Nancy, Rosanna, Patsy, Cynthia, Mary, Kelli,* and *Beatrix* for book suggestions.

Uncle Buck, Aunt Melba, Aunt Evelyn, and *Aunt Mary* for style, charm, wit, and courage.

Cousin Miranda for naming Copper and Jipsey; *Cousin Cathy* for four-wheeling around her horse ranch; *Brett* for horse stories; *Cousin Trooper Chris* for lawman inspiration; *Cousin Shelley* for sharing the creative dream; *Cousin Casi* for keeping me on time and on schedule; *Cousin Chester* for firearm instruction; *Cousin Eddie* for writing and support; *Cousin Ginger, Cousin Crystal,* and *Cousin Kendra* for inspiration; *Dee* and *Stella* for generously sharing their Choctaw heritage.

As always, for *Dean* who knows the many reasons why.

ACKNOWLEDGMENTS

"There is no law west of St. Louis, and no God west of Fort Smith."

—*Red River Reporter,* Texas and Indian Territory

Chapter 1

1883, Delaware Bend, Texas

"*She's a wild woman, a renegade, a lady gone bad.*"

Deputy U.S. Marshal Rafe Morgan sat at a battered table, his glass of whiskey gathering dust, as he listened to the legendary singer billed simply as Lady. She was a stunner, a heartbreaker. And her name was at the top of his "Wanted" list.

Lady's husky voice wove sultry fantasies, enticing, cajoling, promising fulfillment by the light of a silver moon. She stood, strumming a guitar as she mesmerized her audience. Smiling coquettishly, she set one foot on a rung of the stool beside her, revealing white lace petticoats and shapely legs in black lace stockings.

Rafe shook his head, determined to break free of her spell. He felt like all the other red-blooded men in the saloon. More sinner than saint.

A crimson gown set off her auburn hair and golden skin, and showcased her luscious body. She was rumored to be part Indian, maybe explaining why she'd never been caught. A man could drown in her big eyes. Lose his wits and everything he owned. Plenty of men would be willing to pay that price. He wasn't one of them.

Rafe carried a warrant for Lady's arrest. Judge Parker

and Marshal Boles of the Circuit Court for the Western District of Arkansas with jurisdiction over Indian Territory wanted her brought in, dead or alive.

He had tracked her to the Bend, a tough town squatting on the Texas side of the Red River. Outlaws had turned the place into their own heaven on earth, gambling, drinking, and carousing. If a Texas Ranger dared to show up, outlaws could easily escape north across the Red River where Indian law applied strictly to Indians and deputy marshals were limited to federal law. Rafe and other deputies did their best, but still the desperados ran wild.

Rowdy with drink and desire, cowboys, gunslingers, and outlaws stamped their boots, hootin' and hollerin' and clamorin' for more as they joined the refrain of "The Ballad of Lady Gone Bad." They were out of tune, with no rhythm, but enthusiastic enough to shake the rafters.

Lady's performance was so riveting that, while she sang, every man in the place ignored the Red River Saloon's legendary bar. Quite a feat considering the cavorting naked women carved into the mahogany. Patrons couldn't set a glass steady on top, but a lot of them spent time nursing a drink and stroking the handiwork of a down-on-his-luck Eastern tenderfoot who had traded art for whiskey. The shapeliest parts were worn smooth and shiny. Rafe appreciated the famous bar, but it could not compare to the living, breathing beauty on stage.

Lady pursed her lips, painted come-hither red, and glanced around the saloon as she crooned in a sultry voice.

They always curse to lose their horses.
They surely cry to hand over their gold.
But on Lady's trail at the wide Red River,
They better make sure not to ride alone.

Rafe tossed back his whiskey, wishing it was cold as a river in winter. He regretted that the whiskey did nothing to ease his pepper-hot, iron-hard ache for Lady Gone Bad. She teased and tormented men, stoking their fires, but gave no relief. Nobody knew her real name or much about her, but how much trouble could one little lady be?

The Bend was hell on lawmen. Rafe was out of his jurisdiction. But he didn't care. He wanted this arrest. And he had a plan. Wasn't much of a plan, but he didn't figure he needed much of one. He'd buy Lady a drink, lure her outside, and handcuff her. Once on horseback, he'd take her back into Indian Territory and head for Fort Smith.

If Lady didn't give him any trouble, he'd take time on the journey to inquire about his sister Crystabelle. She'd been kidnapped off a Katy train by outlaws. He didn't know if she was still alive, but he couldn't give up hope. He had good informants and better trackers, but so far nothing had led to Crystabelle. She was a delicate lady. He worried about her every day.

As he waited, he studied the patrons. A big man with a long mane of silver hair under a black hat sat at a table with his back to the wall. Two smaller men, one with a blond beard and the other with straight black hair, sat on either side of him. They looked like the kind of trouble that kept lawmen busy.

When he turned back to look at Lady, she was setting aside her guitar. She stepped into the crowd, giving her audience a notion of what it'd be like to get close to her. She patted a bald pate, stroked a bushy beard, and blew a soft kiss as she slowly prowled the room. A low growl, more animal than human, followed in her wake.

She sidled up close to Rafe and leaned down, the décolletage of her gown revealing the upper slopes of her breasts. "Buy a lady a drink?"

He nodded, determinedly staring at her eyes instead of the tantalizing view below. She had unusual, tricolored eyes, a brown center with a band of sage green and an outer ring of forest green. Reminded him of agates. She likely mesmerized men with her cat eyes. But not him. He was made of stronger stuff.

Rafe picked up the whiskey bottle on his table and filled the extra shot glass. He pushed out the chair next to him with a boot. He dropped his right hand down near the Colt .45 Peacemaker he wore on his hip, ready for trouble.

"New in town?" She smiled, ruby lips curving slightly upward. She ignored the drink and the chair.

"Passing through."

She leaned in closer and teasingly walked the tips of her nails up his chest. Breath caught in his throat. Wasn't easy, but he remained stoic. She smelled sweet and tart, like honeysuckle and lemon. He wanted nothing more than to bury his face in that lush bosom. She had a beauty mark just below the right corner of her mouth. He wanted to kiss that dark spot, lick and nibble to her mouth. Mark her all over.

But he was here on business.

"I like to give newcomers a special welcome." She flattened both hands against his chest and stroked upward over his leather vest to his shoulders. "Something they'll never forget."

Suddenly she flipped open the left side of his vest where he'd pinned his deputy badge out of sight. Damn. He should have left it in his saddlebags. But it didn't matter. She was going with him come hell or high water.

She pouted her crimson lips, sighing. "Figured you for a lawman the first moment I saw you. Hoped I was wrong." She jerked the handcuffs out of his vest pocket.

Surprised again, he reached for the handcuffs, but she dodged quick as a cat and stepped back out of reach.

Lady turned to the crowd. "Gentlemen! We've got a lawman with us tonight."

Stamping their boots, the crowd jeered, hissed, and cursed.

Rafe figured he was well and truly shut in the outhouse and tumbling downhill. But he'd been in worse situations and come out alive. He just needed a plan that didn't aggravate the situation.

She held the handcuffs above her head and clicked them together in rhythm. She pointed at her audience, and the saloon filled with deep, raw voices.

She's a wild woman, a renegade, a lady gone bad.

Lady threw back her head and laughed, twirling in a circle as she continued to click the handcuffs.

Rafe wanted to grab her, shake her, and take her to bed. But he couldn't let her get the best of him. "Darlin'," he drawled. "You want me to show you how to use those cuffs?"

She turned to face him. Excitement brightened her agate eyes as she raised one arched eyebrow. "Lawman, you want to play?"

Audacious as only a lady gone bad could be. She was burrowing into his mind, putting down roots like a squatter. He jerked free. She was one little lady whose good luck had turned bad. "Got an iron bed back at the hotel."

"Really?" She stepped closer, handcuffs held against the swell of her deep bosom. "Tell me more."

"Give those back and let's go test how well they work on my bed's railings."

"Got a real high opinion of yourself, don't you?" She

glanced back at the room, shaking the handcuffs. "Gentlemen! What do we do with lawmen in the Bend?"

An angry roar filled the saloon.

Rafe forced his mind back to business, but his body didn't want to follow. He checked the outlaws packing the tables and didn't like what he saw. His situation was turning ugly fast. He had to end the game. He stood up, keeping an eye on the men around him.

She quickly snapped one cuff on his left wrist.

He reached for her, but she slithered aside and snapped the other cuff on a rung of his chair.

As she stepped back in triumph, laughter filled the room.

Rafe hadn't given her enough credit despite the stories of her exploits. And he'd let her cloud his mind. He could quickly break the chair over a table and get loose, but she'd pricked his pride. He sat down and casually leaned against the chair, appearing completely relaxed despite his fast pulse.

She looked surprised, cocking her head to one side.

He patted his leg with his free hand. "Sit here and let's talk about finding my handcuff key."

She shook her head, a smile teasing the corners of her mouth. "You look like a lawman that needs to be taught a lesson."

"Think you're the woman to do it?" He touched his vest pocket, ready to take action if any man made a move toward them.

She sighed dramatically. "I do believe the task has fallen to me."

He patted his leg again. "Sure could use some help finding that key."

"You just don't know when to fold." She turned toward the crowd, her crimson skirt swirling around her. "Gentlemen, he's all yours."

Rafe watched her pretty backside sashay away. Turned out, she'd held all the aces. He couldn't go after her, not with a room full of men ready to jump him. He stood, then slipped the key from his pocket and into the cuffs with smooth familiarity.

A big brute with a beard down to his belt rose in drunken bravado. Somebody shattered a whiskey bottle on the side of a table. The outlaw trio he'd noticed earlier stood up and started toward him.

If they wanted a show, they'd get it. But he'd give as good as he got. He freed his hand with a satisfying click and reached for his Peacemaker.

Chapter 2

"Got trouble," Lady called as she burst into Manny's Livery Stable, tossing back the hood of her forest green cape. Soon night would give way to dawn. She had to keep moving if she wanted to get away under the cover of darkness.

"When ain't you got trouble?" Manny turned from feeding a horse.

"I had to teach a no-good lawman a lesson."

"Was he happy to learn it?"

"Not very."

Shaking his head, Manny spit tobacco toward a spittoon in the corner as he limped forward in faded blue jeans and a red plaid shirt. "How fast you got to leave town?"

"Fast."

"You want Jipsey?" He scratched his grizzled beard, and then raked fingers through his wild mane of black hair touched with silver.

"Please. I've got to change clothes."

"Change from girl to boy, you mean."

"I do what I have to do."

"Can't let the dead rest, can you?"

She paused, her hand on the ladder leading to the hayloft, and looked back. "Copper and Jipsey are all I've got left of Ma and Da."

"Good horses."

"The best! Da thought Copper would outshine any stallion he ever bred. If I don't locate him soon, he'll go lame."

"You'll find Copper before he's put down."

"I better." Tears moistened her eyes. She blinked hard to get control.

"You cryin'?" he asked, sounding astonished.

"Not crying. Mad."

"Don't get mad. Get even." Manny picked up a saddle and bridle. "Make your wishes come true."

"If wishes were horses," she sighed, "I'd have a remuda."

"Copper and Jipsey will give you a line that'll make all the other horses eat their dust."

"Got to find Copper first."

With her guitar strapped over her shoulder, Lady climbed the ladder as fast as her skirts would allow. She took deep breaths, drawing in the comforting, sweet scent of hay.

Her cozy nest upstairs was hidden behind strategically stacked bales of hay. Thick canvas sheeting covered the rough wood floor. A quilt and pillow added comfort, warmth, and beauty. A small mirror, wash basin and pitcher, hand towel, oil lamp, and a trunk to store necessities provided all she needed to survive in the Bend.

She gently placed her guitar in a special case, closed the lid, and set it aside. When she was sixteen, she'd worked an entire year to be able to afford the wonderful instrument. Now at twenty-seven years old, she left her guitar safely at Manny's when she went on the road.

As she peeled off the satin gown she never felt completely comfortable wearing, she remembered the surprised look on the deputy's handsome face. Lawmen counted on women who wore satin to be dumb. She counted on that misconception, but stayed on her toes every moment of every day. No other choice when you ran with wolves.

The patrons of the Red River Saloon would force the lawman out of the Bend. She wished she'd gotten to play with him a little more. He reminded her of a powerful stallion, and she did admire good horseflesh.

Tall, broad-shouldered, narrow-hipped, long-legged. He moved with the natural grace of a wild animal in his blue shirt, black leather vest, and charcoal trousers tucked into black knee-high cavalry boots. He wore his dark hair long, pulled back with a leather thong. A clean-shaven face revealed tanned skin, high cheekbones, and full lips. But most riveting of all were his eyes, a deep, smoky gray.

He was a man to make a woman's blood run hot. Probably why she hadn't resisted her impulse to touch him, tease him. Smiling, she thought about his handcuffs. She liked a man with enough guts to find her amusing rather than intimidating. Unfortunately, this one wanted to put her behind bars.

She stripped off her corset and all the other trappings men doted on. After she carefully folded the delicate fabric, she stored her clothes in the trunk for the next time she played Lady.

For now, she needed to obscure her curves, so she wrapped her breasts to flatten them. She slipped into a loose green, plaid shirt, big black vest, and baggy Levi's. She tugged on fancy cowboy boots, her one concession to vanity. She tied a blue bandanna around her neck, pointed end in front, to conceal her throat and pull over her nose. She pinned up her long, thick hair and covered it with a wide-brimmed hat. Last, she put on leather gloves to protect and disguise her hands. She could pass for a boy if nobody looked too close.

A disguise. All her life was a disguise. The satin and the

blue jeans, the saloon singer and the young boy who rode like the wind. She sometimes wondered who she really was under all the lies. Yet she couldn't let it matter.

Now she was going into danger again, grateful Da had taught her how to use weapons. She quickly buckled on his holster belt, checked that his prized pearl handle Colt .44 was fully loaded, and slipped the revolver into place. She adjusted the weight on her hips. Finally, she slipped a knife into the sheath inside her boot. She was as ready as she was going to get.

When she hurried down to the stable, she focused her mind on the challenge ahead.

Manny already had Jipsey bridled, saddled, and set to go.

"Thanks." She gently stroked the long blaze face of the chestnut. She stepped back to admire the dark red color with white left fore pastern, right fore sock, left hind sock, and right hind sock. The coloring worked well for camouflage. Picking up the reins, Lady swung easily into the saddle.

"Canteen's filled. Cornpone and jerky in your saddlebags."

She leaned over and kissed Manny's rough cheek. "What would I do without you?"

"Swing on the end of a rope."

"Don't even say it."

"Job came in for you."

"Not now?"

"Yep. Hayes Brothers been up to their usual shenanigans."

"Thought they were in Indian Territory."

"Back in Texas long enough to steal two apple pies from Ma Engle's farmhouse near Whitesborough."

"She thinks they didn't gobble them down first thing?"

Manny chuckled. "She bakes the best apple pies in the Red River Valley. Folks know it. Church social coming up. Stood to reason she'd be baking pies and letting them cool on the porch. She was coming back from the barn when she saw them riding off with her pies."

"What does she want them to return? Apples?"

"Nope. She left her reticule out there, too. They grabbed it. Guess they figured she'd have some money."

"She wants that back?"

Manny placed a hand on her boot. "Thing is, Ma had her daughter's funeral jewelry in her reticule. She'd braided that child's golden hair into a flower pin. Ain't worth nothing to nobody but her."

"That's a real shame. But they probably threw her pin away by now."

"She's willing to pay a half eagle to the brothers and one to you, if you can get it."

"That'd be ten dollars. Might be all the money she has in the world."

He nodded. "She only had one daughter. Snake bite last summer."

"This is going to be another one of those times when I don't get paid, isn't it?"

"Reckon so."

"Okay. I'll keep an eye out for the Hayes Brothers."

"Watch your back. Outlaws in Indian Territory are thick as fleas on a hound dog. Deputy U.S. Marshals are busy chasing their own tails."

She pulled down her hat. "Except for the one I left in the saloon."

Manny rubbed his beard. "Lawmen don't cotton to being made fools."

"I'll be careful."

Lady rode Jipsey out of the stable into a dark alley. The night was hot, humid, and oddly bright. The combined odors of liquor, refuse, outhouse, and sweat filled the air.

She heard shouts and gunshots. What were the wild denizens of the Bend up to now?

She urged the mare up an alley and stopped in the shadows. She watched as angry patrons spilled out of the Red River Saloon onto Main Street. Their noise drew others from nearby saloons. Several men stood in the street, holding up burning torches to light the area.

Shouting and shoving, the mob forced a lawman, *her* deputy, down the street. With his hands cuffed behind his back, he struggled to get loose, digging deep ruts in the mud with his boot heels.

When they reached a large tree, somebody in the necktie party threw one end of a rope over a low limb. Two men pushed a hangman's noose down over the deputy's head.

Still fighting to get free, he was thrust onto the back of a horse.

Chapter 3

If the lawman died, Lady would blame herself.

She wanted him out of town. Not dead. He must have made the saloon patrons madder than a downed hornet's nest. Couldn't he tell when men were drunk and spoiling for a fight? The Bend was known for its lawlessness.

Still, it didn't matter how he got on the wrong end of a noose. She had to save him, or she would have one more regret to add to her growing list.

Cursing, she took a deep breath. Outnumbered and outgunned, she needed surprise on her side if she had any hope of freeing him.

She wheeled Jipsey around and rode through alleys to the end of Main Street. In the shadows, she jerked up her bandanna to disguise her face. She made sure her rifle was loose in its leather sheath on her saddle. Finally, she leaned down and whispered in the chestnut's ears. They took off like a shot.

Racing down the street at breakneck speed, the mare's hooves kicked up mud and debris. Lady jerked out her Winchester and aimed over the heads of the lynch mob. She shot high and wide to scatter them.

Startled, the necktie party froze in shock. Not what she

wanted. She clipped a couple of hats. Men scattered and ran for cover.

The deputy sat on a honey chestnut with a flaxen mane and tail. Gorgeous animal. Memorable. Seemed a poor choice for a lawman who might prefer to go unnoticed at times. Maybe he liked flashy. She needed to settle his dancing mount. If his horse bolted, it was all over. She whispered to Jipsey. The mare slowed, nickering loudly until the other horse focused on her, trembling but staying put.

Lady wished for more light so she could see better. She didn't want to hit the lawman and complete what the lynch mob had started. She took careful aim, squeezed off a shot. Missed. She steadied her hands, took a deep breath and held it. Her second shot severed the taut rope.

The deputy slumped forward, noose around his neck, hands in cuffs behind his back. He was agile enough to stay balanced in the saddle as he gigged his mount into a canter.

Grabbing the reins of his horse, Lady turned Jipsey with the pressure of her knees. Together, they thundered back down the street. Shouts and shots dogged their tracks. She leaned low in her saddle to present less of a target. She depended on him being strong enough to hang on to his horse, but nobody could miss his chestnut's pale coat. She hoped the necktie party was too drunk to aim straight, but she never counted on luck.

Safety lay not far away on the north side of the Red River. She headed there. As they left the Bend behind, she kept a firm grip on the other horse's reins. She set a ground-eating pace, determined to cover as much territory as possible in case the lynch mob decided to mount up and follow.

The deputy presented a problem. He wasn't outlaw. He

was law. She didn't want to cast him out of the frying pan into the fire by taking him into outlaw lairs. She also didn't want him to discover hideouts where he might later return and arrest the very outlaws she needed to lead her to Copper.

Yet she didn't have much choice. If caught, she'd swing alongside the lawman. A lynch mob in a hurry would never recognize her as Lady without the face paint and satin gown. They probably wouldn't know she was a woman until too late. If she hadn't been so cocky, she'd have finished her song and slipped out the back door without ever confronting him. Now she was stuck with rescuing the very man who meant to arrest her.

She hit the outlaw trail, tracking back to well-known territory. At the scrub brush near the high banks of the Red River, Jipsey slowed and eased around a blind bluff that carried them out of sight. She reined in the horses and leaped to the ground.

In the gray light of daybreak, she ran back down their trail with a branch. She stopped and listened for sounds of pursuit. Nothing. She quickly brushed away hoofprints with the leaves as she walked backward until she was concealed in the thicket again. No good tracker in bright daylight would be misled, but her efforts might buy them time.

The deputy marshal looked rough. No hat, split lips, bloody nose. They'd done a job on him. Even so, he sat his saddle with the strength bred of rugged, determined endurance.

She patted his knee in reassurance. His muscles tightened in response, sending heat dancing up her spine. She let her hand linger, unwilling to break their connection. Battered and bruised, he still conjured up visions of rutting stallions and mares in heat. If wishes were horses, she'd have met him when she was a real lady. As it was, she could never let their paths cross again.

"Thanks, stranger," he said, voice a rough baritone.

She jerked her hand away, chiding herself for weakness. No matter his appeal, she didn't need extra aggravation. He could never know she was Lady Gone Bad, so she must keep her distance from him.

"Noose off." He leaned down.

She struggled with the rough rope, trying to get the knots to slip open, but she couldn't make much headway. At the same time, she listened for sounds of the necktie party catching up to them. She yanked harder on the rope. He maintained balance with his knees, but it couldn't be easy.

"Hurry," he urged.

"Can't budge it," she said softly, disguising her voice. She lowered her hands, finally giving up. She needed to use her knife, but didn't want to take the time. "Handcuffs. Key?"

"They took it."

She sighed, glancing back toward the Bend. "Can't shoot 'em off. Too loud."

"I can ride."

She patted his knee again, but this time felt sticky moisture. "You bleedin'?"

"Don't matter."

"Like hell. Pass out and you'll fall off."

If she couldn't get the noose or the handcuffs off him, she had to find another way to keep him in the saddle long enough to get across the Red River. First, she'd bind his wound so he stopped losing blood.

As she stepped up to Jipsey, she heard a horse's urgent cry in her head, once, twice, three times. She stumbled, feeling chills cover her body. Epona, her totem horse, was giving an early warning that nobody else could hear. She'd been alerted with that same warning the morning her parents had died. Danger was near.

A moment later came the jingle of harness back down the trail. Actual sound. Not a second to lose. She jerked her lasso off Jipsey, ran to the deputy, and tied him to his mount. "Stay quiet. I'll get us away."

She leaped into her saddle, tugged on his horse's reins, and urged Jipsey forward. She couldn't use Delaware Jim's ferry or the narrow bend in the Red River. They'd be too visible, easily shot in their saddles. She had to take the more dangerous route overland to the east. Along the way, she'd need to find a likely crossing on the shifting sandbars.

And somehow keep them ahead of the lynch mob.

Chapter 4

Rafe felt like a chicken trussed up for market. He bounced along hard enough to break every bone in his body, not to mention losing his ability to ever again please a lady. Or himself. He was so damn mad he wanted nothing more than a chance to settle the score, but first he had to stay alive.

For some reason, a boy had come to his rescue. It rankled. He was the one who rescued people, not the other way around. But he was thankful.

Justice felt sound beneath him. He hoped the gelding hadn't been hurt by the lynch mob. He'd hate to lose Crystabelle's recent gift to him. The gelding had been left with a note by an unknown party at the courthouse in Fort Smith. If the horse was an outlaw joke, he wasn't laughing. But if Justice meant his sister still lived, he was grateful.

Rafe shifted in the saddle, getting a better grip with his knees. The noose felt like an anvil on his neck and shoulders. The handcuffs bit into his wrists. Knife wounds leaked blood. Battered but not out.

He'd survived enough fights to know his height, strength, and quickness gave him an edge, but he hadn't been prepared for the noose. He'd figured he would fight his way out of the Red River Saloon with a few cuts and bruises. He hadn't counted on the Bend wanting to send a message to lawmen by stringing up Deputy U.S. Marshal Rafe Morgan.

He'd been warned to take backup. But no other deputies had been available. He'd been warned Lady was crafty as a fox. But he'd figured he could handle one little lady on his own. He'd been warned the Bend was her playground. But he'd had to see it to believe it. Now he wished he'd heeded the warnings.

Punished by the hot sun overhead, he felt as if his brain was cooking to jerky. He fought the numbness in his knees and thighs by stretching as much as he could. He was dry enough to drink a river. One thought kept him going. He would personally put Lady Gone Bad behind bars.

If they kept riding east, they'd reach Paris. He could get help there at the courthouse from Bill Phillips, U.S. Marshal for the Eastern District of Texas. All they had to do was stay ahead of the necktie party.

Horse-wise, the odds were in their favor. He rode a good mount. The kid sat easy on the back of a dark red chestnut that looked built for speed and stamina. But he had to figure the odds against them, too. Trussed up, he was slowing them down. If the kid was an outlaw, maybe he wanted a deputy to owe him one. On the other hand, the boy might be leading him straight to another outlaw gang. For now, he couldn't do anything but trust the kid and hope to come up aces.

He glanced back. The lynch mob wasn't giving up. He could see their dust cloud, gaining ground all the time. At this rate, they'd never reach a safe haven. If he could get rid of the noose and handcuffs, he could guide Justice and move faster.

"Hey," he called, his voice cracking with dryness. "Stop. Free me."

"Cave ahead." The kid gestured at a bluff. "Get us out of sight."

Relief poured through him like a river, washing to the surface all the aches and pains he'd been holding at bay. He hurt like a house afire and needed to get out of the saddle fast.

Soon the boy led their horses out of the bright sunlight into the shadow of a small cave, dismounted, and untied the lasso.

"Thanks." Rafe coughed out the word, then cautiously stepped down from the gelding, felt his legs buckle, and sat down hard on his butt. "Free me quick."

"Aim to." The kid started working on the noose again.

Rafe forced his body to remain still, but he wanted to rip off the rope with his teeth. He felt a pat on his shoulder from the boy's gloved hand.

"Gotta cut you loose."

"Do it." He waited impatiently, knowing the necktie party was getting closer every moment.

He glimpsed a sharp knife before he felt sawing on the rope, back and forth. Hurt like hell, but he didn't care. When the knife finally cut through stiff fibers, the blade pricked his raw skin. Again, he didn't care. All that mattered was his relief when the noose was finally jerked over his head and tossed to the ground. He took a deep, satisfying breath and stretched his neck in relief.

"Cuffs now." The kid lifted a small packet out of his saddlebag. He squatted down beside Rafe and unrolled a blue cloth bag to reveal a row of picklocks, each in a separate cloth noose.

Rafe watched a gloved hand select a pick. The boy had long fingers, slender wrists. With a few deft movements, the lock clicked open. Rafe jerked off the cuffs, tossed them down, and then rubbed circulation into his raw, swollen wrists.

The kid quickly rolled up the picklocks, replaced them in his saddlebag, and brought back a canteen.

Rafe poured water over his face, took several deep gulps, and sighed in satisfaction. He wet his bandanna and tied it around his neck to cool and protect his raw, sore skin.

"Better get," the kid said, motioning toward the horses.

"Thanks." Rafe held out his hand in introduction. "Name's Rafe." Something about the boy seemed familiar, but he couldn't see much in the dim light and the kid kept his hat pulled low. "Rafe Morgan."

The boy turned over Rafe's hand and put cornpone and jerky in it.

"I can't take your food. Bad enough I drank your water. Put you in danger."

"Eat it on the run." The kid picked up his canteen and headed for his horse, looking like he wore his older brother's clothes.

"Thanks. I'll pay you back." Rafe grabbed his handcuffs and the noose, tossing them into a saddlebag. No easy trail left behind. "What the hell kind of town lynches the law?"

"The Bend." The boy swung up in his saddle like he'd been doing it since birth.

Rafe mounted Justice. "A low-down, conniving polecat set me up. When I catch her, I'll take her to the Hangin' Judge."

The kid set off down the trail without reply.

As Rafe followed, he gnawed at the cornpone and felt his mind click into gear. Details kept him alive. The boy carried picklocks. An outlaw's tool. Cowboys could be overly proud of small feet and fancy boots, but this kid took the cake. Gunslingers wore fancy boots like the boy's hand-tooled design of a rearing horse silhouette, crisp white against blood red. The kid was young, but folks grew up fast in the West. There were lots of ways he could get his own money.

All in all, Rafe couldn't trust the boy. But he owed the

kid for saving his neck. He felt responsible for getting them both into trouble. Rafe was better off in Texas. If the boy was an outlaw, he'd do better in Indian Territory. Might be safer for them both if they parted company.

First, they had to get rid of the lynch mob.

"You got a name?" he asked.

"Kid'll do."

Rafe glanced over at the boy's delicate profile. He was struck by a sudden idea that, like the last piece of a puzzle, put everything into place.

Maybe, just maybe, this clever boy was a girl.

Chapter 5

Lady wished the lawman hadn't said his name. *Rafe.* A name was powerful, too personal to share quickly. *A gift of spirit.* She preferred people know her as Lady rather than by her real name. Ma and Da had trained her not to give up anything easy, especially her name, when she might end up with nothing but that name, good or bad. They knew about losing everything, but they'd started over and worked hard together. Always together.

She blinked back tears as she stopped Jipsey on the edge of the cliff above the Red River. Rafe halted beside her. She pushed down her rising emotions. Some days she felt so tired she simply wanted to join her parents in their final resting place on a peaceful hilltop. But justice drove her onward.

"Justice," he said, patting the gelding's neck.

Startled for a moment, she thought he'd read her mind.

"Easy boy."

She realized the honey chestnut was his justice. She had a much different kind in mind.

The Red River was no friend today. She'd watched for an easy place to cross since dawn. But after recent rains, the river ran high and wide, lapping over sandbars on the way to Louisiana where the clay-reddened water cut south to join the mighty Mississippi River.

Now that the sun was setting in the west, she had to cross. No choice. She couldn't chance the river after dark. Dusk offered protection. She'd be able to see, but the lynch mob couldn't hit their targets so easily in dim light.

"We better get going," Rafe said.

Lady indicated a beaten trail to the river. "I'm headed down. Lynch mob'll tail me." She pointed down the road. "You can make Paris tomorrow."

"What if they catch you or wing you?"

"I'm fast." She kept her face hidden in the shadow of her hat, hoping he wouldn't recognize her face or voice.

"I've seen better crossings."

"Out of time. Dark soon." She didn't understand why he seemed so reluctant to ride away.

"Two guns are better than one."

"Why risk it?" She couldn't believe he wouldn't take the easy, safe way out of their situation.

Rafe pointed back at the dust cloud dogging their tracks. "You saved my life."

"Make it count. Go to Paris."

She set heels to Jipsey and started the slippery descent down the winding dirt trail. She rode under the green branches of pine, oak, sweet-gum, bois d'arc, and other trees. She ducked low so as not to be swept out of her saddle. She caught the sweet scent of wildflowers. Birds stopped singing as she passed under their perches.

When she heard Rafe follow, she cursed under her breath. Why hadn't he taken the easy way out? She fumed as she rode. He was nothing but trouble. Now he seemed intent on being a gentleman who wouldn't let a kid go alone into danger. Felt he owed a debt. What were the odds? A rattler held nothing on a maverick lawman. No telling what he'd do if he discovered her true identity. She had to lose him somewhere in the Red River Valley.

At the bottom of the cliff, she let Jipsey pick her way

into the current, trusting the mare to know the best way to cross. As they splashed deeper into the river, muddy red water quickly rose up to the chestnut's belly. Dead leaves and branches swirled around them. A musky scent filled the air.

Lady heard Rafe's horse enter the water behind her. She urged Jipsey up onto the first long sandbar. Noisy flocks of birds wheeled overhead, gathering for nighttime retreats. Sunlight cast dark shadows across the burnished river.

"Hurry!" Rafe shouted as he rode up. "They're above us."

Shocked, Lady glanced back. Men with Winchesters, at least a dozen, were lining up along the cliff's edge, taking aim as the dying rays of the sun winked on gun barrels. How had the outlaws gotten there so quickly? She'd thought she had more time to get away.

"We're not out of rifle range!" she called, judging the distance with a practiced eye.

"Zigzag!" He gigged Justice forward, cutting back and forth across the sandbar and into the river.

Lady kept pace, counting on their staggered pattern and the fading light to protect them. A shot whizzed past her head, whining like an angry bee. Bullets peppered the water, kicking up small red geysers. She ducked and stayed low in the saddle, urging Jipsey forward. Rafe's gelding pulled away, faster and stronger against the current.

She glanced back at the bluff. Three men were down on their knees, bracing their rifles, narrowing their shots. She desperately needed to get out of rifle range. She urged Jipsey faster.

At the next sandbar, she saw Rafe glance back, slowing his horse to wait for her. She waved him ahead to the far shore, wanting one of them to make it.

Out of the water, she made a bigger target and knew it. She plunged back down, staying low on Jipsey's neck. She was covered in red mud, a slick mess that made staying in the saddle a challenge. She clung to both saddle horn and reins, gripping the mare tight with aching knees.

When she heard Epona give a warning cry in her head, she knew trouble had found her. A moment later, a bullet slammed off Jipsey's saddle, scored a red path across her shoulder, and she went down.

Lady leaped clear of the saddle, losing her hat in deep water. A strong undertow pulled her beneath the surface. She swallowed too much muddy water. She fought her way back to the top, spitting out water and gasping for air. She swam against the current, struggling to regain the sandbar.

She feared Jipsey might be dead or badly injured. But the mare stood on the sandbar, trained to remain calm under fire. Rafe's horse, saddle empty, stood beside her. But he was nowhere in sight. Had he been hit and fallen in the river?

She had to get back to help, but the strong current kept pulling her farther away. Bullets peppered the river all around her. She stopped swimming and tread water to use less energy. The cloth that bound her breasts had slipped down around her waist, getting in her way. She jerked on it, managed to pull it loose, and let it float away. Somehow, she had to reach the sandbar before her strength ran out.

Suddenly strong hands grasped her around the waist. She yelped and struck out, fearing an outlaw had grabbed her.

"It's me," Rafe said. "You're okay."

She felt relief, but then horror. What if he realized she was a woman, much less Lady Gone Bad? She had to get his hands off her, but she needed his help more.

"Got to get out of here." He glanced up at the bluff. "Grab my shoulder."

She gripped hard as he plowed through the river, drawing her beside him. Muscles rippled under her fingers as his arms slashed through water. She was acutely aware of him, dark hair wet and sleek, strong shoulders broad and muscular, long body taut and powerful.

When he reached the sandbar, he lifted her into his arms and carried her to shore. Cradled against his chest, she felt safe, protected, emotions she'd given up so long ago. But she wasn't safe. He was her enemy. And they were under increasing fire.

"Put me down!" She struggled to get away before he realized the truth. She felt his hands slip, slide over the round globes of her butt, the curves of her breasts, the slick surface of her skin.

"Female, like I suspected." He froze, appearing puzzled as he searched her face.

"No!" She struggled to get free, desperate to stop where his mind was taking him.

He rubbed the beauty spot below her mouth with a rough thumb, his puzzled expression giving way to understanding.

She knew he knew. And bit his finger.

"Lady!" he spat out in fury.

She squirmed in his arms, trying to get free, but he held her tighter as he turned back.

And dumped her in the river.

Chapter 6

Rafe reined in Justice on the rich soil of Indian Territory. Mud ran off his body and pooled around him in a crimson tide. He saw it through a red haze of fury.

Lady Gone Bad had tricked him again. All day long he hadn't recognized the infamous outlaw. He felt like a fool. How had he missed her voluptuous body? Eyes like polished agate? Soft, scented skin? She was the damnedest outlaw he'd ever met.

Safely out of rifle range, he could hear steady fire from the bluff on the other side. The necktie party ranks had swollen to over a dozen men. They continued to spray the river with bullets, aim improving as they sobered up.

Only a matter of time before Lady and her horse were nothing but buzzard food. She was getting what she deserved after terrorizing law-abiding citizens and serving him up on a platter for a lynch mob.

A small voice of reason argued she'd come back for him, saved his neck, and gotten him to safety. He was a Deputy U.S. Marshal, not a vigilante. But his anger didn't want to hear reason. His rage wanted sweet, swift revenge.

Lady's mount was down. She wouldn't leave the animal. Did she have some kind of death wish? Maybe she couldn't swim. Pretty quick, the outlaws would decide to take their sport to the river. That'd be the end of her.

Gone. Forever. He felt his anger sizzle, as if doused by water, and go out. He'd hate to live in a world made poorer by her absence, particularly if he was to blame.

Punish her, yes. Kill her, no.

He plowed Justice back into the river, dodging bullets, zigzagging toward Lady. By the time he got there, she had the mare up. He grabbed her around the waist and slung her over his lap, facedown, not caring how uncomfortable he made her. He'd do whatever it took to get them out alive.

A thought flashed through his mind. He was living the dream of every man who'd heard Lady Gone Bad's legend, who'd listened to her sing, who'd watched her strut, untouchable, through a saloon. She was at his mercy, stretched across his lap, her round butt fairly asking for it. He threw back his head and laughed, slapping her rump and feeling hard enough to bust out the buttons of his Levi's.

Lady twisted around to look up at him. "Stop! Are you trying to get us killed?"

Rafe saw her clearly for the first time. No face paint or lip rouge. No teasing seductress. No pretension at being a boy. Instead, she revealed a depth and determination that took his breath away. Lady Gone Bad was a phantom. This was the real woman. She hooked him, so deep and hard it went straight to his gut.

"Jipsey!" she cried out, pointing to the mare. "Can't leave her behind!"

This compelling woman hadn't left him behind either. She was loyal to the bone, for man or horse. He wondered what it took to win and keep that rare kind of loyalty. If it was the last thing he did, he'd make sure she had her horse. He grabbed the mare's reins. He looked back at the lynch mob to assess the danger.

Shocked, he blinked hard, almost unwilling to believe his sight. Deputy U.S. Marshal Lynch'em Lampkin stood with the outlaws, firing his standard issue rifle. Now Rafe knew the real reason the necktie party wouldn't give up. If Judge Parker and Marshal Boles found out one of their deputies was working with desperados, Lampkin could kiss his job, maybe his life, good-bye.

They were in deep trouble, about as bad as falling into a pit of rattlesnakes. A lynch mob would eventually give up. Lampkin could never stop. They had to get the hell out of there.

Rafe set heels to horse, pulling the mare, and rode back into deep water. Bullets zinged around them, splashing into a river turned bloody red in the setting sun. For speed's sake, he rode straight. If the sun didn't drop like a rock below the horizon soon, their chances of getting out alive were slim. He drove hard toward the shore. A bullet stung his arm. Another grazed his shoulder. Lady groaned. He knew she'd been hit, too. No telling how many bullets their horses had caught, but they valiantly kept going.

All at once, the sun went down, making them shadows in a darkening world. The bullets slowed, then stopped. No point wasting ammunition. Shouts and movement came from the cliff. The outlaws were coming down, back to the hunt.

Rafe drove their mounts relentlessly through the dark water, pushing the exhausted horses to their limit. He heard the lynch mob plunge into the river behind them. A chill spread up his spine. Gunfire came again, hitting short and wide. But not for long.

One final push and the horses scrambled ashore, trembling with exhaustion, struggling for breath, lowering tired heads.

Rafe let Lady slide to the ground. He leaped down beside her.

Sunlight still touched the bank. He started to check her for wounds. She waved him away, pointing to the mare.

She was right. If two had to ride one tired mount, they'd never make it. He checked the red chestnut, running hands over prime horse flesh. The mare felt sound, except for a grazed shoulder, maybe other slight injuries. He checked Justice, felt a bullet graze on a muscular hip. Somehow the lynch mob had missed killing shots at big targets.

When he turned back, Lady stood with hands on hips, her hat and vest gone, and her shirt and Levi's plastered to her body like a second skin. Red mud covered her from head to toe, completely bronzing her. She looked like an ancient goddess come to life.

She might as well have been naked, with her long, shapely legs, slim hips, and breasts like two ripe melons. Good enough to eat. Her kisses would taste like lemonade, sweet and tart. He imagined her teeth raking his mouth, teasing and tormenting, urging him on. He wanted to plunder her body, lay siege to each plump, luscious curve with his mouth and hands, pull her down to the bank where he could drive hard and deep between her legs, bodies slick with red mud, sliding and grinding together until they exploded with fulfilled passion.

"Thanks." Lady thrust slim fingers through her long, muddy hair. She smiled at him with pure exhilaration, teeth white and straight in the growing darkness. "We made it!"

For a moment he felt confused, his vision so intense that he thought she was thanking him for gratifying sex. He shook his head. Heart thudding hard in his chest, he knew how a rutting stallion must feel. She was as changeable and volatile as a prairie thunderstorm, but he liked a challenge. If she wasn't an outlaw, he'd be a goner for sure.

They *had* made it, thanks to him. Lynch mob or no lynch mob, he wanted a reward. No glittering gold for him, just straight up, simple, hard-driving sex. Only one woman would do. After all, she owed him.

Then, a shower of gunshots hit the shore, kicking up dirt, seeking soft flesh.

"Better ride," Lady said.

Rafe felt lust seep out of him like a spilt glass of whiskey. No time now for anything but escape.

"Those bushwhackers ought to remember Lady's ballad." She started up the steep, slippery cliff, calmly leading the mare.

Grabbing Justice's reins, he started after her.

Soon Lady's sultry voice echoed across the Red River Valley as if the sound came from everywhere and nowhere at once.

She's a wild woman, a renegade, a lady gone bad.

Rafe felt the magic of her song, an ancient power that raised the hair on the back of his neck. He was heading into Indian country where American rules applied only to a limited degree.

They better make sure not to ride alone.

The lynch mob stopped, rifles went silent, horses grew still, as if all the breath and will had gone out of them.

Rafe looked up at the top of the cliff. He expected to see Lady's dark shape. Instead, a white mare reared and pawed the sky before setting hooves to earth and disappearing into darkness. He was reminded of the rearing horse on Lady's boots.

He exhaled, realizing he'd been holding his breath. Wild horse. That was all. He checked the sky. Not enough moon to make a difference. Maybe a campfire had illuminated the horse. Not likely. Taking a deep breath, he did what he always did when in Indian Territory. He accepted that not all was knowable.

When he reached the cliff top, Lady sat on her mount, waiting, watching, listening.

"Did you see that white horse?" he asked.

She raised her eyebrows in surprise.

"Guess not." Maybe he hadn't seen the mare either. "Lynch mob stopped." He swung into his saddle, checked to make sure he had his Colt and Winchester. "But they'll be coming after us."

She turned away from the river.

"Hold it."

She looked back.

"Ma'am, you're under arrest."

She laughed.

Chapter 7

"About time you were brought to justice," Rafe said, pulling handcuffs out of his saddlebag.

Lady put her right hand on the Colt .44 hugging her hip, but doubted the pistol would fire after her swim in the river. She figured he knew it, too. Still, she had a knife in her boot, come to that.

"Easy or hard makes no never-mind to me." He held out the cuffs. "Good thing I carry a second pair. I've got a key."

"You'd have better luck if you traveled with the usual team of deputy marshals, cook, and covered jail wagon." She straightened her shoulders, sitting up higher in the saddle. "As it is, you're fresh out of luck. I'm *not* going in easy."

"Warrant stipulates bringing you in, dead or alive." He held out the handcuffs. "Snap them in front so you can ride easier."

"Damn the Hangin' Judge. Thinks his word is law."

"It is. No petition goes to a higher court."

She shivered, imagining how the rough rope of a hangman's noose would feel around her neck, followed by a hard drop into empty air. *No.* She couldn't allow that to happen. She had to get justice for her parents, but time was running out.

Rafe rattled the handcuffs. "Let's get a move on."

Jipsey shied to the side, sending unease rippling up through Lady. She glanced down at the dark ribbon of river below, then back at him. "You've got bigger trouble than me."

"We're out of range and reach if we keep moving."

"I wouldn't be so sure—" She stopped her words in mid-sentence as a single pinpoint of light flashed in the north, three equal times. She glanced down at the river. Light answered, three more times.

"What is it?"

"Hell and damnation!" she hissed, turning Jipsey east. "Got to get out of here."

"Not so fast—"

"Didn't you see the signal lights?" She pointed north, then south.

"Friends of yours?"

"If they are, they won't be once I'm caught helping you."

"I know outlaws keep lookouts and send signals all over Indian Territory, but this appears too convenient. Did you set a trap?"

She snorted. "Stay if you want and discuss the matter with the night. I'm gone before I'm caught between two outlaw bands."

As she drummed her heels against Jipsey's sides, she saw him quickly tuck the handcuffs back in his saddlebag. The mare exploded from standing to running, and she left him behind.

Lady reveled in the power of a blooded horse between her thighs and a wild wind against her face. But she knew Jipsey couldn't keep going at top speed, not after the long, hot day.

As she raced toward scrub brush and the distant tree

line, she heard the hooves of Rafe's horse pound a staccato beat behind her. Soon he matched her pace, side by side, flying through the night. She glanced over at him. Danger made her blood run hot. His, too, from the look of him. She grinned. He threw back his head and laughed. Fine pair they made. Separated by law. Bound by peril.

She looked back. Half a dozen outlaws were eating up the distance, most likely on fresh mounts that could run them down. She'd counted on even odds with the lynch mob, but now the odds were on the other side. She hated trying to win from a down position.

Still, she never counted on easy or fair. Some days you had to create your own luck if it didn't fall your way.

When they made scrub, she hit a narrow trail that wound back toward trees that grew along a creek emptying into the Red River. Blackberry vines hooked her Levi's, and then tore loose. She caught the scent of overripe persimmons. As she slowed Jipsey, she let the mare pick her way through any hidden dangers such as armadillo holes in the ground or downed tree limbs that could cause a horse to break a leg.

Lady watched the sky, a sooty gray broken by the black silhouettes of ancient trees. Thick with limbs and heavy with leaves, the tree line created a sky road that ran north, deep into Choctaw Nation. Squirrels and birds used the upper road. Indians, too. But she was horse-bound and could do no more than use the trees as camouflage.

Alone, she had a better chance of losing the outlaws. Two horses and two people were harder to hide. The last thing she needed with her was a lawman set on escorting her to Judge Parker, infamous for hanging Indian Territory outlaws. Yet they were a long way from the court in Fort Smith, Arkansas. She'd find an opportunity to lose

Rafe along the trail. For now, she had to find a way to keep them alive.

No place to run, not with tired mounts. No place to hide, not with outlaws hot on their trail. Too dark for an ambush, not that she wanted to kill anybody by picking them off from the bushes or hurt horses by pulling a taut rope across the trail to trip them. Outnumbered, and riding spent mounts, they were getting into more trouble by the moment.

She turned in the saddle and glanced back. The outlaws hadn't made the cutoff into scrub yet. No sign of the lynch mob either. Now was the moment to fish or cut bait.

When she brought Jipsey to a halt, Rafe rode up and stopped beside her. She pushed back her hat and looked him in the eyes. "Any ideas?"

"I'm wracking my brain. If we don't get off this trail, we're sittin' ducks."

"You're used to backup."

"With enough deputy firepower, we'd get those desperados under control."

"I'm used to going it alone." She nodded in the direction of the outlaws. "I've got an ace up my sleeve."

"You plan to sing?"

"If I thought it'd help, I would." She dismounted, letting the reins dangle to ground tie Jipsey. "Don't know if this'll work or not, but it's worth a try."

"I'm ready for a good plan. Need help?"

"Hold the horses. They may spook." She opened a saddlebag, rummaged around inside, and pulled out a small burlap bag. "Better keep them facing north."

"Come dawn, we could play hide and seek. Use our Winchesters from a distance." He leaped down and picked up Jipsey's reins, holding both mounts side by side.

"I'd hate to leave a trail of dead outlaws. There'd be reprisals. And I'm not sure we'll make it to dawn."

"Let's try your plan first."

"If something happens and I don't get back, I'll trust you with my horse." She swallowed hard, pushing down pain that tightened her heart at the idea of leaving Jipsey and not finding Copper. "She's a fine mare."

"Tarnation!" Rafe jerked his Winchester from its saddle sheath. "I'm not sending you into danger alone. Horses be damned."

"We need them if we're going to stand a chance of getting away without a bloody battle. Those outlaws know they've got backup coming. Once that lynch mob gets here, they'll have enough rifles to cut us to bits."

"I'll tie the horses to a tree."

Maybe this was her last chance to see Rafe, or maybe she wanted one final time before throwing herself into danger again. Either way, she took a moment to watch as he led the horses off the trail. Cast in gray light and dark shadow, he appeared long, lean, and dangerous, like a cougar on the prowl. She felt a sudden hunger, a shift in her soul, a nameless longing. Maybe she'd been alone too long. But he wasn't the man for her. He was a man to escape as quickly as possible. And yet, she wished with him she'd come up aces.

For a long time now, longer than she could ever have imagined, she'd worked best alone. She wasn't sure anymore if it was by choice or necessity, but she didn't need or want his help. Still, she remembered a time when a shoulder to cry on and a warm, comforting hug had been the cornerstones of her life. Gone now. All gone. Forever.

She'd be well away before Rafe finished with the horses. He'd be safer there. She tossed the burlap bag over her shoulder, holding it steady as she quietly jogged back down the trail.

When she neared the end of the brush line, she knelt and crawled on her knees until she could see the open plain of high grass that stretched to the Red River. No movement in that direction. But when she looked west, she saw dim shapes and heard the outlaws coming fast. They took dangerous chances by pushing their horses in the darkness.

No time to lose. She felt her heart beat a fast staccato as she dropped the burlap bag to the ground. When the sound of hooves striking ground grew closer, she slipped off her gloves and tucked them behind her gun belt. She gently pulled delicate objects out of the bag. She laid the various shapes and sizes across the beaten path that led from plains to thicket. She arranged the objects in three rows, larger in front and smaller in back. Finally, she pulled and prodded fuses into easily accessible positions.

Taking a deep breath, she moved behind the largest bush near the trail. She remained close enough to touch a horse's hoof should an outlaw get that far. She reached into the burlap bag and pulled out the last object, a tin of matches. She opened the tin, perfect for keeping matches dry no matter the weather, and selected three matchsticks. She closed the tin and put it in her pocket. She held the matches, phosphorous tips upright to stay dry, and waited for the desperados.

As the pounding of hooves shook the ground with impact, she struck a match across the bottom of her boot. Cupping the small flame with her palms, she knelt over the objects directly in the path of the oncoming horses.

The fire fizzled out. Shocked, she looked up, saw the huge, looming shapes and heard the harsh breath of laboring animals. Yet she couldn't let the danger stop her. She struck another match, cupped the flame, and leaned down almost flat against the ground. She quickly lit first one fuse, and then another.

Hoping against hope not to get pounded into the earth, she struck the last match. With shaking hands, she lit fuses until the first object exploded into the starry night.

Chapter 8

"Chinese fireworks!" Rafe dropped down beside Lady, taking cover from the onslaught of brilliant color and deafening sound.

Only one other time had he seen blue, green, red, and yellow ribbons and flowers streak into a night sky accompanied by bursts of what sounded like rifle fire. White smoke drifted upward, and he caught the sharp stench of burnt gunpowder.

The outlaws' horses reared in fright, bucked off their riders, and thundered away from a sight that had to be as terrifying as a violent storm. The desperados were left on foot without rifles.

"Clever!" Rafe chuckled as he clasped Lady's shoulder. She'd been smart to recognize spooking the horses would throw the outlaws into a tailspin.

Lady glanced at him, smiling as she picked up her burlap bag. "Bought us a little time."

"Let's go!"

As they ran back down the trail, light and sound faded to a few staccato bursts. He guarded her back, knowing he kept her alive only to take her to a court notorious for handing down stiff sentences.

She was a mystery, the kind a man could spend a lifetime unraveling, but he feared she wasn't a woman to make old bones. If she ended up on the gallows, she'd take her mysteries to the grave. He hated the thought and his part in it. But she couldn't be allowed to hurt innocent people. Maybe she'd simply be sent to jail for a good long while.

But that wasn't his problem now. He had to live long enough to get her to Fort Smith. More importantly, he had to let Judge Parker and Marshal Boles know that one of their deputies was working both sides of the fence. Rafe had never liked or trusted Lampkin, not exactly bad blood but close enough. Now he knew why.

He glanced back down the trail, still dark and quiet. But for how long? They had to get in their saddles and get out of there. Fort Smith was too far away. As soon as possible, he'd head for Paris, where he could report Lampkin and send a telegram to Marshal Boles.

When they reached the spot where he'd tied their mounts, the horses were nowhere in sight.

Puzzled, he looked around, wondering if he'd missed the place, or something worse. "Tarnation. Think somebody stole our horses?"

"Jipsey's not one for being tied."

"Think she used her teeth to get free?"

"Either that or her hooves."

He laughed outright at the idea. "One thing is for sure, you're dang entertaining."

"That's what all the men tell me."

He turned serious. The thought of rutting outlaws doing what he wanted to do with her made him mad as hell. "We need to get out of here."

"Suppose Jipsey taught your horse, too?"

He rounded on her. "You've spun one yarn after another since I met you. Smoke and mirrors. Is nothing real about you?"

"You believe life is black and white, don't you?" She

put her hands on her hips, giving him a hard stare. "It's not. Life comes in shades of gray."

"Your world. Not mine." He looked down the trail, irritated that she kept distracting him, challenging him, goading him. "We'd better walk if we don't want to be caught. We can get those outlaws and our horses later."

"I'd rather ride." Lady put two fingers between her teeth and whistled three quick bursts of piercing sound.

Jipsey trotted out of a thicket. Justice followed.

Rafe just shook his head, figuring he ought to be glad the white ghost horse hadn't pranced out, too. Some days a man had to go with whatever was put in his path and not question providence.

Lady stroked Jipsey's nose. "Coming?" She put her boot in a stirrup and straddled the mare.

"Where'd you get fireworks?" He sheathed his Winchester and mounted Justice. "Saddlebags are for necessities only. Why the extra weight?"

"Payment for a job."

"Not too many people keep fireworks lying around."

"Guess I was lucky." She headed Jipsey down the trail.

"That's for sure." He followed, realizing she wasn't going to tell him more about the fireworks. Most likely outlaw trade. "We need to find a cave or somewhere to shelter and rest the horses."

"Come dawn, they'll track us. Wish it'd rain."

"And wash out our tracks." Now that he had a little breathing space, all his aches and pains, cuts, and bruises were hurting like hell. "Wish we had a hidden cabin with a soft bed and plenty of food."

"Sounds good." She glanced back over her shoulder. "You hit? Bleeding?"

"Bullet grazes."

"Me, too. We need to take care of our wounds."

"Get away first."

He rode up close behind her, horse nose to horse tail. No good answers to their situation came to mind. All he knew to do was keep moving forward.

In the distance he heard a rumble that vibrated through the air, growing closer and louder. He glanced back. What now? He hoped the outlaws didn't have a canon. Six-shooters and rifles were bad enough.

"Hurry!" he called. "They may be catching up."

Chapter 9

When the first fat, wet drops of rain splashed Lady, she hooted and hollered with glee. "That'll stop those sidewinders in their tracks!"

"Can't believe it," Rafe said. "Night was filled with stars. Not a cloud in sight."

"Maybe Jipsey and Justice did a rain dance while we were off shooting fireworks."

"Guess a storm blew up from the south."

"That's one way of thinking about it." She stopped Jipsey while Rafe rode up beside her.

He lifted his face to the sky, ran a hand through his damp hair, and then glared at her. "Only way to think about it."

"You're stuck in the mud. No imagination." She glared right back, feeling so relieved that rain was washing away their trail that she was ready to strike out at anybody handy to release her pent-up tension. Rafe was annoying enough to fit the bill.

"I can imagine you standing in front of Judge Parker," he snapped, his voice rough with irritation.

"Just what I said. No imagination."

"Enough to catch the infamous Lady Gone Bad."

"But not enough to know you're caught as well."

"I'm not. That's your big head talking," he said.

"Who's leading who?"

"I can lead."

"But can you take us to a warm, dry, hidden shelter with food for the horses and us?"

"You better mean that."

"Did the horses do a rain dance?" she pushed, wanting him to let go of his expectations and step into her world of possibilities.

"Lady, you're straining your luck."

"Yes or no?

"Hideout, yes or no?"

"Horses, yes or no?"

"Tarnation! You could drive a man crazy. On the chance there's food and shelter nearby, the dang horses could have done anything when we weren't looking, including a rain dance."

"Yes."

"Yes, what?" he asked, wiping water from his face.

"Yes, I'll take you to my hideout if you promise to stop talking about taking me to the Hangin' Judge."

"Okay. That's settled. Now let's get the hell out of here before we drown. Rain's coming down cats and dogs."

"Maybe a few possums, too."

"Raccoons and beaver. Herd of crazy critters."

She laughed, abruptly feeling lighthearted at his agreement, their banter, and the narrow escape. Maybe he was a man as well as a deputy. Somebody with a heart as well as a gun. He might even be a friend as well as an enemy. Time would tell. She just had to make sure they got that time.

Glorying in the rain, she felt the grime and fear and anger wash away with the slick mud and musty scent of the Red River that clung to her.

She was tired, so deep down tired her bones hurt. Aches and pains from the long ride, the graze of bullets, and lashes from branches rode her, relentless and inescapable. All she really wanted was a long, hot soak in a tub with plenty of soft lavender soap. Thoughts of a huge, sizzling steak, bison, deer, steer, she didn't care, made her mouth water. She'd follow the meat with a piece of fresh baked apple pie or blackberry cobbler. Better yet, the whole pie itself. She could almost taste it all she was so hungry. She licked fresh rainwater from her lips, then tilted back her head and drank from the weeping heavens.

But she had to stay focused, or she'd never be able to find her hideout through overgrown trails. She kept a few places stocked here and there, always hoping no desperado or black bear found her caches. She never knew when her foresight might be all that stood between life and death.

As she peered into the dark, stormy night, she searched for signs to mark her way. Nothing obvious that might alert others, but a slash she'd left in tree bark or an unusual boulder.

Lightning flashed, followed by thunder that rumbled like a herd of running horses. Grateful for the light, she finally saw a large, familiar rock. She turned off the trail. Twisting and turning, wet branches and clinging vines slowing her pace, she continued until she grew unsure. In the darkness, visibility down to almost nothing, she was moving forward mostly by instinct alone. At least she'd led them off the main trail, so they were safer than they had been since the Bend.

She stopped Jipsey, looking around, trying to see through the heavy rain.

"Lost?" Rafe asked, riding up beside her.

"Need some light. Waiting for the next lightning flash."

"Hope you're not taking me on a wild goose chase, or planning to lose me in this mess of a night."

Lady glanced over at him, felt more than saw him, and realized he was probably going against his lawman experience, deputy marshal training, and male instincts to trust her enough to follow her. But why? He'd been in trouble from the moment he met her. She guessed he still wanted to arrest her. But why did she keep helping him? Safety and strength in numbers, she supposed. Guilt, too. She'd set him up and her conscience wouldn't let her rest till she'd gotten him to safety. After that, he was on his own. And she was free, as much as she ever was with images of death and destruction seared in her mind.

Lightning flashed, brilliant bursts of white light that revealed a slash she'd left on a tree trunk.

"This way." She pointed east.

"Hideout better be near. I'm sloshing in my boots."

"Near enough."

She urged Jipsey into a thicket, pulling back branches, and then holding on till Rafe grabbed them behind her. If she'd let go, the heavy limbs would have knocked him out of his saddle. Part of the time, she had to ride bent over Jipsey's neck to avoid low-hanging branches. It was slow going, creating a trail through the underbrush, but it was also the safest way to avoid detection. Between the downpour washing away their tracks and cutting their own trail, she doubted anybody could find them.

She peered hard through a curtain of glittering rain, clinging greenery, and lightning-split darkness. She finally made out the silver gray wood of an abandoned stagecoach station that she'd turned into a hideout. She felt weak with relief.

She looked back, grinned, and pointed at what was visible of the building through the overgrown bushes that protected it from prying eyes.

Rafe joined her, glancing around the area. "Safe?"

"Better go in loaded for bear." She never entered a hideout without her Colt .44 drawn and eye at the ready.

He nodded. "I'll check first."

"I'm right with you." She hoped everything was as she'd left it, prepared for her to hunker down until whatever storm was chasing her had blown over and forgotten her existence.

"Wait. One of us needs to be here in case there's trouble." He eased out of the saddle and splashed down into ankle deep water.

"I'll go. I know the place." She dismounted, too.

"Let me earn my keep." He took several steps forward. Lightning flashed. "Is that a stable back there?"

"Ramshackle but usable."

He tossed his reins toward her and drew his Peacemaker. "If you'll take care of the horses, I'll check the building."

She caught the reins, exhaustion and pain washing over her in a giant tide that she'd held back by sheer force of will. Now that they were hopefully safe, she desperately wanted to let down and catch her breath.

Still, she watched Rafe's back as he headed for the station's front door.

Chapter 10

Rafe was glad to be out of the saddle and on the move. He'd had enough of following Lady, depending on her while knowing she could be leading him into a trap. He hoped she was telling the truth, but hope didn't keep a man alive. Neither did trust. He'd check out the building before he even thought about letting down his guard.

He splashed through water, figuring the rain would cover any sound he made. He flattened his back against the rough wood near the door. He waited, listened, heard nothing suspicious, felt nothing contrary, so he reached out, twisted the white porcelain knob, and thrust open the door. He waited again, but still heard nothing. He leaped up, stepped over the threshold, and dropped to a crouch, senses stretched out to catch any hint of danger.

He waited, not moving, for the next flash of lightning so he could see into the dark depths around him. When light came, followed by rolling thunder, he made a quick inventory of the small, square room. A single rope bed covered by colorful quilts, one rocking chair, two straight-back chairs, one table with a lantern and a tin of matches on top, and a thick layer of dust. She hadn't been there in a while. Neither had anybody else.

A second door led out back. Good thing, too. He hated to be trapped in a place without at least two exits. Remembering the layout of the room, he quickly crossed to the back door. He stepped to one side, flattened his back against the wall, and jerked open the door. He waited. Lightning flashed. He glanced out back, saw a stable, door sagging open. Place looked empty, too.

Satisfied, he turned back into the room. She'd tacked horse blankets over the front and back windows so nobody could see inside. Place smelled dusty and musty, but a moist breeze blew through the open doors, drawing in clean air.

He holstered his Peacemaker, rolling his shoulders to ease the tension as he walked to the front door. He stopped in the doorway. Lady and the horses appeared no more than shadows in the slanting rain. Even so, he'd been intent on her long enough that he could read the tiredness in the way she leaned into her mare. *Vulnerable.* Not an emotion he'd associated with her till now. He felt protective. He even wished whatever had set her on the outlaw trail had never happened. Felt like a fool. If ever a woman had chosen her way of life, she had to be Lady Gone Bad.

Still, a warmth uncurled in his gut, remembering her sassy smile in the saloon tormenting every man in sight, struggling to save her mare in the river, rising up like a clay goddess, every curve slick with red mud, and riding hell-bent for leather across the plains. Heat hit him like a thunderbolt. He grew hard as a bois d'arc log. Craved her. Didn't do him a damn bit of good to imagine shucking off her clothes, running hands up her smooth bare flesh, feeling her wet heat on his tongue. But he did it anyway.

Might as well roll over and show his belly, let her see his eagerness like a stray puppy. He snapped off his thoughts. She wasn't a woman for him, so no point in tormenting himself.

He had to keep his mind on business. He gave Lady a

thumbs-up, and watched her start around the cabin with the horses.

Stepping outside, he let the rain cool his body, dampen his fever pitch to glowing embers. He figured a man never, ever lost his heat for Lady.

When Rafe felt more under control, he went back inside. He walked to the table, struck a match on a table leg, and lit the lantern, adjusting the flame as brightly as possible. Took the edge off the night. Made the place a little more hospitable. Like a rendezvous for lovers.

What he needed was a swim in a cold river, but he figured he was up the creek without a paddle. He might as well settle in for a rough ride and make the best of it.

He picked up the lantern and set it just inside the back door. They'd have some light, but not enough to give away their position while they bedded down the horses. He slogged over to the stable that had once housed enough horses to keep a stage line running from Missouri to Texas. With the Katy railroad now cutting across the Choctaw Nation to the west, much of the through travel went that way. Eastern Indian Territory still relied on local stages and horses to get from one point to another.

When he caught the sweet scent of hay and oats, he noticed that both horses had their noses stuck in feed buckets. "How'd you pull that rabbit out of a hat?"

"Keep oats in old pickle barrels. Hay bales in the loft."

"Good idea."

"Got a few places like this scattered about. I can go without food, but not my horse." She rubbed Jipsey between the ears. "Empty barrel outside to catch rainwater, too."

"Plenty tonight." Lady might starve, but not her horse. He didn't want to admire her, but he kept doing it anyway. Didn't matter. Worst outlaw could have a few good points. If she had to hang, he'd be there to see her off to a better life, even if he felt like part of him was dying on the gallows, too.

"Let's get this tack in the house." Lady unbuckled Jipsey's cinch, and then lifted off the saddle.

"Let me do that." He wanted her to see he could be more than a burden. He reached out and tried to take the saddle from her. She resisted, pulling back. They tugged back and forth. "Lady, let go. I'll curry the horses."

"I take care of my own horse." She jerked hard on the saddle, trying to free it.

"For once, let me do something to help." He tried to wrest the saddle away, but she pulled against him. She was a lot stronger than a man would guess.

"Will you let go?" she hissed between her teeth.

"I'm trying to help."

Lightning flashed overhead, close enough to almost set the stable on fire. Thunder cracked so loudly that both horses flinched, threw up their heads, and kicked back with hind legs.

Rafe jerked away from the flashing hooves, taking Lady with him as he sent them flying out from under the roof and into the yard. They landed entwined under the heavy saddle, water running in a steady stream around them.

All ceased to matter except Lady, so warm and wet and close. He caught her scent, sweet and tart. This time he decided she smelled like lavender and cinnamon. She faced him, breath warm on his cheek, long hair twined around his arm, a long leg nestled against his thigh. If he'd been hot before, now he was molten. Yet he felt tender, understanding her tiredness, worry, care for her horse. If he hadn't tried to help, everything would be okay.

"I think," she said, putting a hand between them and pushing weakly against his chest. "I got hit, kicked maybe. My head. I feel woozy."

"Hell, I'm sorry." But he wasn't sorry that she was pinned close to him, not thinking clearly enough to struggle. "Stay still. Let me get the dang saddle off us."

"Don't curse my saddle," she said, words slurring. "Handmade special for me."

"I'll be careful." He rolled his eyes as he hefted the saddle off her with one hand and tossed it into the water. He gently probed her skull for injury. Even though he should be thinking like a doctor not a lover, he took pleasure in touching her.

"Ouch!"

"Got a knot there. Probably getting bigger by the minute."

"Let's finish up . . . the horses."

"For once in your life, you're going to do what somebody else tells you to do." He stroked down her head to her back, feeling her hot curves in sharp contrast to the cool rain on his skin.

"Horses first."

"I'm taking you inside. I'll deal with the horses."

"No." She raised her head, groaned, but sat up, using his chest for support. "Da always said, 'Horses first, Sharlot, horses first.' Mustn't let him down."

"Who's Sharlot?"

"Slip of the tongue," she said, pushing hair back from her face, teeth worrying her lower lip.

"But you said Sharlot." Rafe sat up beside her, concern about her injury warring with his need to know more.

"Doubt it."

"You did so." He gripped her hand, delicate but strong, willing her to trust him. "Is that your real name?"

"I'm Lady Gone Bad, nothing more, nothing less. No past, no present, no future." She jerked her hand back, turned away, and pushed up on her knees.

If he hadn't known better, he'd have thought he heard

anguish in her voice, maybe seen tears on her cheeks. But with the rain and the lack of light, he couldn't be sure of anything. Except that he had to know more about her. "Sharlot?"

She looked back at him, no hesitation.

"Beautiful name, *Sharlot.*" Off guard, tired, injured, she'd given him an ingrained response to what must be her real name. "Suits you, too."

"Lady suits me fine."

"Let's come to an understanding here. I'm Rafe. You're Sharlot."

"No. You're Deputy. I'm Outlaw."

"I don't want to keep calling you Lady. I want to use your real name."

"I want to get the horses fed and get out of this rain." She stood up, swayed, regained her balance, and stood defiant on shaky legs. "At the rate we're going, we'll catch pneumonia and do the lynch mob's job for them."

"Best get you dry then." He caught her by surprise, sweeping her up into his arms and heading for the back door. She weighed more than he expected, but on second thought, that wasn't surprising for a horsewoman. She must be solid muscle under her soft, sleek skin. His heart pounded at the thought of her riding him until they both collapsed in sweat and satisfaction.

"Stop!" She hit his chest with her fists, and then groaned in pain, clutching her head. "Put me down!"

"You're not doing your injury any good fighting me." He strode over to the building. "Like I said, for once you're going to listen to somebody."

"Horses."

"Trust me. I'll take care of them." He stepped inside the building, trailing water across the floor as he carried her to the rocker. He gently set her down.

She leaned her head back against the chair and closed

her eyes. "Feels so good. World stopped spinning." A slight smile touched her lips. "If I can just rest a moment, I'll help you with the horses."

"I told you that—" He stopped, realizing she'd fallen asleep, head nodding forward in exhaustion. Wet, hungry, hurt, she'd fought him to keep going, but her body had rebelled against her iron will. Good thing, too.

He'd let her rest while he finished with the animals. Soon they both had to get dry, get food, get some rest.

Yet his body didn't care about that. Felt like he'd been poker-hard since the first moment he saw her. And his situation wasn't getting any better. He'd be best off sleeping with the horses. Alone here, he'd be thinking only about getting her onto that rope bed.

He stepped out into the rain, hoping like hell neither band of outlaws knew about the hideout. At least nobody could read his mind and figure out he was a goner for Lady Gone Bad.

Chapter 11

Lady woke with a start, feeling disoriented and confused. Head hurt. Body hurt. Wet all over. She sat in what must be a rocker. Groggy, she opened her eyes a slit to get her bearings.

And almost fell out of the chair. A tall, lean, but oh-so-buck-naked man with his back to her was pulling blue jeans up over his taut, muscular butt. He stood near a table where a single lantern cast a spotlight of golden glow over him while the rest of the room faded into shadows.

She ogled his long legs and perused his fine ass. His back and broad shoulders were thickly muscled. Sleek, tanned skin marred by old scars the color of muscadine wine and fresh crimson wounds spoke of a tough, perilous, predatory life. Dark hair hung loose about his shoulders. She wished she could see his face.

The sight of him bypassed her brain and inflamed her body with hot, dangerous desire. She wanted him with a single-minded intensity that thrust everything from her mind except getting her hands on his hard body. When he buttoned up his blue jeans in front, putting into play the thick muscles of his arms and back, she wanted to howl in frustration.

If he'd been performing in a saloon for ladies, he'd have

earned a fortune. As it was, she was ready to buy him a drink, or anything else he was willing to sell. A man shouldn't be allowed to be so gorgeous. He might take advantage. She was ready for him to do just that, what with her nipples puckering to pebbles, her inner core turning molten, and her skin aching to be stroked.

Yet she could be only so appreciative. She felt like hell. She squeezed her eyes closed. Couldn't stand the light, or the sight. Made her head pound even harder. Felt like she'd been kicked by a horse. Sleep tugged at her again, or maybe she'd been dreaming all along. She floated down into a fantasy where she lassoed her man, slipped a bit in his mouth, and rode him hard.

When she woke up again, teeth chattering with cold, she felt smothered in wet, clammy clothes. Pain pounded in her head like a blacksmith striking an anvil. She couldn't stand the lantern light and kept her eyes squeezed tight. She had to get warm, but felt too tired and too hurt to move.

"Cold," she muttered, her body shivering. "So cold."

Next thing she knew, strong arms lifted her up against a warm body that smelled of sage and leather. Delicious scent. Luscious heat. Wondrous strength. She snuggled, rubbing her face like a contented cat against a bare, muscular chest. If she was still in a dream, she didn't want it to end. She felt safe and secure.

As she was carried across the room, she felt woozy with the movement, so she kept her eyes shut. She tried to collect her thoughts, but they skittered away like wild horses. Darkness claimed her again.

When consciousness returned, she was sitting on the side of a bed, head pounding, body freezing. She took deep breaths to hold down the nausea. No dream, surely.

Strong hands unbuttoned her wet shirt, swiftly, efficiently, and tossed it to the floor. Chills pebbled her flesh, causing her nipples to harden. She quickly crossed her arms over her breasts.

Thoughts raced around in her pounding head. Was she drunk? Had she allowed somebody in the bar too much freedom? She shivered from the chill, the pain, the confusion. If this wasn't a dream, she had to get up and escape, but her body didn't want to obey her.

Next her boots, socks, Levi's, and drawers were stripped away. She was completely naked. And vulnerable.

A soft quilt quickly went around her, wrapping her in blessed warmth. Next strong arms tugged her against a hard chest. When a gentle kiss pressed against her lips, she heard the warning cry of Epona in her head. She was in danger of succumbing to a man, letting him get too close, kiss her, hold her in his arms, see her completely naked.

Clarity rang like a bell in her head. The Deputy! She shoved him away and leaped to her feet, holding the quilt around her like a shield. She swayed, but regained her balance.

"What are you doing?" she demanded, even more alarmed when she saw that he was half naked, too.

"Horse kicked you. You're wet, hurt, cold." He stepped back, giving her space. "You were fading in and out. I had to get those sopping clothes off you and get you warm."

"What about that kiss?" She clinched the quilt with her hands, trying not to succumb to the pain pounding in her head.

"Looked like you needed one."

"What!"

He smiled, shrugged, failed to look innocent. "Body heat. Can't build a fire. Somebody might see it, even in the rain."

"Were you taking advantage? You knew I wasn't thinking straight."

He sighed, running a hand through his still damp hair. "You think a woman has to be out of her mind to want me?"

"If you think every woman wants you, you must be shy a few marbles."

"Must've lost my mind wantin' anything to do with you."

"If you recall, I pulled your fine ass out of the fire."

"My fine what?" He grinned, crossing his arms over his bare chest.

"Nothing." She didn't know how she'd gotten into this argument. All she wanted to do was crawl into bed and sleep for a week. Maybe then her head would stop pounding like a drum.

"You peeked when I changed clothes, didn't you?"

"I was asleep."

"The whole time?"

"You're changing the subject."

He stepped closer. "If you're still cold, I can warm you up."

She frowned, not up to fencing with him. "Why don't you go put on a shirt?"

"Something bothering you?" He gave her a smoldering look with his smoky gray eyes. "Something I can do to help?"

"Go take a walk outside and cool off in the rain."

He chuckled, standing there, long legs spread wide, muscular chest lightly furred, big bulge in his Levi's. He looked like a man way too pleased with himself and his effect on a woman.

She wanted to hit him, or worse, toss him on her bed and have her way with him. But he was the enemy. She'd made a mistake because she was hurt. Once she could forgive herself, but not twice.

Yet Rafe was a stud, a prize stallion worthy of the name.

And she'd just gone into heat.

Chapter 12

Rafe lost his swagger when Lady turned pale, swayed, and sat back hard on the bed. Once more, he felt like a fool. But he had an excuse. Holding her close, seeing her naked, kissing her lips had addled his mind to the point where he wasn't thinking straight.

She was tired, hungry, and injured. He ought to be helping her, not entertaining thoughts of a tryst with a wanted woman, no matter how much she set his cock on fire.

"Okay." He took control of the situation, if not his body. "I'll take care of us."

She glanced up, pulling the quilt tighter. "Horses?"

"Dry, fed, and plum tuckered out."

"Asleep then."

"Brought our stuff in here. Saddles, blankets, saddlebags, rifles. Put our Colts on the table. Give everything a chance to dry out tonight."

"Good."

"Ought to see to our wounds."

"Salve in my saddlebags."

"We treat each other's injuries. Keep it professional."

"Deal."

He walked to the table and started to open her saddlebags, but he felt her gaze on him and glanced back.

"Over here. I'll get what I need." She adjusted the quilt to free one arm, giving a quick glimpse of soft flesh.

He looked away, not needing any reminder of her lush body. Course she didn't trust him. No telling what kind of stolen goods, along with Chinese fireworks, she carried with her. He set her saddlebags on the bed and stepped back from temptation.

"Thanks." She rummaged around before she pulled out a small dark blue jar with a white metal top. She held it up to him. "Best in the world for a quick heal."

"No label." He unscrewed and lifted the lid. Pungent odor almost took off his head. "What in the hell is that stuff?"

"Old family recipe."

"Strong enough to shoo horseflies."

"Horses do like it."

He slammed the lid back on the jar. "Don't you have any people medicine?"

"That's it."

"Works?"

She nodded, wincing as she put a hand to her head and squeezed her eyes shut.

"Don't mean to be a bear," he said in a gentle voice.

She opened her eyes and held up her hand. "Let me rub salve in your wounds. You'll feel better. And the smell goes away."

"Thanks." He handed her the jar.

"Come closer."

He turned his back and knelt in front of her. He was putting a lot of trust in an outlaw. Yet they'd ridden long and hard together. In that time, he'd come to understand that she lived by her own code of honor. She wouldn't try to hurt him, not when he was vulnerable. He'd stake his life on it. And he was.

She started with the abraded ring around his neck, gently applying salve. When she moved on to the bullet graze on his right bicep, he took a deep, steadying breath. She rubbed the salve slowly into one wound after another, even the old scars. He felt almost instant relief from the pain, but she was causing blood to rush south and lodge in his cock. If she didn't stop soon, he was going to ruin his only dry pair of blue jeans.

He gazed out the door at the rain, trying to cool down. *Outlaw. Outlaw. Outlaw.* He chased the word around in his head like the answer to his salvation or the doom of his existence. No matter how he twisted his mind, he couldn't turn his body. He remained ready for action, long, hard, and hot.

"There," she said. "Feel better?"

"Yes. Thanks." She'd eased one pain, but caused another.

Lady leaned forward, holding the quilt in front while letting it slide down to reveal her back. "Got a bullet graze back there. Can you reach it?"

He'd be happy to help her, more than she'd ever know. He sat on the bed and tried not to think about what he really wanted to do. Instead, he focused on her injuries. A bullet had burned across one shoulder blade, another had cut lower on her side, and one had grazed a bicep. He hated to think how close she'd come to death.

"You're lucky," he said, voice tight.

"We both are."

"Hold still. This may sting." He dipped a forefinger in the salve and gently massaged her painful wounds, drawing out the process as long as possible.

"Appreciate it," she said in a husky voice. "Feels better already."

Her voice brought him back to reality. No more touching. He screwed the lid on the jar, tucked it in his pocket, and stood up.

"Ruined my shirt," she said. "Don't know what to sleep in. Everything's wet."

"You can use my dry shirt." The thought made him even harder, if that was possible.

"What will you wear?"

"Don't need one tonight. My other shirt will dry by tomorrow."

"Thanks."

He stalked over to his saddlebags, jerked out his blue chambray shirt, and tossed it to her. "I'll take first watch. Check the horses and put salve on their wounds."

"That's good. You want me to fix food?"

"No. You need sleep."

She pulled two packages out of a saddlebag. "Here's cornpone and beef jerky."

He walked over to the open back door. "You go ahead and eat. I'll get some later."

"Okay. I'll put it on the table for you."

"Looks like the rain is letting up."

"Rafe?"

He glanced back at her wrapped in the colorful quilt, clutching his shirt. The sight made his heart beat way too fast.

"Thanks for the help. Wake me when it's my turn to watch."

"Get some rest."

He leaped out back, not caring if he got wet all over again. Last thing he wanted was to sleep in the same room with Lady Gone Bad, not when she wore nothing but his own damn shirt.

Chapter 13

Lady sat at the kitchen table, the toes of her right foot wedged under a too short table leg to keep the top level as she cleaned her Colt .44. Ammunition lay strewn about a half-eaten can of beans, spoon sticking out of the top. She'd cleaned her Winchester and the long barrel gleamed in the early morning sunlight streaming in through the open front door of the station.

She felt logy headed from her hard night's sleep. She'd stumbled out of bed, no Rafe in sight, checked on the drowsy horses, and relieved herself in the bushes. Back inside, she'd changed out of his shirt into her own damp blue jeans and stained shirt. She'd pulled her hair back into a tight chignon and was ready to go.

At least she wasn't quite as tired as the night before, but she still felt as if she'd been run over by a team of mules. A dull throb and a knot the size of a hen's egg reminded her of the kick to her head.

She'd already packed her saddlebags. Weapons were now top priority. As soon as she loaded them, she'd saddle Jipsey and be on her way. Rafe wouldn't have gone far, not without his horse. Maybe she could get away before he returned and possibly caused trouble. She'd folded his shirt and placed it on the rocker, pushing away a reluctance to part with it, or him. When he didn't waken her for guard duty, she'd slept with his scent all night long. Now she felt as if he'd somehow crawled under her skin along with his smell of sage and leather. She didn't want or need the distraction.

As she spun the cylinder in her six-shooter and reached for cartridges to reload, she heard Epona's warning cry in her head. She glanced up as Rafe stepped inside, a dark, menacing silhouette that filled the doorway.

All the air seemed to leave the room, sucked into his presence. She felt her heart speed up, a fast thud in her chest that left her breathless. She could smell him, sense him, see him with an intensity that belied rational thought. She wanted nothing more than to throw herself into his arms, seeking his lips for a kiss that would drown the aching sorrow of the past, fill the lonely hunger of her soul, and warm her future with heat and passion.

Instinctively, she stood up, feeling a silly smile spread across her face just at the sight of him. Hope swelled in her heart. Maybe life held more than the quest for justice and the fulfillment of her parents' dreams. Perhaps life held something special for her.

"Rafe." She tasted his name on her lips like blackberries and sweet cream. "I guess this is where we part ways." Yet some young place in her heart held out hope that someone would, at last, remain with her.

"Ready to go?" He stepped into the room, boot heels thudding against the wooden floor. Beard stubble accented his strong jaw, giving him the appearance of a desperado.

No warm welcome. All business. No longer in silhouette, she could see the expression on his face, closed, severe, dangerous. Smile fled to frown. Instinctively, she gripped the Colt .44, wishing she'd already loaded her weapon. She fumbled with a bullet, glancing down to see what she was doing although she'd been trained to work in the dark.

"Don't load."

She looked up at him as she pushed a cartridge home and spun the cylinder. One chance, at least, if she needed it.

Sunlight glinted on metal as he pulled an object from behind his back and tossed it on the table, scattering bullets everywhere.

She knew some women might associate metal with a gift of jewelry, rings, or necklaces. Rafe didn't disappoint. He'd chosen bracelets. Trouble was, his gift came with a key. "Handcuffs?"

"Put them on. You're under arrest."

She sat down hard, feeling all her hopes and dreams rush out. Epona's warning had come too late. "You said you wouldn't mention the Hangin' Judge again," she said, reminding him of his promise.

"And I'm keeping my word on that."

"Rafe, I saved your life." She held down her anger through sheer force of will. She must think clearly if she had any hope of turning this to her favor.

"You dang near got me strung up."

"Just a game gone wrong."

"More than that when you're on the business end of a rope."

"You'll never get me out of Indian Territory alive. Fort Smith is a long ride from here. All the outlaws have lookouts."

"We're not going to Fort Smith."

"But that's Indian Territory's court." Confusion warred with anger, making her wonder if she understood anything about him.

"I've got more than one fish to fry." He pointed at the handcuffs. "I'll let you off easy. You can cuff your hands in front."

"But we've been through so much together." She stared at him, trying to find the gentle healer or ardent lover in the hard-faced man confronting her.

"We may be a lot of things, but right now, you're an outlaw and I'm a deputy with a warrant for your arrest."

"Can't you saddle your horse and ride out? Forget you ever saw me?" She gave negotiation one more try.

"No."

Taking a deep, shuddering breath, she looked down at the pistol in her hand. One bullet stood between her and arrest. Could she shoot Rafe? Would he shoot her?

"Don't try."

Beneath the steel in his voice, she heard the slight thread that still connected him to her. She pointed her Colt .44 at his heart. "I've got one shot. Doubt I'll miss at this range."

"Give the court a chance. You're a woman so—"

"Rafe, I can't let you take me in."

"I can't let you go free."

"If you want to live, walk out of here right now."

"Lady . . . Sharlot—"

She caught his tell, a slight narrowing of his eyes, before he lunged at her. She adjusted her aim, going against everything she knew and had been taught, to hit him in the arm, not the heart, as she squeezed the trigger. Yet her six-shooter dry-fired, pin hitting empty cylinder. She rapid-fired as he came at her, but she kept hitting empty. Just as he reached her, grabbing the handcuffs, she finally hit home. A loud bang filled the room and smoke stung her nose as she braced against the recoil of the six-shooter. But the bullet didn't stop him, even though it grazed his shoulder, gouging a red path across his flesh.

Growling, he jerked the Colt .44 from her hands, slammed it on the table, pulled her hands together in front of her, and handcuffed them. When he stepped back, he glared at her with steel gray eyes.

She frowned. "No fair using brute strength."

"Hell! I didn't pull my Peacemaker on you." He glanced

down at his arm where blood stained his torn shirt. "You tried to kill me."

"You're not getting any more of my salve. You can hurt all the way to Fort Smith." She was as mad at herself as at him. If she'd taken true aim, she'd be free now. But he'd be hurt. Maybe dead. She couldn't stand the thought.

"We're not going to Fort Smith."

"Liar! You're taking me to the Hangin' Judge."

"I'm taking you back to Texas."

"Texas?"

"Closest U.S. Marshal is in Paris. We're going there."

"But why take me there?"

"I'm not letting you out of my sight." He sighed, put fingers to his wound, and held out his hand stained with crimson. "You're more trouble than any dozen outlaws."

"That's because I'm righteous."

"You're anything but that." He hesitated, his gaze searching her face. "Would you really have killed me?"

"I'm usually a dead shot."

"Pulled your aim?"

"Wish I hadn't."

"When I finally get you to Fort Smith, you'll probably get some jail time, nothing more."

She felt a sickening drop in the pit of her stomach. She had not a moment to spare. Copper was already on borrowed time. If she didn't find the stallion soon, he'd be put down. If that happened, she'd never get a chance to save him or get justice for her parents.

"Let's load up and get out of here."

"Rafe, please, you don't understand." She tried one last time to reason with him. "You've got to let me go."

"Save it for the judge. I've heard it all before."

"Not *my* story." If he'd been a reasonable man who would listen to her truth and believe her, she'd have told him why she rode the outlaw trail, why she risked her life, why she had no time to waste. But he was a lawman. Without any shred of proof to back up her claim, he'd laugh at her, at the very least. To him, she was an outlaw, nothing more, nothing less. He thought he had the proof to back up his truth, his claim, his right to judge her. But she hadn't survived this long without a few tricks up her sleeve. He'd learn that a woman who couldn't get justice as a lady threw all caution to the wind when she turned bad.

"We'll make Paris by nightfall."

Chapter 14

Rafe rode into Paris, leading Lady on her horse. He didn't trust her not to find a way to sneak off in the crowd of people and animals, so he kept her tethered to him. She was as wily as a coyote, and he didn't want any more trouble.

Paris, a county seat, was up and coming with a courthouse, two hotels, a schoolhouse, and other buildings. After the fire of 1877 destroyed ten acres of the downtown district, residents had lost all faith in clapboard and rebuilt in brick. The Texas and Pacific Railway station looked busy. Thousands lived in Paris, but most of the settlers in the area made their homes on small cotton farms in the rich black gumbo land of the Red River Valley.

Rafe would have liked nothing better than a hot meal and an even hotter bath, topped with a shot of whiskey. Lady appeared about as dirty and tattered as he felt. He thought they must be making a sorry looking pair as they rode up the street. If he'd had the time, or thought he could keep Lady under control, he'd have booked a room at the finest hotel in town, eaten, bathed, and then rested his weary body overnight. But that might lead to weakening his resistance to her. One more of her hot kisses would about make him forget his mission.

His job came first. As quick as possible, he needed to

send a telegram about Lampkin's double life to Judge Parker and Marshal Boles. If Marshal Phillips was in his office, Rafe would alert him, too. The U.S. Senate confirmed U.S. Marshals, who hired their own local deputies. Like Rafe, Lampkin worked for Boles, but Phillips ought to know, too, so he could be on the lookout for trouble.

Rafe nodded to people he passed. He'd gotten used to being out in the country on his own and wasn't sure he much liked the hustle and bustle of town life. People made for complications. They could not be trusted and their motives were often unclear. Neighbors could turn to enemies in the blink of an eye. Guess their shenanigans kept him in business, though, so he shouldn't complain.

"At least let me get a bath and put on clean clothes before you slam a jail door shut behind me," Lady said, kneeing her mare closer to him.

Rafe glanced over at her. "I'd like nothing better myself, but I can't trust you." No more Sharlot. He had to think of her as Lady, a dangerous outlaw not a desirable woman. It helped with the guilt, too.

"I need a bath."

"You can get one in jail."

"With an audience?"

"I'll set it up for you. String a blanket for privacy."

"Look!" She pointed at a store front. "Let's stop at that mercantile with ready-made clothes. You could use a new hat."

"No time." But she was right. He needed one.

"Won't take long. I'll get some soap."

"I don't trust you not to make a break."

"I'm weaponless. You're ruining my life. At the very least, you could give me five minutes to buy a bar of soap."

"You're always dangerous. And I'm not ruining your life. You made the choice to—"

"Forget it." She looked away. "You've got no idea how to treat a lady."

"You really know how to twist the knife in a man." He groaned. "I know I'm going to regret this, but if we stop, do you promise not to do anything except buy soap?"

"Yes!"

"You won't try to escape?"

"No!"

"Okay. You like the looks of that store?"

"Harris Mercantile. Look at that gorgeous crimson gown in the window."

"Are you sure red is the color for jail?"

"I'm Lady Gone Bad. What other color would I wear?"

Rafe stopped in front of the store, squinted down both sides of the street, evaluating the men, the weather, and the lay of the land. Satisfied all appeared safe, he got down, and tossed both horses' reins over the hitching post. He gazed up at Lady. The sight of her made his heart beat fast. She was no-good, ornery, bad luck, but the most fascinating and desirable woman he'd ever met. Best thing he could do was get her out of his life.

She lifted a leg over the saddle horn, and then slid out of the saddle. He caught her around the waist, felt her curves slide through his hands, setting him on fire. When she firmly planted both feet on the ground, she grinned up at him, a challenge and a dare. He stared at her, unable to make his hands do anything except hold her close, knowing it was most likely for the final time.

"Take it easy, Deputy," she purred, sounding like Lady Gone Bad even though she looked bedraggled and down on her luck. "Don't want to get too attached now."

He dropped his hands, but kept one hovering over his Peacemaker. "We can do this easy, or we can do this hard."

"Mmm." She winked at him. "Decisions. Decisions."

"You want soap or you want to go to jail? Either way, I'm not putting up with your antics."

She bit her lower lip, pouted, and then flounced up the wooden steps. He followed, his gaze riveted by her sashaying hips. Much time around her and a man would age fast. Almost be worth it.

He opened the front door for Lady and watched her sail into the store as if she owned it, wearing handcuffs and all. He glanced around. Place carried the usual groceries, such as cured meats, sugar, coffee, cheese, crackers, dried fruits. He saw a big selection of dry goods like denim, calico, and gingham fabrics, plus dress patterns, hats for men and women, and some clothes. He'd check the guns and ammunition that filled one counter. He might even pick up a luxury like peppermint stick candy.

While he was there, he could use some new duds. He'd toss what he was wearing and start over. Life with Lady could be hard on a man in more ways than one.

"I want that red gown in the window," Lady said, walking toward a trim, dark-haired woman in a blue gingham dress.

"You've got good taste. I'm Mrs. Kay Harris, proprietor and owner. Let me know what you want and I'll make sure you get it."

"You have a wonderful selection." Lady looked around. "I don't think I've ever seen so many clothes before."

"I carry more ready-made clothes than any other store in town," Mrs. Harris said with pride. "If you're on the move, I'll even order from a catalog and you can pick it up here. Naturally, I add a small handling fee and you pay in advance."

"That's good to know." Lady smiled. "And convenient."

"We're in a hurry," Rafe said, giving Lady a steely look. "Thought all you wanted was a bar of soap."

"That was before I saw this lovely merchandise."

"Sir, would you like something, too?" Mrs. Harris asked, eyeing Lady's handcuffs and Rafe's clothes, but saying nothing about her customers' appearance.

"Might as well," Rafe said. "Levi's, shirt, socks."

"Hat?"

"Yes." He was sick of the sun beating down on his bare head. Damn the necktie party for trampling his favorite hat. No telling how long it'd take him to get a new one broken in just right. At least it was his hat, not him, lying back in the Bend's mud.

"Preference in color?" Mrs. Harris indicated a stack of plaid shirts in a variety of colors.

"No." He suddenly felt like a bull in a china closet, ready to rampage if they didn't get done soon. At least he could solve his hat problem quick as greased lightin'.

"Blue," Lady said. "Plus, wrap up a gray shirt, charcoal trousers, and gray neckerchief to go with it."

"I don't want to look like a dandy," Rafe said, wondering if a shirt was worth an argument and quickly deciding it wasn't.

"You won't. Besides, it goes with my red dress." Lady pointed at the lingerie. "I also need chemise, drawers, corset, and petticoat for the gown."

"Certainly." Mrs. Harris eyed Lady up and down. "Fortunately, you are of a size that all will perfectly fit you."

"Good."

"By your leave," Mrs. Harris said, clearing her throat, "I must say you've come to me none too soon for clothes. Would you by chance need a key for your bracelets?"

"I've got the key," Rafe said.

"And he's not giving it up easy," Lady added.

"No doubt. Some men do like control." Mrs. Harris quickly took the crimson gown from the window, pulled out lace trimmed muslin underwear, set it out for Lady's decision, and then continued to select other items.

Rafe grumbled to himself, but he wasn't going to get into the fact that Lady wore handcuffs because she was under arrest although that seemed obvious. Let them have their little joke. He didn't want to embarrass Lady by stating the truth, but he had to wonder if she was a woman who could blush.

He tried on several hats. Most were the wrong size, too flashy, or cheap enough to fall apart in the first storm. He settled on a gray John B. with a high crown, wide brim, and a snakeskin band with a silver buckle. Stiff and pricey, but right as rain. He hoped Mrs. Harris picked the correct sizes because he wasn't trying on anything else.

Tugging the Stetson down tight on his head, he glanced impatiently at Lady as she toyed with one bit of fluff and then another, probably delaying going to jail. He got hot at the idea of seeing her wearing nothing but underwear, hard thinking about stripping off her finery, and finally burned imagining his hands on her luscious, naked body.

Trying anything to get his mind off Lady, he opened a jar of peppermint sticks and sniffed the tangy aroma. "I'll take some of these."

"Just a moment and I'll be happy to help you," Mrs. Harris said. "How many do you want?"

"Couple dozen ought to do it. Three boxes of .45 ammunition, too. Better throw in some beef jerky, coffee, cheese, and crackers."

"Certainly, sir."

"I need something practical, too," Lady said as she looked in the glass-fronted cases of merchandise. "I'll take that forest green split riding skirt with the matching blouse. And I need a new hat."

"Perfect for horseback." Mrs. Harris picked up Lady's choices.

"She may not be riding horses for a while," Rafe said, "but she'll look good in it anyway."

"Don't count your chickens before they hatch," Lady snapped, trying on a beige hat. She exchanged it for a bright red one. "Oh, look at that ruffled crimson blouse. I must have it, too."

"Excellent taste." Mrs. Harris quickly stepped away from them as she sorted and added up merchandise. "Just one moment and we'll be all done here."

By the time she had all of their purchases wrapped in paper and tied with string, Rafe wondered where he was going to put so many packages. He supposed he could tie them to the saddlebags till they reached the jail.

"Sir, the total is—" Mrs. Harris said.

"Almost forgot." Lady set down a bar of lavender soap, tossing him a quick grin. "I'm paying." She struggled to pull a coin purse out of her pocket.

"No, she's not." Rafe shouldered Lady aside and set several gold pieces on the counter. "That ought to cover it."

"Yes, indeed, sir." Mrs. Harris smiled, sliding the gold pieces toward her. "Please come back often to shop. I get in new merchandise weekly." She nodded toward Lady's handcuffs. "I carry some lovely jewelry you might want to consider on your next visit."

"Thanks, I'll keep it in mind." Lady tossed Rafe a narrow-eyed look. "You can carry our packages, too." She walked to the front of the store, flung open the door, and stepped outside.

He grabbed their merchandise and followed in Lady's wake. He knew she was mad at him for buying her clothes, but he liked the idea of dressing Lady Gone Bad on his dime. Maybe one day he'd buy her a gold locket or something pretty, but he had to admit, no two ways about it, she looked mighty fine in handcuffs.

He stopped in the doorway, looked carefully down both sides of the street, didn't see any trouble, and stepped into the sun.

Lady waited for him a few paces away. She was reading wanted posters stuck to the building wall. Maybe looking for her own. Suddenly, she jerked down two posters. She glanced at him, then down at the posters as if comparing his face with what was on the paper.

"You'd better take a look." She held out the wanted posters.

"You still trying to buy time?" He clattered down the steps, tied half the packages on his horse and the other half on her mare.

She followed him. "I'm serious. Take a look."

He turned around, grabbed the posters. "Okay." He might as well keep her happy a little longer, so he read, "Wanted Dead or Alive: Lady Gone Bad." He looked from the drawing to her face. "You don't admire your likeness? I admit it doesn't do you justice."

She glanced about, edging closer. "The other poster!"

"Wanted Dead or Alive: Rafe Morgan." He stopped, looked hard at the poster, reread the words, and realized his jaw had gone slack in astonishment.

She jerked the posters out of his hands and swung up on her mare. "Let's get the hell out of Paris."

Chapter 15

"You think I've got a yellow stripe down my back?" Rafe glared, body rigid, hands fisted.

"No," Lady snapped. "I think we're both in danger of hanging for no good reason."

"We're going straight to the jail, to put you behind bars, and set this misunderstanding about me straight."

She shook the wanted posters in his face, handcuffs jingling. "You believe they'll trust your word over your poster?"

"I'm a Deputy U.S. Marshal."

"Not now! You've been stripped of your badge and your image is on a wanted poster." She waved the posters. "Look, you're not listed here as a deputy marshal."

He rocked back on his heels. "Lampkin! That dirty, conniving rattlesnake."

"Let's get out of here." She pulled her hat low to conceal her face, and dropped the wanted posters in the dirt.

Rafe shook his head. "I can't run away. I'm not made that way. I need to explain that Lampkin is the turncoat, not me. He lied. Set me up." He gave her a hard stare. "You'll explain about the Bend, the outlaws, everything."

"Why should I help you stay out of jail when you're so determined to put me in it?" She turned Jipsey north as she looked back at Rafe. "We're sitting ducks here. You coming?"

"You're using this as an excuse to run." He grabbed his reins and leaped into his saddle.

"Run?" She laughed. "Not me." She wanted to drum heels against the mare's sides and leave Rafe and Paris in her dust as fast as four hooves could take her, but that'd be drawing too much attention. She urged Jipsey forward at a sedate pace.

Rafe rode up beside her. "I'm thinking we'll be better off in Fort Smith."

"Not me. We're both hunted now. Lot of miles to Arkansas."

He glanced around, his right hand hovering over his Peacemaker.

"Eyes everywhere. Indians. Outlaws. Citizens." She tried to ease the itch in the center of her back, feeling as if she was the target of somebody's rifle, wanting him to feel it, too.

"Deputy marshals and lighthorsemen," he said.

She smiled, shrugged. "I doubt we've been recognized. We're so dirty and scruffy our own mothers wouldn't know us."

"Justice," he said.

"Pretty showy." She kept watch in every direction, alert for anything out of the ordinary. "You pick out that chestnut your own self?"

"Gift."

"Lady friend?"

"Sister."

"Your sister gave you that horse knowing you're a lawman who needs to fade into the background?"

"Long story."

"I'd like to hear it."

"Not now."

"For a law and order type of man, I'm beginning to think you shelter a lot of shady secrets."

"Unlike you."

"We all do what we have to do." She glanced around, clearing her head, sizing up opportunities. If she got Rafe arrested, she could escape, but to do that she needed to draw attention to him. Unfortunately, that'd put her in the calaboose, too. She had to come up with a better plan. Now that he was in a pickle, maybe she could use him to help her. At the very least, he sure as hell wasn't taking her in to the law, not with his own neck on the line. If he didn't realize that fact now, he'd come to that realization pretty quick. She just had to keep him from doing something stupid before reality hit him.

Rafe glanced back at the courthouse, half turning his horse in that direction.

She kicked his boot to draw his attention to her. "What really makes us obvious are these bracelets. And think, if you get put in jail, how are you going to clear your name?"

"Damn Lampkin's hide."

Heads turned, watching them.

"Look, let's take it easy till we get out of Paris." She gave him an encouraging nod, hoping to bolster his confidence in her. "Better yet, till we cross the Red River. Once we're in Indian Territory, we'll be safe. You can tell me about this Lampkin. We can figure out a plan."

Rafe narrowed his eyes to a squint, drilling her with a long, steady, assessing look. He gave a curt nod. "Never in a million years would I have thought I'd be taking the advice of Lady Gone Bad."

Chapter 16

Rafe sat in an outhouse. Dim light slanted in through the quarter moon cut in the gray wood of the closed door. Golden light from a kerosene lantern illuminated ladies lingerie in the popular Wish Book, Montgomery Ward's impressive 240-page, 10,000-item mail order catalog. Rafe had plenty of wishes. And, at the moment, most of them involved Lady. While he contemplated which lacy undergarment would look best on her luscious body, he listened to her splash around naked as a jaybird in a galvanized tin tub just outside a ramshackle hay barn.

She had more tricks up her sleeve than a seasoned gambler, a fact he was coming to appreciate. Once he'd made up his mind to run from the law with her, they'd ridden hard out of Paris, determined to put as much distance as possible between them and their wanted posters. Safety lay on the north side of the Red River, but with tired horses and night coming on, they'd decided to play it smart and cross the next morning. That left them in desperate need of a safe haven. Once more Lady had come through with a plan. Now they were hidden in a lonely spot just south of the Red River.

For the first time since meeting her, Rafe had a little space and time to gather his wits, strength, and focus. He wished he was using it to good purpose, but about all he could conjure up were images of Lady putting on a show in that tin tub.

She sang while a mangy bird dog howled a few octaves higher. Quite a duet. Felt like he ought to buy the dog a drink.

He couldn't decide whether to be mad or glad. True he had more time with the most fascinating woman in the West, but on the other hand, he was up the creek in a leaky boat. He hoped he could trust Lady, at least enough to forge a trail so convoluted no lawman could follow them. He also hoped they could trust the couple who owned the place where they were hiding out. Lady had said she'd done the farmers a favor once and they'd be glad to help. Seemed they were. He sure couldn't complain about the fried chicken, mashed potatoes, gravy, green beans, biscuits, and blackberry cobbler. He'd eaten his fill until he couldn't hold another crumb.

The couple had given them permission to use the barn on the far side of their property, and their dog had accompanied them. He wondered how Lady could engender so much trust when she was a known outlaw. It made no sense. But since he'd met her, not a lot in his life had made any sense. Now his own face was on a wanted poster. He couldn't hardly bear thinking of the consequences, but he must address them sooner or later. Not just yet though.

He finished his business, set the catalog aside a few pages lighter, picked up the lantern, and eased open the door. Moonlight brightened the evening. Frogs sang lustily in a nearby pond. Lightning bugs flashed on and off as they chased each other. The scent of wild flowers filled the air. It was a night made for lovers.

Even though he and Lady were on opposite sides of life, it didn't mean he couldn't appreciate her attributes. Not that he trusted her. That'd be like not heeding a rattler's warning. Still, a man in his position would be a fool not to get help where he could find it. He'd taken the handcuffs off her, but he'd stowed them in his saddlebags next to her arrest warrant.

An evening like this reminded him of home and his sister Crystabelle. Twenty-nine now, he'd been old enough to remember fear and hunger during the Civil War, but also the warmth and security of a winter fire in a snug log cabin in the Kentucky mountains. When his father went off to war, Rafe had become the man of their small family. Half-grown with skinny arms and legs, he'd hunted, fished, chopped wood, anything to help keep them alive. They'd made it, but like so many good men, his father never came back.

Lonely and alone, his mother had insisted they follow her sister to Arkansas and then on to Texas. Both his mother and aunt had died of chickenpox. He'd been left to raise Crystabelle alone. She was three years younger than he. He'd known she needed more than he could offer, so he'd made enough money to board her at the Bonham Female Academy in Texas. She had graduated and taught there a few years before deciding to spend a week that summer in Fort Smith to be near him.

She'd never made it. Kidnapped by outlaws, she'd disappeared into the wilds of Indian Territory. No matter how hard he'd tried, he'd learned nothing more about her or the men who'd taken her. He'd planned to see if Marshal Phillips had gotten any word in Paris, but that hadn't happened. Another reason to curse Lampkin.

What gave him hope that Crystabelle still lived was the horse. She'd either had Justice delivered to Fort Smith to let him know she was alive, or the outlaws who'd taken her had delivered the gelding as a stab in the eye. He had to find out which was the truth. She was all the family he had left. He loved her. But he felt guilty, too. If she hadn't been coming to see him, she'd still be safe in Bonham.

Maybe this crazy wanted poster business was a blessing in disguise, putting him in a better position to find Crystabelle. Lady knew outlaws and their hideouts. If Crystabelle was being held hostage by desperados, Lady stood a good chance of leading him to his sister. Not that he was on Lady's good side, not after arresting her. Still, he'd been known to sweet-talk a woman. If that didn't work, threats and incentives might do the trick.

Following the lure of Lady's voice, he walked quietly toward her, figuring she wouldn't hear him approach while she sang.

Some old rounder come along,
Took my sugar babe and gone.
I ain't got no sugar baby now.
No, I ain't got no sugar baby now.

Rafe snorted, shaking his head at her words. One thing for sure, Lady would never be short of sugar.

He heard the cock of a pistol about the time he saw Lady raise her six-shooter with one hand while crossing her other arm over her naked breasts. That still left a lot of exposed flesh to tantalize a man.

Damn dog growled low in his throat, almost as threatening as Lady herself. He couldn't decide whether to run for cover or grovel at her feet as the best thing he'd seen since Lulu the Naked Lady had emptied men's hearts and wallets when she'd stopped off in Fort Smith on her Sensational Tour of the Wild West.

"Get your hands in the air," Lady commanded, aiming her Colt .44 at his midsection. "And identify yourself."

"It's me." Rafe raised the lantern so she could see his face. "Don't go off half-cocked and kill me."

She lowered her six-shooter. "Thought you'd be a while."

"I got inspired." He walked closer, wanting to see more.

"Did you sneak over here to ogle me?"

"Thought crossed my mind."

"Well, stop it."

"If you'll share your bath, you can ogle me."

"You're so dirty no woman would want to share a bath with you." She set aside the revolver, and patted the dog on his boney head.

"Some women *like* dirty."

"Only in men's minds." She pointed past the dog. "Please hand me my towel. This rascal drug it off."

Rafe wished the dog had run away with the towel. He picked it up and stood over her. With the lantern in his other hand, he could see that water lapped just under her breasts, only partially obscuring everything below. When she looked up, he followed the smooth line of her exposed throat to her full lips. Hunger burned in him like a demon. He was ready to fall to his knees if he could just get his mouth, hands, body on her.

The dog growled as if reading Rafe's mind, and stood up in a threatening position.

"Call off your dog." He stood his ground. Last thing he needed was a dog bite.

"You disturbed our duet. Makes a dog cranky."

"Makes a man cranky, too."

She chuckled, acknowledging his allusion to sex. "You seem to be getting over your sudden transformation from lawman to outlaw."

"I've been distracted, what with riding hell-bent for leather, eating enough vittles to choke a horse, and listening to you warble in your bath."

She sighed, patting the dog's head. "Down boy."

"Me or him?"

"Both." She held out a hand for the towel. "I'm used to men ogling me, but normally I'm dressed and it's business. No time for games now and you know it."

Reluctantly, he tossed the towel to her, keeping a wary eye on the dog. Maybe he wasn't playing games anymore. Maybe Lady had gotten so deep under his skin he'd never be free of her. He didn't like the idea, couldn't afford to even imagine it. He was determined to cool down, think with his mind, not his cock.

"You want to use my bathwater, or do you want fresh? I can heat some more water on the campfire, but it'll take a while."

She might as well have grabbed his cock and jerked hard with both hands. The idea of getting into water that had caressed her naked body, lapping at her openings, almost sent him over the edge.

He swallowed, finally able to speak. "No need. This'll do."

"Think so?"

"Yes."

"Look away."

He reluctantly averted his eyes while she got out of her bath. When he glanced back, the towel wrapped around her body only emphasized the jut of her breasts and the swell of her hips.

"If you don't mind lavender, you can use my bar of soap. It's on the ground. I'll go get you one of the wash-rags and towels they loaned us."

"Thanks." He set the lantern beside the tin tub.

"Dog'll guard you."

"I'd feel safer if you were here with your six-shooter." He tried to sound needy, not hard to do when he was about to bust his buttons.

She hesitated, glanced around, and then looked back at him. "I don't think anybody can find us here, but maybe you're right. Best to be cautious. I'll be right back."

He watched her sashay, barely covered by the towel, into the barn and out of sight. Dressed up in satin, some women might promise more than they could deliver. Not so with Lady. In satin or out of it, she delivered in spades.

Quickly unbuttoning and jerking off his shirt, he was as ready to get into her bathwater as he was into her bed. Maybe he could at least persuade her to wash his back.

Chapter 17

Lady sat outside the circle of lantern light that cast Rafe in a golden glow. She had her legs tucked to one side, Colt .44 near her right hand, and the dog's head resting on her knee. A coyote yipped in the distance, and was answered by several companions. Familiar sounds, comforting in the same way Rafe's splashing in the water and the quiet country night soothed her, reminding her of happier times.

She'd always liked sitting with Ma and Da on the back porch of their ranch house on an evening when chores were done and night had fallen. They'd been lazy together, full of good cooking and tired from a day's satisfying work. She could almost smell the pungent aroma of Da's pipe and hear Ma's knitting needles click as she knit by touch alone. Maybe a horse would snort, whinny, or kick a board in the barn, and then all would be peaceful again.

Horses. Everybody knew Indian Territory had the best horses, stolen or otherwise. Da was good as a Comanche at breeding, raising, and training the beautiful beasts. And that was saying something since the Comanche knew horses like the back of their hands. People arrived from far and wide to buy from Da, but he was choosy about who he let lead away one of his family, for that was how he regarded every living being on the ranch.

Family. Ma was kind to all who came her way. At home, she always had a scrap of food for a stray dog, chicken, or motherless critter. She never criticized Da when he turned away good gold for a prize horse if he thought the buyer might be mean to animals. And he never asked enough when he thought the buyer would be kind.

Home. Ma and Da had provided enough food to eat and clothes to wear, for they gardened, raised chickens, cooked, canned, sewed, and hunted. Gold bought the extras like books, sugar, salt, shoes, metal goods, and a little extra in case of hard times.

When Lady looked back on those golden days, she couldn't imagine how life could have been any better. They'd loved and laughed all day, every day. Sure, they'd had problems, but they'd solved them together.

Da had been training her to take over with the horses someday, but at that time she couldn't imagine a moment when he couldn't or wouldn't want to work with his beloved animals. She still found it hard to believe her parents were gone. Sometimes in the dead of night she'd wake up and all would seem normal, but then the pain of their loss would wash over her. Nothing was the same, nor ever would be again.

Da had always said she'd been given a divine gift, that Epona, Goddess of Horses, spoke in her ear, and he cautioned her to never give Epona a reason to withdraw the special totem power. Ma believed Spider Grandmother had spun a web around her daughter's throat at birth, granting the powerful medicine of a golden voice to weave and share the people's stories. They'd impressed upon her that she had a responsibility never to squander her gifts and to always respect her totem power.

Tears filled Lady's eyes. If Ma hadn't been Indian, of Choctaw and French heritage, and forced West into Indian Territory . . . If Da hadn't been American of Irish ancestry and gone West in search of freedom and land for horses . . . If she hadn't been picking blackberries when Da turned down one outlaw too many . . . If not for all those ifs that made them vulnerable, yet blessed with love and plenty, she'd still be Sharlot Eachan. She'd be a well brought up young lady, the apple of her parents' eyes, not Lady Gone Bad, a notorious outlaw and dance hall singer.

Yet all would be worth her fall from grace if Epona helped her locate Copper's trail, and Spider Grandmother spun a gossamer web of deception that allowed her to rescue the stallion and achieve justice. She must make it happen. She must remain free. And to achieve both, she must enlist the support of this lawman.

Deputy U.S. Marshal Rafe Morgan. She should hate him for putting her in handcuffs, making her feel vulnerable, turning her into a prisoner, trying to put her behind bars. But she didn't hate him. She couldn't. He had saved her life. In doing so, he'd lost the life he knew, a good life as a respected lawman.

Luck had turned in her direction. Maybe Epona, maybe Spider Grandmother, wove the magic of him, sending him into her upside-down life. With him beside her, the tables had turned and she finally had an acceptable hand to play. Play it she would.

She'd put on her new split-skirt and blouse. She felt good, clean, fresh after all the hard days on the trail. Cuts and scrapes, aches and pains didn't matter so much now that she was well fed, clean, safe, and free.

Rafe had been the bane of her existence since she'd first met him, but if she wanted to be honest with herself, he was a surprising pleasure, too. She mustn't let him know that fact. After all, she was the elusive Lady Gone Bad, notorious for tormenting men in Texas and Indian Territory until she got her way. One lawman on the run couldn't be that much trouble to bring to heel.

"Rafe," Lady said, not trusting herself to look too closely at him when he was naked a few steps away. Maybe she didn't trust him either, not when so much boiled between them. "I want to ask—"

"How about—"

"Excuse me," she said, "You go first."

"A spot on my back hurts. Feels infected. But I can't reach it."

"You want me to wash it for you?"

"Appreciate your help." He held out the soap and washrag.

She holstered her Colt .44, patted the dog on his head, and knelt beside the small, round tin tub. Rafe sat with his knees almost under his chin. He smelled like lavender, a scent that was surprisingly sensual on him. She wanted nothing more than to caress the hard muscles of his bare chest, run her fingers through his thick hair, burn hot kisses into his skin so he'd be branded forever.

Instead, she took the soap and washrag. "Lean forward so I can get a better look." She wasn't letting this excuse to touch him go to waste. "I better wash your entire back."

"Thanks."

She soaped up the washrag and gently rubbed the inflamed wound on his shoulder blade. As she washed his back, she felt inflammation move from him to her, causing her body to burn.

"Feels good."

Felt good to her, too, but she had to focus on her goals, not her desires. Time was running out for Copper. She desperately needed to get their plans in place. "I wonder what you're going to do about your wanted poster."

"I wonder the same about you."

"A lot rides on what we do next." She hesitated, and then plunged ahead. "I guess my bark is worse than my bite."

"How so?"

"I'm not really an outlaw." She felt his back muscles tense under her hand.

"I've heard that before." He started to turn toward her in the tub, but couldn't. "Come around here where I can see your face."

"You think I'd lie?"

"Let's just say I want to see you."

She set down the soap and washrag. She moved around so she faced him, lantern light on both their faces. She needed to read his expressions, too.

"Now what do you want to tell me?" Rafe asked, his eyes a steely gray.

She wished she could trust him with the complete truth, or even think that he'd believe the truth. Instead, she had to tell him something that he would hopefully accept. "Truth is, I'm riding the outlaw trail to find a young stallion that was stolen from me. His bloodline is vital for my future plans."

"A horse?"

"Not just any horse. Copper is unique, but he's got a problem. He's wearing one special horseshoe to correct a hoof. He'll outgrow that shoe soon. If it's not changed, he'll go lame and be put down."

"Won't somebody notice the horseshoe before that happens?"

"Not likely."

"You've been putting your life on the line for a horse?"

"Yes. He's family."

"You're willing to go to jail for this animal?"

"I can't go to jail! He'll be dead by the time I get out."

"Can't your parents, or brothers and sisters, find this horse?"

"No." She felt tears burn in the back of her eyes, but she refused to let her pain show.

He shook his head, but didn't say more about it. "You've been breaking the law."

"Prove it."

"You either break the law, or you don't break the law. There's no in-between."

"I consort with lawbreakers. That doesn't mean I break the law." She struggled to find a way to reach him, to make him understand. "I'm trying to find Copper's trail. I gather a little information here and there, among outlaws, among horse thieves."

"You mean you sing to liquored-up men who'll tell you anything to get and keep your attention." His eyebrows drew together in a frown.

She looked down at the sleeping dog to control her temper, then glanced back at Rafe. "What about that Lampkin who set you up?"

He ran a hand through his wet hair. "Lampkin's a Deputy U.S. Marshal like me, but I saw him riding with the lynch mob."

"He shot at us?"

"Yep." Rafe snorted in disgust. "I couldn't believe it at first cause he's one of Marshal Bole's favorites. Problem is, he knows I saw him. He knows I'll turn him in. He's aimin' to put the noose around my neck, not his."

"If you'd ridden straight to Paris and not come with me—"

"I'd never have known Lampkin was working both sides of the fence."

"But you'd be safe now. No reward on your head."

"Figure Lampkin set that up, too."

Lady quickly thought through her options. "I'll help you if you'll help me."

"What do you want?"

"If you'll keep me out of jail and help me find Copper,

I'll help you get the information you need to clear your name."

"How can you do that?"

"I get information from outlaws, remember."

Rafe rubbed his jaw, considering. "True. But if we help each other, you've still got to face Judge Parker."

"Let's make that part of our deal. Once your name is cleared and we find Copper, you can arrest the outlaw who stole my horse. After I've helped you, perhaps Judge Parker could see his way to clearing my name."

"I doubt he'd be against it, not if you helped bring two criminals to justice. I'd put a good word in for you, too." He gave her a hard stare. "But you'd have to mend your ways. No more consorting with outlaws."

"When I have Copper safely back, I'll have no reason to." What she didn't say was that when he caught the horse thieves, he'd also be arresting her parents' murderers. Justice, finally.

"I hope you mean it. Some people can't give up the excitement of being bad."

"I'm just a simple girl at heart."

He shook his head, chuckling. "Nothing simple about you."

She smiled, relieved that they'd struck a good bargain.

"Why don't you sing a song for me?"

She gave him a slow, sultry smile, and sang the first line of a ballad about finding true love.

Chapter 18

For once, the Red River came up aces. As Rafe glanced down from the bluff above, midday sunlight burnished the river crimson. He checked their back trail, remembering their past wild ride. This time was different. No necktie party. No raging water. No deadly bullets. And nobody followed them.

He glanced over at Lady. She held her chin high in determination. He felt the way she looked. Come hell or high water, they had to achieve their goals. No choice. No turning back. No second chances.

He was glad to be riding on a good night's sleep and a full stomach. They'd given the peppermint sticks, plus some coffee and sugar, to the kind couple for their hospitality. After that, they'd rearranged what was left of their purchases into feed sacks and tied them over their saddlebags. He wished they were traveling lighter, but they'd probably need the stuff they'd bought in Paris before all was said and done.

At dawn, they'd crossed into Indian Territory near the Boggy River, which meandered across one corner of Choctaw Nation to empty into the Red River.

Lady wanted to follow the Boggy north to Clear Boggy Creek. He let her lead, but it didn't sit well with him. He knew his way around, but not into outlaw hideouts. He felt uneasy depending on her. For that matter, everything about his situation made him uneasy. But there was no help for it.

He didn't say anything. She didn't either. Silence suited them. Too much rode beneath the surface. He didn't want to break their truce by asking unwelcome questions. He figured she felt the same way.

Truth was, he didn't trust Lady's story completely. Yet she'd struck a chord when she'd referred to the horse as family. He played his cards close to the vest, too. Crystabelle was never far from his thoughts. He'd stay on the lookout for her in outlaw hideouts.

Trust was a hard won commodity. It had to be earned. Maybe in time, he and Lady could come to trust each other. Maybe not.

By late afternoon, he was ready for a break. The horses were snatching bites of tall grass as they followed a narrow trail, so he knew they were ready, too. Lady rode ahead, intent on her mission. Driven. He wondered what or who really drove her. He'd seen the pain in her eyes when he'd asked about family. He wondered if one of the outlaws she'd consorted with meant more to her than she let on. Was she out to get revenge for a missing lover? A husband? No way to know.

So far, their mounts appeared to have no bottom, but he didn't want to push too far and find out different. A big oak tree up ahead with limbs spreading across the stream appeared a likely place to hole up for a spell.

"Lady," he called, "let's take a break."

She glanced back, looked where he pointed, and broke trail.

As he followed her into the shade of the oak, birds shrieked in protest and rose into the air. A white-tailed jack rabbit leaped into the bushes and disappeared. Rafe circled the tree, checked the area for tracks, for danger. All appeared safe.

He dismounted and led Justice down to the river. While the gelding drank, he kept his eyes wary and his hand by his Peacemaker. No point taking chances, particularly in Indian and outlaw country.

"Want to break out the cornpone and jerky?" Lady asked, stroking Jipsey's neck as the mare drank deeply.

"Sounds good."

"We ought to arrive at Boggy Saloon about sundown. No point getting there any sooner. Place would be deserted."

"Which outlaws go there?"

"Depends."

"On what?"

"If it's a favorite watering hole, or somebody just happens to be in the area."

"They'll be dangerous."

She nodded, looking Rafe up and down. "They don't cotton to strangers."

"But you'll take care of that."

"They won't ask your name. Nobody'd be that foolish. But they'll expect you to use an alias."

He considered a different name, absently rubbing the persistent itch of the rough, raw hanging mark around his neck. He looked out across the river, dark green in the shade of the spreading oak. Frogs jumped off the bank and splashed into the water. Justice stamped a hoof and swished his tail at buzzing flies.

"Any ideas?" Lady asked.

"You've had more experience at this than me."

"True blue John Law, right?"

"Been doing my best."

"I'll let them know you're a fast gun, strong arm."

"And your man?" He glanced over at her, tossing a quick smile to challenge her. "Why else would I be with you?"

She studied the stream. "Maybe I needed some help."

"Not likely. You're Lady Gone Bad."

She shrugged. "You could be family. A cousin. We'll see how it plays out."

He grinned, imagining how he'd play it. "What about my name?"

"Seeing as how you're John Law, let's call you Fast John."

"Fast John?" He snorted in disgust. "That's not clever. Lady Gone Bad and Fast John? Hardly seems fair."

She chuckled. "We don't want to be too smart, do we?"

"I get a song, too?"

"Let me think about that one." She winked, smiling as she led Jipsey to a grassy area and dropped the reins.

He followed her, wishing all the world would disappear. With enough time alone with Lady, maybe he could figure out the real woman behind the masks that appeared to come and go so easily with her. He felt sure the kind farmers wouldn't have recognized her as a dance hall singer, a scrappy boy, or an outlaw. They'd thought she was a helpful cowgirl.

"On second thought," he said, letting Justice graze beside Jipsey, "I don't want you to write me a song. No telling what you'd say."

"We're talking about Fast John." She grinned. "Would that be with pistol in hand?"

He eyed her warily.

"Would that be mighty impressive to a man, or kicked out of bed by a woman?"

He groaned, shaking his head. Trust Lady Gone Bad to

come up with a clever play on words that was sure to make a man's head spin.

She laughed, cleared her throat, and sang.

Quick John, Slow Johnny,
Apple of the ladies' eyes.

Rafe laughed hard. He could get used to having her around. Life would never be dull. When she joined his laughter, he wanted nothing more than to prove just how slow and attentive John Law could be. He'd have her singing, all right, but it'd be to his tune, not hers.

Chapter 19

Lady grew more alert and cautious as they neared the notorious Boggy Saloon nestled near the apex of the Boggy River and Clear Boggy Creek. On one side, the Boggy gurgled its way downstream. On the other, tall trees vied with grass high enough to tickle a horse's belly. She could smell wood smoke even though the night wouldn't be much cooler than the day. Probably somebody was cooking up a mess of pinto beans and ham hocks. Not as good as farm food, but saloon patrons would contentedly chow down on filling fare as long as whiskey kept flowing down their gullets.

She glanced over at Rafe. He'd pass as a gunslinger now that he wore his fancy gray shirt, gray neckerchief, black leather vest, charcoal trousers, and black boots. He'd buckled his Peacemaker low on his right hip. At the barn, she'd used a pair of scissors she'd borrowed from the farmers to cut his hair short. He'd let his mustache grow in dark and thick. With his transformation complete, he appeared even more daring and dangerous than usual.

She had to admit Rafe excited her, now more than ever. A shame they were at cross purposes, or he just might be the man to finally make a believer out of Lady Gone Bad.

She hoped that nobody would connect Fast John with Rafe Morgan. If somebody recognized his flashy horse, he'd just have to explain that he'd stolen the gelding from some no-count John Law.

Anything could happen at the Boggy Saloon because anybody might show up. In case there was trouble, she'd opted to wear her Levi's since she could move easier in blue jeans and draw her Colt .44 faster from her hip. Still, she needed to appear as Lady Gone Bad, so she wore the ruffled, low-cut crimson blouse from Paris. Matched her red boots, too. That'd satisfy her audience.

"Let's go in with attitude," Lady said, glancing back at Rafe.

"I never saw you go anywhere without it." He rode up close beside her, his black boot strafing her red one as their horses moved forward together.

"Just doing what works." She shrugged. "If somebody talks about cashing in his six-shooter, please ignore the fact that he's referring to a bank holdup."

"And if I recognize a face from a wanted poster, I'll try to resist cuffing him and taking him to the Hangin' Judge."

"Don't even think such a thing. When you get into your role as gunslinger, you must stay there. Live it. Breathe it."

"I'm not used to playing parts like you."

She pulled Jipsey to a halt so she could stare into Rafe's eyes. "Listen! If any one of them catches a whiff that you're not who you're supposed to be, we're both dead. They won't question us. They won't give us a trial. They won't let us walk out. They take no chances."

"I know. They put me on the wrong end of a hangin' noose just for looking at you."

"You were sniffing around their turf ready to make an arrest."

"Set their backs up, didn't it?"

She rolled her eyes, shaking her head at the way he downplayed the situation.

"And you didn't help matters." Rafe jerked a thumb toward her.

"I saved your neck, so it all evens out in the end."

"If you say so."

"I do." She gave him a hard look. "They're tough, no doubt. But we're not shrinking violets either."

He grinned, mischief dancing in his gray eyes. "Not by a long shot."

"You ready to brave the bears in their own den?"

"Might as well." He glanced toward the saloon, then back at her.

She nodded, her heart speeding up, anticipating battle, fingertips tingling with excitement. "Let's go."

As the sun descended in the west, Lady led Rafe across packed ground to the front of the saloon, long shadows stretching away from them. The place looked like a rundown farmhouse, its rough hewn logs grayed with age. Two large rooms were connected by an open dog trot under a single shake-shingle roof. Two square windows darkened with soot seemed to watch their approach. Smoke curled up from a river-rock chimney.

Several horses were tied to the hitching posts in front. She checked them over, pleased to see the Hayes Brothers' sorrels were already there. If she got Ma Engle's funeral jewelry from them, she could focus on Copper. She only hoped they hadn't thrown it away.

She stopped Jipsey at the hitching post in front of the saloon half of the building. The other half held a dozen bunks so patrons could sleep off liquor and fistfights or hide from the law. Rafe eased up beside her. They exchanged a meaningful look, nodded, dismounted, and adjusted their gun belts.

So far, so good. Lady took a deep breath. Not too busy. Maybe they could get in and get out without causing trouble. But she was prepared, always prepared, for the worst.

As she walked into the shadow of the dogtrot, the doors to the saloon and the bunks stood open, letting out the stench of liquor, tobacco, and sweat. Gulping one last breath of clean air, she stepped up the two sagging wooden steps to the saloon, feeling Rafe right behind her, warm and strong. She hesitated a moment, waiting for all eyes to find her.

The Boggy Saloon didn't have a woman's touch, not even close. Floors had long ago turned dark with grime, tobacco that had missed spittoons, dried beans, and spilled whiskey. Men sporting face-hiding whiskers and filed-down pistols sat at tables playing poker and downing whiskey.

Everything in the room had been hacked from nearby trees, and then put back together in the shape of tables, chairs, and a bar made from one long tree trunk split down the middle. Time had turned the wood dark. Hands had smoothed off the rough edges.

The Hayes Brothers, two broad-shouldered giants with wild, black hair and beards, wearing red plaid shirts, black wool trousers with suspenders, and heavy work boots, leaned against the bar. Each held a shot glass.

Saloonkeeper Crowdy, a rangy Cherokee with high cheekbones and a square jaw, set down two blue porcelain coated tin bowls loaded with beans and two spoons. He added a bottle of whiskey.

She'd known Crowdy since she was a kid. No telling his age, not with his smooth, walnut-tinted skin and thick black hair. In the past, he'd dropped by the ranch and helped Da with the horses. She trusted him to never reveal her true identity.

Crowdy glanced up and saw her. "Hey, Lady! Lady Gone Bad." He motioned her inside, a slight smile curving his lips. "Look here, b'hoys, best treat in Indian Territory."

Lady plastered on her famous smile, bright and white with just the hint of a tease, and stepped into the room. All activity stopped. Drinks and cards were dropped to focus on her. She put a hand on her hip, and chuckled, a low, seductive sound.

"Lady . . . Lady . . . Lady."

She heard her alias go round the room, watched the men's eyes brighten with excitement, and felt the usual responsibility not to disappoint.

For a moment, she couldn't quite recall her role. Rafe's fault, she realized. He'd insisted she be real with him, even wanted to know her real name. She'd gotten into the habit of reality. She'd even been finding the way back to herself, little by little. Now she must thrust truth aside and be what these men, and others, wanted her to be. Tears blurred her vision. Ridiculous as it seemed, she felt like a damsel in distress. She had an impulse to turn around, bury her face against Rafe's strong chest, and make Lady Gone Bad go away.

Shocked, she stood completely still, smile plastered in place. She couldn't allow Rafe to make her weak, forget her duty, run away with fear. Nothing mattered except justice. She must achieve it no matter what price she had to pay.

"Hey, boys," Lady said, blinking back tears and letting her voice drop to a low, sultry tone. "I heard there were some handsome hombres holed up here at the Boggy. I just had to stop by and see for myself."

Behind the bar, Crowdy nodded, keeping dark eyes on the crowd.

Lady made a show of looking around the room, judging each man in turn. "Let's see." She put a forefinger to her chin, and then cocked her head to one side. "I do believe the rumors are true. I've just got to spend a little time here."

"Dang fools," Rafe whispered behind her.

She pretended to ignore him, but wanted to clamp a hand over his mouth to keep him quiet. She could only hope nobody heard him. "Any handsome hombre here willing to buy a lady a drink?"

"Free drink for every song you sing," Crowdy said, holding up a shot glass and pointing the open end toward her.

"You mean, you want me to work for my whiskey?" Lady batted long eyelashes and pouted crimson lips.

"Land sakes, mosey over here," Burt Hayes said. "Share our bottle."

"Choc, too," Bob Hayes added.

"You're so kind." Lady smiled, shuddering at the thought of strong Choctaw beer as she let her gaze travel over each man again. "I might even sing a little song, if nobody objects."

"Lady . . . Lady . . . Lady."

"Later, boys. Let me wet my whistle first." And then, as if just remembering, she moved aside and held out a hand toward Rafe.

He stepped up into the saloon.

"Who's that?" Crowdy hissed, picking up his shotgun and pointing the business end toward the open doorway.

"Fast John." Lady smiled, intentionally keeping her hand away from her Colt .44 by fluffing her hair with her right hand to indicate neither she nor Rafe meant trouble. "I met him in the Bend. Likes to play cards."

All eyes fastened on Rafe like an eagle sighting prey. Hands dropped to six-shooters. Crowdy cocked his shotgun.

"I told Fast John he might like to cool his heels for a bit in Indian Territory," Lady said, implying Rafe was running from the law. "And I told him everybody at the Boggy likes to play poker."

Despite her brave words, she felt her heart beat fast, wondering if the outlaws would shoot first and ask questions later.

Chapter 20

"Indian Territory looks a mite more hospitable than Tombstone." Rafe kept his voice firm but friendly. He couldn't show weakness, or aggression either. He walked a narrow ledge. One he'd trod before.

"Come from there?" Crowdy broke the standoff, but kept his aim.

Rafe smiled down at Lady, put his left arm around her waist, and tugged her close. "Got nothing like Lady Gone Bad out there."

"'Course not." She gave him a surprised look, but then patted his chest and gazed adoringly up at him, a twinkle of mischief in her eyes.

"They've got some lookers, some talent, but nothing like this little lady." Rafe covered her soft hand with his right one, felt her heat caught between his chest and his fingers, and wished their act was for real.

"Not much on sharing." Crowdy glanced around at the outlaws.

"Don't blame you, not one bit," Rafe agreed. "But Lady here put the bit in my mouth and took to leading me around. Isn't that right, darlin'?"

"Fast John is a difficult man to resist." She snuggled closer, plastering her body down his length.

"Got to know how to treat a filly right." Rafe felt the tension in the room ease down a notch, so he knew the outlaws were buying their story.

"Looks like you know a thing or two," Crowdy said, setting down his shotgun.

"A man don't like to brag—"

"Sweetie here keeps me happy." Lady tapped Rafe's chest with the tip of her forefinger.

Rafe raised her hand and planted a kiss against her soft palm, lingering to let her feel his warmth and his mustache. He could get used to this game real fast. He pressed her palm to his cheek. When he heard her soft intake of breath, he smiled. Maybe she could get used to it, too.

"Heard they're filling up their Boot Hill," Burt Hayes interrupted. "That true?"

Rafe pressed Lady's hand back to his chest. He nodded. "Helped them out a little my own self."

Every eye in the place checked Rafe's Colt .45, obviously trying to count the notches.

"Ever cash in your six-shooter?" Bob Hayes asked.

"Not my kinda odds." Rafe looked down at Lady. "I like to play another game."

Lady gave a coquettish giggle. "Fast John does like his games." She glanced up at him, arching an eyebrow. "And he knows how to play them."

"Just doing the best I can, darlin'." Rafe smiled down at her.

"You hire out?" Burt interrupted again.

"Depends." Rafe glanced at the man, figuring if he had trouble it'd come from the brawny Hayes Brothers. Jealousy could eat at a man, causing him to act stupid and dangerous.

"Acknowledge the corn," Bob said. "You fast?"

"Fast enough, so far." Rafe shrugged as if he didn't care

one way or another. He looked at Lady again, but kept his senses alert for any sudden movement from the outlaws. "I've been told on occasion I can be too slow."

"Or just right." Lady giggled again and managed to blush a pretty shade of pink.

Rafe watched her in amazement. She was a better actress than any he'd ever seen on stage. If he hadn't known the truth, he'd believe she was enjoying flirting with him just as much as he was enjoying holding her close.

"Think I did hear of a Fast John out Tombstone way," one of the poker players said. "You that John?"

Rafe shook his head. "Not me. We called him Slow Johnny after he got planted on Boot Hill."

Everybody laughed.

"If that ain't the beatingest," Burt said, shaking his shaggy head. "Stand you a drink."

"Thanks." Acceptance didn't come easy, but he'd gotten a measure of it. He glanced at Crowdy. "First, I'll buy everybody a round."

Lady led him over to the bar where Crowdy pulled out a bottle of amber liquid and started to pour.

"Sing us an all-fired good song." Burt put huge hands completely around Lady's waist, lifted her up to the bar, and set her down.

Lady smiled and patted Burt's whiskers.

Rafe saw red, bit his tongue, and refrained from throwing a punch. The outlaw was testing him, but he wouldn't be drawn into a power play for Lady or a position in the pack. That was a losing game.

"Burt, if you and Bob just can't wait, I'll give you that song." Lady slanted a glance at Rafe, raising a brow to let him know she realized the Hayes Brothers were trying to get under his skin.

Rafe relaxed, patted her hand, and smiled. "Go ahead, darlin', shake the rafters."

"I know all of you can relate to lost love." Lady glanced around at the men. "A Choctaw maiden wrote this song after her father and brothers were killed in a raid. I'd like to share it."

Patrons of the saloon grew quiet in anticipation, cards laid down and drinks set aside.

Lady gave a mournful smile, ducked her head, and then looked back up as she sang.

All men must surely die,
Though no one knows how soon.
Yet when the time shall come,
The event may still be joyful.

Rafe watched the outlaws lean toward Lady, faces rapt, breath still, nodding in understanding that their own lives might be cut short. She'd picked the right song for these outlaws living life on the edge in Indian Territory.

He realized he'd been here before, back at the Red River Saloon. Lady had captured hearts, maybe even minds and souls there, too. She had that kind of power when she sang. Difference was that then she'd simply been a name on an arrest warrant and a pretty face on a stage. Now she meant much more. Seemed like a lifetime ago, but it wasn't long at all. Somehow she'd wormed her way in close to his heart, set his body to aching for her, and turned his life upside down.

She wasn't called Lady Gone Bad for nothing. A man would be a fool to think he could trust her, depend on her, even love her. Rafe was skirting that fence a little too close for comfort.

Yet they were bound to each other on a lot of levels, circumstances, goals, lust, and maybe more he didn't realize at the moment. He felt as if she had spun a web of danger and deceit, and he'd been caught in her beautiful but deadly silk strands. Fanciful. He didn't know why his mind had turned that way, but her voice woke men in ways that led them down paths they might not otherwise follow. And that power made her one dangerous lady.

He picked up his shot glass, tossed back the whiskey, felt it burn all the way down, and knew a little relief. Lady had a way of putting a man on edge, but he mustn't go there. He had to be smart. Gather information to clear his name and find Crystabelle. Nothing else mattered.

As Lady began another song, he glanced around the room. He wasn't popular, not by a long shot. The outlaws thought he was a poacher, at the very least. Burt and Bob gave him narrow-eyed stares. He might even have to fight somebody to prove Lady belonged to him. But till then, he'd be happy to watch them turn green as grass with envy.

Chapter 21

So far so good. Lady felt relief for a lot of reasons. Rafe was carrying off his role as a gunslinger and the outlaws, for the most part, were accepting him. Word would spread, and next time they would get less of a challenge. At least she hoped so.

She'd been surprised when Rafe had played up his part as her lover. She wished she'd been more surprised when she'd responded so quickly, easily, and naturally. But that sensual song of theirs had been building toward a crescendo from the first moment they'd met. She just needed to keep it under control. Life was already too complicated, too hard, too dangerous. She had no room for a heartbreaker.

For now, first things first. She must deal with the Hayes Brothers, and she didn't want Rafe to interfere. He needed a distraction, something to do, while she got her job done.

She finished another song, and then picked up a shot glass of whiskey, indicating that she was through singing.

When the outlaws broke out in clapping and catcalls, she smiled, bowing her head. "Go on back to your games. I'll sing again in a bit."

After a lot of grumbling, the men turned back to their cards.

"Thank you," Crowdy said.

Lady raised her glass to him, and took a tiny sip. She pretended to drink more than ever went down her throat. She didn't like the taste and she had to keep her wits about her.

Rafe smiled at her. "Beautiful voice."

"Thank you."

"Nobody sings better'n you," Burt said. "Like to hear you warble in the Bend. Bob, too."

"Thanks." She put a hand on Rafe's shoulder.

"What can I do for you?" he asked.

She held out her hands. "Help me off the bar."

"Any time." He put hands around her waist and lifted her down, letting his hands linger for a moment, holding her close.

"Appreciate it." She could feel his heat and her body responded with a fire of its own. When he placed a kiss on her cheek, then trailed his lips to her ear, she shivered.

"How long before we go?" he whispered.

"Now, Fast John," she said, pushing at his shoulders playfully. "I know you want to play a few hands of poker."

He gave her a searching look. "I do. If you don't mind?"

"Of course I do, but go ahead."

He winked at her.

She watched him walk toward a table, pleased he'd understood. He'd marked her for everyone to see. Her ear still felt hot, as if burned by his touch. She felt vitally aware of him, too aware, and couldn't seem to stop watching as he pulled out a chair and sat down at a table with the grace of a panther.

Forcing her mind to business, she turned back to the bar and glanced over at the Hayes Brothers. They watched her. She toyed with a lock of hair, letting a smile play about her lips.

"How you boys been doing?" she asked.

"Better now," Burt said.

"Full chisel," Bob added.

"I've wanted to talk with you two."

Burt grinned, revealing strong white teeth. "All you had to do was whistle."

"Seen anybody ride by here on a copper-colored stallion?"

"Nope," Burt said. "You lookin' for one?"

"I like that color," she said.

"You'd look good on any horse," Bob added.

"Thanks." Lady smiled and leaned forward. "A little bird told me you two recently had a hankering for apple pie."

Burt and Bob glanced at each other, appearing sheepish.

"That true?" she asked.

"Not likely," Burt said.

"A lady's reticule went along with the pies. Know anything about that?"

"Don't sound like nothing an outlaw worth his salt would turn his hand to," Burt said.

"But apple pies are plum tasty," Bob added.

Lady had to keep from smiling. The Hayes Brothers were notorious for their antics, but didn't have a mean bone in their bodies. "Little bird'll pay a half eagle for a golden bird pin in that reticule. Funeral jewelry."

Bob whistled, a short burst of approval. "Looks like dang grass."

"Shut up!" Burt hissed.

"Tell you what." Lady pulled a half eagle out of her pocket, twirled it on the bar top, and then covered it with her hand. "Little bird already paid me, so suits me fine if I get both ends of the deal."

"Let's see that gold," Bob said.

Lady held the coin out between her thumb and forefinger, and then folded it into her palm again. "I'm willing to make an even exchange, one for the other."

"Shucks," Burt said. "Mighta picked up somethin' like it on the road."

"That'd be a lucky break." Lady smiled. "Want to check to see if you've got it in a saddlebag?"

Burt glanced around the room, then at Bob. "Go see if the horses didn't eat that thing."

Bob grinned. "Outhouse calling me anyway."

Lady watched the big outlaw walk out of the saloon, and turned back to his brother. "How long since you've been in the Bend?"

"Couple days. Didn't see you there."

"I was a little occupied."

Burt frowned. "Stranger give you trouble, let me know."

"You're so kind. Anything new going on in the Bend?"

"Place is hopping mad about that lawman, the one who tried to arrest you. He got clean away."

"Are they looking for him?"

"Like a duck on a june bug. They lay eyes on him again, they'll settle his hash."

"They get his name?"

"Nope. Did you?"

"No."

"Dash!"

"Yeah." She glanced back at the doorway and saw Bob step inside.

He made the floor shake as he hurried over and dropped the pin on the bar. "That it?"

Lady picked up the piece of jewelry, knowing an untold number of hours had been spent weaving hair to make the beautiful pin. Ma Engle would be so happy to have this remembrance of her daughter back. "Far as I can tell."

"Pony up," Bob said.

Lady set the half eagle between the brothers, knowing

she'd never charge Ma Engle a dime for retrieving the pin. "Now don't you boys spend that all at once."

"You're considerable of a woman," Burt said, smiling. "You lay eyes on me like you do Fast John, and I'll drop every dime I've got on you."

"You're sure a sweet-talking man." She slipped the pin into her pocket.

"I'm not talkin' malarkey." Burt leaned toward her, heat in his dark eyes.

"You flatter me." She stepped back from the bar, needing to get away from them before things got out of hand. She glanced over her shoulder.

Rafe glared at her, and then looked down at his cards.

"I'm no seven by nine," Burt said. "That gunslinger don't treat you right, you skedaddle to me and I'll see he gets what for."

Lady felt her smile freeze on her face. Last thing she needed was for Burt Hayes to think she found him of personal interest. But she couldn't make him mad either, or do anything to set him against Rafe. She had Ma Engle's pin. Now she needed to find a way to ease out of the saloon.

She smiled at Burt. "I bet you'd like to hear another song."

"You want me to put you back on the bar?" he asked hopefully.

"Thanks, but no," Lady said. "I'll just walk around."

As she moved away from the Hayes Brothers, she felt their gazes hot on her back. She just might have stirred up a hornet's nest.

Chapter 22

Rafe kept an eye on Lady and an eye on his cards. With divided attention, he'd been steadily losing, but that probably wasn't a bad idea considering the company. He held another rotten hand and didn't feel like bluffing his way to a win. Instead, he nursed his whiskey and watched the saloon.

After dark, Crowdy lit kerosene lanterns, setting two on the bar and another two on the fireplace mantel, so yellow light brightened the smoky interior. Nothing helped the lingering afternoon heat stoked by too many sweaty bodies and too many crackling embers in the fireplace. Place reeked to high heaven, but nobody else seemed to care.

Rafe kept hoping Crystabelle would walk in the door. If Lynch'em Lampkin stepped inside, he could confront the turncoat. So far, plenty of outlaws, many of them Indian, had arrived, but none that could help him solve his problems.

Worst yet, he couldn't arrest a single one. His badge was rolled up in the toe of a sock and stuck in the bottom of his saddlebag on the back of his horse. It'd stay there till he got his name cleared. Normally, he could've shut down the Boggy Saloon with a whiskey warrant. In Indian Territory, it was against federal law to sell or give alcohol to

Indians, but that didn't mean firewater wasn't readily available.

For lawmen in Indian Territory, whiskey bootleggers weren't the only problem. They were sworn to protect citizens against cattle rustlers, horse thieves, murderers, timber thieves, land squatters, card sharks, and prostitutes serving the railroad towns. A lot of times, it was a thankless job, but other times, a man with a badge made a big difference in saving lives and helping folks, Indian and American alike.

He studied Lady again. He was beginning to realize that sometimes a woman could do a better job than a man. She could go places a man couldn't go, Men would tell a woman like Lady a secret they'd never tell another man, or take her places they'd never show another man just to impress her. All in all, men could turn stupid around a clever woman like her. She'd been mining that gold field to her advantage. It was just too bad she worked on the wrong side of the law.

Cold facts didn't ease the hot emotions that were building in him. Lady had better be getting plenty of information as she flirted with the outlaws, moving from table to table. Yet he suspected she was simply enjoying herself, enjoying seeing him steam with jealousy, enjoying the attention. Truth of the matter, he was getting madder by the minute. He wasn't used to sharing Lady, seeing her dally with other men. He didn't like it one bit. Besides that, two cardsharps were cheating at his table.

But he had to hold on to his temper. He was there to get a lead on Crystabelle, and Lady's horse. He couldn't ask directly or he'd give away their game. He needed to slide in sideways. Horses were always a safe bet to introduce a name.

"Any one of you see somebody ride through these parts

on a stallion the color of a new penny?" Rafe asked, glancing at the other players. "A lady I know, name of Crystabelle, is looking."

"Sorrels are a dime a dozen around here," one outlaw said, frowning at his cards.

"Lady with a name like that can ride me any day," another added, chuckling.

All the outlaws laughed, nodding in agreement.

Rafe wanted to punch the outlaw for the insult, but he stayed his hand. By now, he figured he wasn't going to get what he wanted, either Crystabelle or Lampkin, so he was ready to go. If Lady didn't signal she wanted to leave pretty soon, he was more than happy to drag her kicking and screaming out the door and to hell with her adoring audience. Not that he would really do it, but he'd had enough. He couldn't sit still a moment longer.

He tossed down his cards and motioned for another man to take his place at the table. Felt good to stretch his legs as he walked toward Lady, carrying his shot glass and nodding to outlaws. She stood by the fireplace, talking with the Hayes Brothers. When he reached them, Burt and Bob glared at him, but Lady smiled and winked. He counted on her to be playing with the brothers, not really liking them. But he couldn't be sure.

"Hey, sweetie," Lady said, tucking a hand around his arm and squeezing. "You like it here?"

Rafe nodded. "Gave up my seat so somebody else could have a turn at losing."

She leaned into him and patted his chest. "Isn't he the sweetest thing?"

Burt and Bob rolled their eyes.

"Thought you might be ready to go," Rafe said.

"Good idea." She glanced over at the brothers. "Burt and Bob here are trying to persuade me to join them at Robber's Cave."

"Up near Cherokee Nation," Burt explained. "Men are driving a powerful lot of horse flesh to a meet up there."

"Horses'll be some pumpkins," Bob said.

"Sin to Crockett not to go," Burt added.

"What do you think, darlin'? I'd like a look myself." Rafe glanced down with a nod to let her know he wanted to go. He'd like nothing better than an entry into Robber's Cave with its famous Stone Corral, a favorite hideout for outlaws when they were pushing horses down Robber's Trail from Missouri to Texas. Place was so defensible it had never been breached by lawmen.

"I've been thinking about a stallion," Lady said, cocking her head to one side as if considering the possibility. "I bet you're thinking there might be a few horse races, too."

Rafe managed to look liked he'd been caught out, a little boy with his hand in the cookie jar.

"If you'll sing, Lady, we'll pass the hat," Burt said. "And we'll pass the word you're gonna be there. Men'll come out of the woodwork to hear you."

"Won't be out nothing for that stallion," Bob added.

"Oh, I like that," Lady said, her smile full of mischief.

Rafe frowned as he drew Lady closer. "She wouldn't pay for a new horse anyway."

Lady hit his chest lightly with her fist. "I've told you before that I take care of myself. And that means buying my own horse."

Burt and Bob guffawed, shaking their heads.

"No man tells Lady Gone Bad what to do." Burt looked at her with respect.

She smiled at the compliment. "He's right. But not to worry, there are plenty of other ways you can please me." She reached up and stroked Rafe's cheek, letting her fingers linger.

Rafe captured her hand and pressed a long, hot kiss against her palm as he looked down into her eyes. If he wasn't mistaken, she felt the blaze between them as much as he did. When he got her out of the saloon, he planned to find out for sure and stoke that flame.

"You're one lucky hombre." Burt gazed wistfully at Lady.

She withdrew her hand and smiled at the brothers. "Now you know you are two of my favorites."

"Balderdash!" Bob said, but he appeared pleased by her words.

"I do believe you're trying to flatter me into singing again."

"Wouldn't hurt my ears none." Burt grinned, winking at her.

"One more song for the road, and then we're gone." Lady stepped in front of the fireplace and began her famous ballad.

She's a wild woman, a renegade, a lady gone bad.

Rafe watched her, struck again by the easy way she handled a crowd. She could make a man feel like he was the only one in the room. No wonder the Hayes Brothers doted on her.

He heard a commotion at the doorway. A big man with a long mane of silver hair under a black hat shouldered his way into the saloon. He looked prosperous in a navy suit, white shirt, forest green vest, and a Colt .45 tucked in a front holster on the belt around his waist. Two smaller, wiry men, one with a blond beard and the other with straight black hair, wearing dark trousers, dark shirts, red bandannas, and Colt .45s on belt holsters for quick draw, walked at his side.

Rafe felt his heart sink. He couldn't believe the three men who'd been the ringleaders in getting him strung up in the Bend had found him here. He quickly tugged down his hat and stepped to the side, putting the Hayes Brothers between him and the newcomers.

Even with his transformation from deputy to gunslinger, he didn't trust the men not to recognize him. He needed to get Lady and get out before he ended up with a noose around his neck again.

He rearranged his neckerchief, tying it tighter and higher to better conceal his neck. The rough, red bruise would be a dead giveaway. He caught Lady's eye and motioned with his head. When she glanced at the newcomers, her eyes widened, and then she quickly looked at him, nodded, and skipped to the refrain.

Rafe leaned toward Burt. "Who're those men?"

"You don't know?" Burt appeared astonished. "That's Zip Rankin and part of his gang, Pecos Pete and Heck Humby. Rattlesnakes don't come any meaner."

"They hang out here?"

"Nope. They go for fancy, not the sticks."

"What do you think they're doing at the Boggy?" Rafe felt his heart race.

"Guess they were in the area," Burt said.

"Where else you gonna wet your whistle?" Bob asked.

But Rafe still questioned why Zip and his men were out of their neck of the woods. He could only hope it had nothing to do with him.

Lady finished her song, bowed her head at the applause, and quickly joined Rafe. "Ready to go?"

He nodded, tossing back his whiskey and setting the glass on the fireplace mantel. He folded his left arm so she could tuck her hand around his elbow, but he left his right hand free near his Peacemaker.

"Robber's Cave meet is about—" Burt started to say.

"Lady Gone Bad!" a big voice boomed across the room.

"You're not leaving, are you?" Zip Rankin headed her way.

"Oh, no," Lady muttered.

"What's wrong?" Burt asked, brows drawing into a frown.

Rafe saw an opportunity and took it. He leaned close to the two brothers and hissed, "Zip insulted Lady in the Bend."

"He didn't!" Bob clenched his fists.

"That sidewinder!" Burt lowered his head.

"She'd like to avoid him," Rafe added in a low tone.

"I can't," Lady whispered, squeezing Rafe's arm, "but let me do the talking."

"Lady, what a pleasant surprise to see you." Zip reached them, smiling, a gunslinger on either side of him.

The room grew quiet, all eyes on them. Crowdy stood stock still behind the bar, watchful. Zip and his men obviously struck fear even in the hearts of desperados.

"Hi, Zip." Lady held tightly to Rafe's arm.

"I see you're with a companion." Zip's voice held disdain. "Texans not good enough for you?"

"Fast John is just in from Tombstone," Lady said, ignoring Zip's barb.

Zip looked intently at Rafe. "Lady, you going to introduce us?"

"Zip Rankin, Pecos Pete, Heck Humby." She placed a hand on Rafe's chest. "Fast John."

Rafe nodded, keeping his face in the shadow of his gray hat.

"Something familiar about you," Zip said. "We meet before?"

"You been in Tombstone?" Lady asked, giving the impression she was ready to leave.

"Wait a minute." Zip held out a hand. "You know who's riding that honey chestnut tied out front?"

"No point asking me." Lady lowered her hand, stepping away from Rafe as she shrugged. "You're the one knows horses."

"Looks like a gelding I admired in the Bend."

Rafe knew Lady was giving them room to fight in case Zip put two and two together, namely a deputy marshal and his horse right there at the Boggy.

"Why don't you ask the boys?" Lady said, gesturing around the room.

"I will." Zip gave Rafe another narrow-eyed look. "You sure we haven't met?"

"Nice seeing you, Zip, but we've got to go." Lady stepped forward.

Zip and his men didn't give ground.

"What about a song for me?" Zip asked.

"Wish I could oblige, but it'll have to wait."

"One song won't cost much time," Zip said. "Fast John's not a man to hold out on the rest of us, is he?"

"Lady says she's got to go." Burt moved up to Lady's side.

"She's done singing," Bob agreed, flanking her other side.

"If you want trouble, you've come to the right place." Zip glanced around the group. "Like we say in Texas, God made some men big and some men small, but Sam Colt made us all equal."

"Nobody wants trouble," Lady said. "We just need to be on our way now."

"Zip says when you leave," Pecos Pete snarled, his voice flat and deadly.

"And, Lady, he ain't done with you," Heck added.

Rafe itched to intervene, but he hoped they could talk their way out of the situation. He glanced around. Crowdy had his shotgun on the bar. Outlaws looked ready to choose sides. Wouldn't take much to set off a room full of liquored-up, fully armed patrons who liked to fight about as much as they liked to drink.

"Lady Gone Bad can whip her weight in wild cats." Burt thrust out his chest.

"Right now she's catawamptiously chawed up." Heck hooked his thumbs in his gun belt.

"She's a huckleberry above your persimmon," Bob insisted.

"Lady is an all-fired, lick-spittle, ass-backward, golderned, pisspot, strumpet adventuress." Pecos Pete tucked his thumbs under his armpits and looked proud of his description.

Everyone else gaped at him in astonishment. Outlaws muttered across the room.

"Nobody talks about Lady that way." Burt reached back with a clenched fist and hit Pecos Pete square in the nose, blood spurting. Pete dropped to the floor and lay still.

Heck leaped forward, but Bob popped him in the head with a meaty fist and Heck dropped down beside Pecos Pete.

Face twisted in fury, Zip went for his six-shooter. Rafe drew first, flipped his Peacemaker over, and cold-cocked Rankin with the butt of his gun. Zip went down hard and lay still.

Lady looked at Rafe in admiration. "Guess that put the *fast* in Fast John."

"Thanks." Burt clasped Rafe's hand. "He had me and Bob in his sights."

"Make 'em think twice before insulting Lady," Bob said. "Or throwing down on us."

"Appreciate the support." Lady motioned toward the door. "But we'd better get out of here before they wake up, or their friends—"

Several outlaws descended on them, cussing and swinging fists, as the room erupted in shouts and fights. Friends of Zip Rankin slugged it out with Lady's defenders. Burt and Bob laid in with their fists, knocking bodies about as they made a path toward the doorway for Lady and Rafe.

They were halfway across the saloon when somebody grabbed Rafe by the ankle and jerked him down. A knife flashed. He felt a slash burn his ribs. Another body piled on top of him. He struggled to get free. Felt another cut. He heard Lady scream. Hit a man senseless and sat up.

Next thing he knew he smelled smoke. Place was on fire. Somebody must have upset a lantern. Burt and Bob were holding their own, laughing as they knocked heads together, but smoke dimmed the saloon. He had to find Lady and get her to safety.

He saw her at the bar, tossing Crowdy gold eagles. She threw the lamp in her hand onto a pile of broken furniture. Flames shot up. She gave Crowdy a handshake, and turned to the doorway.

Rafe blinked in astonishment. He never knew what Lady was going to do next. Didn't matter. He had to save her. He leapt over several bodies, dodged a fistfight, grabbed Lady's hand, held on tight, and made for the exit.

"Everybody out. Now!" Crowdy shouted.

Dazed outlaws went on hitting each other.

Crowdy shouted again, firing a blast of his shotgun into the ceiling. "Get out now!"

There was a stampede for the door.

"Quick!" Lady said. "Let's go."

"I'll watch your back." Rafe drew his Peacemaker.

They ran for it.

Lady swung onto Jipsey's back, throwing him the reins

to Justice. He caught them and swung up on the gelding's back. They thundered into the darkness, Lady in the lead.

Behind them, orange flames licked up into the sky, turning night into day.

He urged Justice faster.

Chapter 23

"You almost got us killed." Lady drew in ragged breaths, so angry she could hardly see straight. By moonlight, she guided Jipsey off the trail at a huge lichen-covered rock that jutted up from rocky ground, marking the path to Medicine Spring.

"I almost got us killed?" Rafe said in amazement.

"You cold-cocked Zip."

"He was about to recognize me."

"But he'll have it in for you now. Me, too."

"He didn't see me."

"Somebody did and they'll tell."

"Maybe not. Lot of confusion." Rafe rode up beside her, voice tight, back rigid, hands clenched. Justice shouldered into Jipsey, causing the mare to dance sideways. "You started the fire."

"Saved your sorry hide." As Jipsey sidled back toward Justice, Lady felt her boot brush against Rafe's leg. A sensation like liquid fire, maybe anger, raced away from the spot. Yet it wasn't anger. To her surprise, the feeling defused her fury.

"You burned down Crowdy's saloon," Rafe said.

"Place was a tinderbox and I paid him."

"No need." Rafe slapped reins against his thigh and struck her, too. "I was holding my own."

She flinched, angry again. "Against a saloon full of outlaws? And Zip?" She jerked Jipsey's reins to get distance from Rafe, the intensity of her emotions causing the mare to buck.

"My kind of odds." He glanced at Jipsey. "Looks like your horse knows more than you do."

"She doesn't like the smell of smoke."

"Then you better get cleaned up. You reek to high heaven."

"Thanks so much," she said sarcastically, patting Jipsey's neck to calm the mare. "If I hadn't set the place on fire, we'd probably be six feet under." She caught the acrid scent of smoke wafting from her clothes, cursing his truth.

"Too bad we were still inside."

"Gave them something to think about besides you and the Hayes Brothers, didn't it?"

"They didn't care about me. It's all about you." He glared at her while Justice sidled back to Jipsey, causing boot to rub against boot. "You need every man drooling over you, don't you?"

"Jealous?" she taunted. Staying mad at him was all too easy when he made remarks like that.

"Trying to keep us alive."

"If you were doing that, you wouldn't watch me like a hawk and let every outlaw I interview know you're spoiling for trouble."

"Interview! Snuggling up to desperados doesn't look like interviewing. It looks like—"

"Enough!" She threw him a disgusted look, feeling the heightened emotions and fast heartbeat that came on the heels of a close brush with death. "I'm doing what I have to do."

She rode over to Medicine Spring, a pool of water known for its curative qualities, nestled in a cascade of rocks surrounded by thick greenery under tall trees. A sharp medicinal scent swirled from the mist rising over the water into the night air. She felt the shelter of trees enclose and protect her. Moonlight transformed the water into liquid silver.

She glanced around the area, looking for any dangerous animals that might have come to drink water. All appeared safe. She listened, as she had since they'd left the Boggy Saloon, for pursuit. Nothing, so far. Not too many people knew about the spring. More Indians than Americans. She felt her shoulders relax. "We should be safe here."

"Dang, it stinks!"

She sighed. "Medicine water."

"I'm not getting in that stuff."

"It will help heal your wounds."

"Or kill me." He flashed a big, white grin, eyes dancing. "A real lady would kiss my injuries and make them better."

"A real lady wouldn't give you the time of day."

"I've been known to spend a day or two with a lady." He raised an eyebrow, eyes full of mystery and mischief about what he meant.

"Just a day or two?" she teased, unable to resist his naughty grin.

"That's all it takes with me."

She laughed, enjoying their banter even though she was trying to stay mad at him. "Maybe I better have a word with those ladies."

She slipped a leg over the saddle horn and slid down, catching her weight with both feet. She pulled Ma Engle's pin out of her pocket and tucked it in her saddlebag. She unbuckled her gun belt, hung it over her saddle horn, and then leaned back against Jipsey to pull off one boot and then the other, stuffing her socks inside. Finally she wiggled her toes and felt the night air cool them.

Felt wonderful. She wished she could shuck all her

clothing, but Rafe was watching and somebody might be trailing them.

After Rafe dismounted, they led their horses down to the pool to drink. She wanted to get into the water and ease her aches and pains, but animals always came first. When Jipsey was full, she led the mare over to the tree line where grass grew tall and green. She slipped off the bridle and hung it over the saddle, so Jipsey could easily eat. Rafe followed with Justice.

Now she could take care of herself. She hurried over to the water, eased down the slippery bank, and then curled her toes in the soft, warm mud, feeling it draw tension from her body. She hadn't been here since the last visit with her parents, but she wouldn't think about them now.

When she reached the shallow muddy side, she knelt to bury her hands in the healing mud, feeling a slight tingling move up her arms into her shoulders to ease accumulated aches and pains. Needing even more, she pushed up her sleeves and rolled up her Levi's, and then rubbed handfuls of mud over her bare skin. She sighed with pleasure as she lay down, rested her head against the bank, and let all her worry and fear and anger melt down into the earth.

"Dirty girl."

She glanced up at Rafe, eyes half-closed, too relaxed to bother to reply. As he walked to the edge of the pool, he tried to pull off his shirt. She could tell the fabric stuck to his wounds.

"Hurts like hell." He glared at her. "Save your life. This is how you thank me. Stinking water."

"Who saved who? You ought to thank me." If he was to receive the benefit of Medicine Spring, he needed help. "This feels great. The water is so warm."

She slipped into the deeper end toward him, and then emerged, mud sliding down her body in a gush, wet clothes plastered to her, revealing every curve and valley as if she had risen straight from the earth.

Rafe stopped, frozen at the sight of her, and then eagerly stepped forward. His boots sank into mud. He looked down, looked up, and grimaced. "Stinking water. Muddy boots."

"Time for you to get dirty, too." Dripping on him, she grasped his shirt, stiff with dried sweat and blood, slit from several knife cuts, and slowly undid buttons, letting the backs of her cool, damp fingers brush against his bare flesh. He felt hot enough to start a fire, or ignite one in her.

"Dirty sounds good," he said, voice rough and husky as he stood still in front of her.

"Buttons can be so pesky." She moved upward, freeing another button, seeing more of his chiseled chest, feeling his heat cascade over her.

"Right lady makes them easy."

She glanced up at his face, wondering if she was the right lady as her fingers stilled on a button, hands nestled against him. She felt springy chest hair and shivered at the sensation.

"Lady, you can unbutton me any time." A slight smile teased the corner of his sensual mouth.

"I might just need your help with buttons myself sometime." She reluctantly unbuttoned the last one, and then slowly pulled open the front of his shirt to reveal his bare chest.

"Now?"

With one fingertip, she gently touched the raw, red circle around his neck, knowing it must be painful. "Now we better take care of your wounds."

He shrugged out of his shirt, frowning with pain, and roughly tossed it aside. Naked from the waist up, his hard muscles appeared sculpted out of stone. Tall and lean, he stood with the unconscious grace of a predator, a mountain lion or a gray wolf.

Taking a deep breath, she wondered if Rafe knew he looked like the answer to a maiden's fervent prayer. He was that, truly, but much more. They'd ridden hard together and survived danger. For now, they were bound together by a quirk of fate, each desperately needing the other's help. But it didn't make them friends. Lapsed enemies, perhaps.

From the first moment she'd seen him, she'd felt an almost irresistible sensual tug, as if he'd lassoed her. She'd fought that feeling with anger, deception, and power plays, but he'd kept reeling her closer till she'd burned for want of him. Now she felt irritated, all her senses heightened by their narrow escape. She wanted to give back some of his tender torment.

"I'm sorely in need of a woman's touch." Rafe ran a single fingertip up her wet shirt sleeve, and then tipped her chin so she'd look at him.

"Can't get your boots off?" she asked, voice low and sultry.

"I'd appreciate your help."

"We don't want your wounds getting infected." She pointed at the bank. "Sit down. I'll start with your boots."

"I've better places you could start."

"Do you now?"

"You bet."

Shaking her head, Lady gave him a little push and nudged him back until he sat on the bank.

He held out a foot, smiling mischievously up at her. "After my boots, there's nothing left but my Levi's."

"How many buttons on them?"

"Just enough for you."

She knelt in front of him, slipping slightly on the muddy

bank, and grasped his boot in two hands. "You know we wouldn't be here if you'd minded your manners."

"They were messing with my woman."

She snorted. "I'm not your woman. We were playing roles." She gave a hard tug and his boot popped free. She tossed it onto dry land behind him.

"Role or no role, I'm happy to take care of you." He reached out, gently nudging long strands of hair behind her ears. "Fire singed your hair. Here in front. You smell like fire."

"You smell like smoke just as much as me."

"More. You're fanning my flames. Want to put out my fire?"

She tossed her head, ears burning where he'd touched them, and her dripping hair fell away from him. "I want—"

His eyes lit with hope and he touched his lips with the tip of his tongue, as if already tasting her.

"Your other boot."

"Sure now?"

"Boot."

He nodded, bracing his hands in the mud and raising a long leg as he held up his right foot.

She tugged, but the boot didn't budge. She pulled harder, but still the boot stuck tight. She stood, bent over, put all her weight into it, and tugged as hard as possible. The boot came off with a snap, jerking him forward and sending her back. She slammed into the water, felt its warmth close over her, and came up gasping for air as she found the bottom of the pool with her feet. She pushed hair back from her face, opened her eyes, and tossed the boot onto the bank.

Rafe was struggling to sit up, covered in mud except for his head.

She laughed at the sight, not ladylike at all, but big guffaws that exploded from her chest in waves. She felt as if all her pent-up frustration and worry and fury were rolled into one, released by ridiculous laughter that would not stop. Might never stop.

"Don't laugh at me. Not funny. You did it on purpose," he said, his voice rough with repressed laughter. He grabbed her arms, dragged her up out of the water to him, but slipped in the mud on the bank, taking them both down. They rolled across the bank, limbs twined together, gathering mud as her laughter filled the night.

Rafe stopped their movement and held her tightly against him, slick body pressed to slick body.

Tears burned her eyes. Breath caught in her throat. She hiccupped.

He rocked her, murmured comforting words. "There, that's better. We're in this mess together."

Laughter died in her throat. Had she been running, always on the move to outdistance her mess of fear, anger, and pain? She hated the idea. Hated him more for making her witness her own weakness. She jerked away. "Back there at the Boggy. Don't ever scare me like that again." She stood up, anxious to get away, get back in control.

"I'm not letting you off that easy." He clasped her hand and jerked downward.

Thrown off balance, she slipped in the mud and fell against his broad chest, pushed up, fingers sliding across slick muscle, feeling him tense, his breath catch in his throat. All her pent-up emotions came pulsing out to her fingertips, making them so sensitive that she felt as if she were touching right to his very core as she explored his chest, drawing spirals in the mud as she reached each hard tip of nipple. He groaned.

A deep sense of satisfaction, power, and need swept through her, igniting her body. She twined a leg across him, felt his hard, hot reaction to her, and rocked against him, desperate to relieve the ache in her molten core, desperate for him to feel the same torment.

"You haven't let me thank you for saving my life back there," Rafe said, voice rough with emotion as he plunged a hand into her thick mane of hair.

Chapter 24

Rafe kissed Lady, slow and tender at first but gathering steam as banked embers caught fire and blazed. He relished the feel of her soft, plump mouth as he nibbled and licked from one delectable corner to the other.

She'd made him needy like no other woman. Now she deserved to feel some of his frustration.

He combed long fingers through her hair, gliding over a sensual layer of slick mud, imagining himself sliding over, under, and into her, creating enough friction to set both her and the pool of water on fire.

When she moaned, he caught the sound on his tongue, thrusting between her lips, tasting sweet and tart, feeling smooth and firm, driving deep, filling her, dancing with her tongue, realizing she was responding to him. That knowledge sent a wave of heat through him that made him so hard he hurt. He couldn't get enough of her, quick enough.

He gently laid her back onto the soft bank and stroked her breasts through fabric clinging like a second skin. When he slid a hand over her heart, he felt the wild pounding echo the tempo of his own. Fingers slipping and sliding as he massaged in circles, he felt her nipples harden to taut peaks.

"I want to thank you everywhere," he said, voice low and husky. "I want to feel your skin against mine."

She spoke no words, only her eyes like polished agates talking urgently to him. She slowly raised her blouse in a smooth, graceful motion, exposing full, round breasts with rosy tips straining against a white chemise turned translucent by a thin, wet layer of mud.

Rafe hesitated as he savored the fact that Lady Gone Bad belonged to him alone. At the Red River Saloon, he couldn't have imagined this moment, but now that it had come, he couldn't imagine anything else. He gazed down at her. She wore no corset, needing nothing to enhance her natural tantalizing shape. She wore no jewelry, needing nothing to add to her beauty. She wore no face paint, needing nothing to emphasize the perfection of her appearance.

If a woman had ever been made to be worshipped by men, she had to be the one. He was ready to worship her in the only way he knew how, body to body.

In the light of the moon, she looked all satin and silver. She regarded him steadily, no words necessary.

Transferring her wrists to one hand, he used the other to push up her chemise so her breasts were completely exposed to him. He splashed warm water over them, sensitizing her as the mud slid away. He took his time savoring what he had wanted the first moment he saw her on stage, tormenting every man in the saloon. Only now he tormented her, setting mouth to nipple, sensitizing with teeth and mustache, while he kneaded the other breast with his free hand.

She whimpered, a sound caught between pain and pleasure, made musical by the quality of her voice. She reached out and stroked down his slick chest, pausing to tease his nipples into taut beads, caressing the straining muscles of his chest, soothing the shallow knife wounds. When she reached lower still, touching his hard, hot shaft through his trousers, he grabbed her wrists and thrust her hands up over her head so he could stay in complete control.

"No, ma'am. Not yet. I'm thanking you right now."

He thumbed open the waist of her Levi's, pulled loose the bow on the waistband of her drawers, and buried his tongue in her navel, nipping at soft flesh with his teeth. As he popped one button of her jeans after another and slowly eased them down with her drawers, he followed with his mouth, making his way toward the burning heart of her. In response, she squirmed, hips moving, thrusting up against him, sighs and moans increasing in intensity the lower he pressed kisses to her hot naked flesh.

Desperate to taste her, to give her a pleasure she'd never forget, Rafe let go of her wrists, grabbed her blue jeans and drawers, and then jerked them down to her ankles. She gasped as warm water washed over her, sloughing off the mud to reveal luminous skin. Another jerk completely freed her. He pulled the chemise up over her head, tossed the soft muslin aside, and she lay nude.

"Beautiful." He marveled that she lay spread before him like a feast for the starving.

"Rafe," she said, reaching down to grab the top button of his trousers. "I want to touch you, too."

"Nope." He shook his head regretfully, pushing her hand gently aside. "Not done thanking you yet."

He was rock hard, needing a release so bad his teeth ached. But that wasn't his goal. He'd keep on his trousers, no matter how tight, how uncomfortable, how miserable.

He started with her toes.

He licked and nibbled, using his hands to stroke up small ankles to firm calves, massaging, teasing, titillating. As he moved upward, he changed from hands to mouth, tasting every inch, memorizing every curve, sensitizing every valley until he reached her core. He hesitated, wondering how he could hold out and pleasure her first when his prick was so hard he felt ready to burst. But he wanted her to ache for him, to need him like he needed her, to never be able to forget how she felt at this moment. For that, he could delay his own pleasure.

He cupped her tight little ass with both hands, raising her upward. She slowly spread her legs for him, revealing the triangle that was her heart. The place he wanted most to be. When he leaned closer, he smelled not medicinal water but tantalizing lust. He dipped his tongue to her nub, licked, tasting tangy juices. And he was a goner.

All thoughts, all plans fled his mind as his body took over, needing her as much as she needed him. He used his tongue as he would his shaft to delve deeply into her hot, molten core.

When he felt her hands in his hair, urging him deeper, harder, he gripped her round butt. He massaged as she clinched her muscles and moaned, softly at first and then louder as she crested the wave, back arching, and shuddered with release after release under his expert touch.

Satisfied, he tugged her against his chest, lying down, pressing soft, sex-scented kisses to her lips, and she shuddered again.

"Now you're my woman."

She pulled away, chuckling, and stretched like a contented cat. Reaching between his legs, she caught the bulge that ached with explosive need for her.

"Think again, Deputy," she crooned. "Feels like you belong to me."

Chapter 25

To prove her point, Lady stroked and massaged till Rafe groaned and reached up for her. She pushed him back with the other hand, so she could toy with the dark hair that tapered downward from his chest and tease his belly button with a fingertip. She smiled in satisfaction at his needy reaction.

"You wantin' some thanks, too?" she asked, her voice barely above a whisper in the stillness of the night.

"Lady, that's not thanks." He groaned again. "That's torture."

She chuckled, a low vibration deep in her throat. "Payback then. You've been an awful lot of trouble." She slapped his chest, feeling the sting against her palm. "Bad!"

Rafe grabbed her hand and pushed it down with the other, pressing both hard against his crotch. "You lookin' for trouble?"

She smiled, a slight tilt to one corner of her rosy lips. "You the man to give it to me?

"What do you think?" He sat up, a lock of dark hair falling above his right eye as he stared intently at her.

"Not sure." She leaned forward, allowing her full breasts to swing outward, tips brushing against the coarse hair of his bare chest. She shivered, feeling her nipples tighten into taut peaks. "Prove it."

Still holding her hands in place, he reached out, touched the tip of one breast, and pinched, lightly and then harder.

She moaned as the painful pleasure swept straight to her core, making her hot and wet. She caught a quick breath. "You call that trouble?"

He pinched again, and then covered both breasts with large hands, squeezing and massaging as he pressed hot kisses across her face, rasping with his mustache to sensitize her delicate skin. When he captured her mouth, he plunged deep inside to pillage and plunder while he released her breasts to wrap hands around her shoulders and pull her hard against his broad chest as if he could bear no distance between them.

Caught between hot and cold, pain and pleasure, guilt and innocence, she rode his passion with her own burning desire. She felt consumed by their wild and wicked lust. And she wanted nothing more than to feel him thrust inside her, stallion to mare.

But in the next moment, she heard an owl hoot high in a nearby tree followed by the distant jingle of a horse's bridle. Passion fled. She shivered as she pushed against Rafe's chest, but he was too deep in passion to notice. She hit his shoulder.

"What?" He raised his head, voice slurred, breath fast.

She looked down. She was stark naked, no pistol, boots, nothing. Defenseless. How could she have dropped her guard, especially so quickly after the saloon fight? One word for it all. *Rafe*.

"Are you having second thoughts?" he asked. "I'd never force you."

"Shhh!" she hissed, listening hard. She'd been trained to notice the slightest change of sound in a forest. No owl.

Eerily quiet, as if all the wildlife had scattered or gone to ground to avoid danger. But she definitely heard the muted clip-clop of a horse headed their way. "Better get your shirt." She glanced at the pool of water, so enticing a moment before but now a place of entrapment. "I'll find my clothes."

"What's going on?"

"Somebody's coming," she whispered. "Let's get out of here."

"You sure?"

"Listen."

He cocked his head, gave her a quick nod, then picked up his shirt and went after his boots.

She located her underwear, blouse, and Levi's, and quickly rinsed off the mud in the water. She rolled her clothes into a ball so they wouldn't drip and leave a trail. She grabbed her boots. She glanced around. Impossible to cover their tracks, too much churned up mud from hooves, boots, and bare feet. All they could do was get out of sight and arm themselves.

Rafe joined her at the tree line. They hurried to the horses. He slipped into his wet shirt while she pulled on her chemise and drawers, sodden fabric clinging like a second skin. She hid her other clothes behind a rock, and then jerked her rifle out of its sheath. Face grim, Rafe buckled on his gun belt, quickly adjusting his Peacemaker on his hip.

When she heard the steady cadence of a horse's hooves drawing close, she gripped Rafe's arm. He nodded, and put a hand on Justice's nose to keep the gelding quiet. She did the same with Jipsey. She didn't want their mounts communicating with the approaching horse and giving away their hidden position under the trees.

A little later, she heard someone step down from a

horse, saddle leather creaking in protest. The person quietly walked around the area, most likely tracking, stopped as if listening, and then walked back to the horse. Whoever it was couldn't miss their trail, but maybe would think they'd moved out earlier.

She kept her breath shallow, watching the ground, stilling her thoughts, holding her body motionless. She pretended not to be there and hoped Rafe knew to do the same thing.

"Lady?" a man called out. "Lady Gone Bad!"

She stayed frozen. He sounded familiar, but she couldn't place his voice. He'd trailed them at night to a little known spot. Not easy. Doubtful he was American, so most likely Indian. Zip rode with a tracker, Heck Humby. She could only hope she didn't have to deal with them. She stilled her thoughts again, determined to give nothing away.

"Crowdy here."

Relief raced through her. Not Zip or his men. She took a deep breath and glanced at Rafe.

He raised his eyebrows, questioning the newcomer.

She nodded okay. "Crowdy, you alone?"

"Yep."

Lady needed to make a decision fast.

"Trust him?" Rafe whispered, jerking on his boots.

"Yes. But better be cautious. Zip might be forcing Crowdy to lure us out into the open."

"Get dressed," Rafe hissed. "I'll scout around Crowdy's back trail, see if Zip is hanging back there, and come up on the far side."

"He'll know."

"Don't matter. We'd be fools to do otherwise."

"True. He'll expect it." She set aside her rifle. "Go. I'll talk from here and distract him while I dress."

Rafe wrapped fingers around the back of her head, held her tight, and pressed an ardent kiss to her lips. "When we're done with Crowdy, we're picking up where we left off."

She raised an eyebrow. "You do like to live dangerous."

Chapter 26

Rafe didn't find anybody else lurking around Medicine Spring. Crowdy hadn't tried to lynch him yet, so that was a point in the Indian's favor. On the other hand, Crowdy had been selling whiskey and beer in his saloon. That was a federal crime. If Rafe had been wearing his badge back at the Boggy, he'd have been obligated to take the saloonkeeper to jail. As it stood, Rafe needed as many friends as he could get on the other side of the law, so he'd reserve judgment about Crowdy's character.

"Saloon burn all the way down?" Rafe asked as he stepped away from the tree line and walked toward the pool.

Crowdy glanced up, hands cupped from drinking water, where he knelt beside his horse. "Tinderbox. Went up fast."

"River and creek contain the fire?"

"Yep."

"Everybody get out alive?

"Yep."

"Too bad," Lady said, walking toward Medicine Spring from the other direction. "Zip always makes trouble."

"Thinks he's big boss-man," Crowdy said.

Lady chuckled. "Like all these independent cusses in Indian Territory are going to let him boss them around."

Crowdy nodded, face somber.

"Any of them come this way?" Rafe joined Lady near the edge of the pool, noticing that she looked good in the green blouse and split-skirt she'd gotten in Paris. He felt a deep satisfaction that he'd paid for it, as if that fact made her belong to him more. He wished like hell they hadn't been interrupted, but he figured they had to be neighborly now that the saloonkeeper was here.

"Scattered. Mad as wet hens," Crowdy said.

Lady chuckled again. "They're always spoiling for a fight."

"Are you going to rebuild?" Rafe asked.

Crowdy stood up, led his horse to a grassy area to eat, and then walked back with a blanket folded over one arm. "Why?"

"Business."

"Bound to happen." Crowdy shrugged. "Fire cleanses."

"Crowdy did the best he could to keep the place clean," Lady said.

"Like Indians," Crowdy agreed.

"Most Indians make a point of keeping themselves and their belongings clean." Lady shook her head. "But a lot of Americans coming into Indian Territory never bathe, carry vermin, and spit on tobacco on floors. They bring in deadly diseases, too."

Rafe nodded in understanding. He'd seen a lot of that in jails and saloons. Baths weren't exactly easy to come by. Some men swore a bath would break their health, so they never let soap and water touch their skin, much less their clothes. Indians had died in the thousands because of European diseases like smallpox and cholera. But he didn't know what that had to do with burning down a saloon.

"Place was crawling with vermin," Lady said. "Eating the timbers, infesting the beds, stinging the patrons."

"Fire cleanses," Crowdy said again.

"I can see that," Rafe agreed, "but it was still your business and most men wouldn't mind a few bugs."

"Next Young Moon," Crowdy said.

Rafe didn't know what that had to do with the fire, so he didn't say anything.

"New moon," she explained, "is considered the most propitious time for beginnings."

"So you're going to rebuild," Rafe said, not much liking the idea that once he wore his marshal's badge again, he'd have to return and arrest the saloonkeeper.

"Ashes feed green shoots," Crowdy said.

"He's free to get on with his life now," Lady said.

"Wait a minute," Rafe said. "Let me get this straight, are you or are you not going to rebuild?"

Crowdy smiled, a slight twitch to his lips, and gave Lady a sidelong glance. "Gold in pockets. Horses on horizon."

Lady laughed. "Long as I've known Crowdy, he's wanted to raise horses. Looks like he's finally going to do it."

"Big meet at Stone Corral," Crowdy said. "Plenty of horses there."

"You going?" Lady asked.

"Not a bad idea," Crowdy said.

"Hayes Brothers told me they'd pass the hat if I sang there."

"I'd like to see Robber's Cave," Rafe added.

"Fact is, I'm plum broke." Lady winked at Crowdy. "You took the last of my money."

"Helped lighten your load," Crowdy said, a touch of humor in his voice.

Lady chuckled. "You did that, all right." She glanced at Rafe. "Maybe we'll go on up there."

Crowdy slanted a glance at Rafe. "Outlaws'll swarm Robber's Cave. You sure you want to go?"

Rafe hesitated, for a moment thinking that maybe somehow Crowdy knew he was a lawman and was giving him a warning. But no, the Indian just looked normally somber. "No reason not to see the place."

"Saloon gone. Outlaws gone. No lawmen," Crowdy said.

Rafe glanced at Lady, again wondering if maybe Crowdy *was* giving him a warning after all.

She shrugged as if she didn't know either.

He guessed there was no way to know the truth of the matter, not without asking Crowdy point-blank. Might not do any good anyway. At least the former saloonkeeper was no longer selling whiskey. He wouldn't be wanted by the law. Left Rafe off the hook for arresting one of Lady's friends.

"The Boggy Saloon is in your past now," Lady said. "I'd like to see all those horses. I'm looking for a good stallion."

"Mare better," Crowdy said. "Stallions like wind. Mares like gold."

"I've got my mare. Jipsey. Now I need my stallion."

"You'll find him," Crowdy said.

"Crowdy's a perfect example of why the best horses are in Indian Territory," Lady said, glancing at Rafe. "A lot of Indian wealth is valued in horses."

"Good idea," Rafe agreed. "If you've got a horse, you're alive. If you're on foot, you may be dead."

"Smart man," Crowdy said, humor underlying his words. "You got vittles?"

"Guess you lost everything in the fire," Lady said.

Crowdy nodded.

"As a matter of fact, we've got some good food we bought in Paris."

"Big place." Crowdy said. "Went there once."

"Never again?" Lady asked.

"Like it best here." Crowdy sat down by the water and wrapped his blanket around him. He pulled out fixin's from a leather beaded and fringed bag tied at his waist. "Smoke?"

"Don't mind if I do." Rafe sat down beside him.

"I'll get the food," Lady said, rolling her eyes, "while you two brave warriors keep watch."

"Don't build a fire," Rafe warned, reaching out for tobacco. "Wouldn't want to attract any desperados."

"Not likely," Lady said. "Plenty here."

Chapter 27

As she crossed Beaver Creek at dusk in the Kiamichi River Valley, Lady wanted nothing more than to step down from Jipsey and rest her weary body. Maybe her mind was making her feel tired because she'd pondered all day what to say to Rafe, or maybe she just felt the aches and pains from the day's journey. Either way, she still didn't know how to begin telling all that she wanted to explain.

She'd hoped to have Crowdy on the journey to Robber's Cave, but he'd told her that he had business in Delaware Bend. Maybe she'd see him at Stone Corral, maybe not. Now that he was free of the saloon, he'd live life on Indian time, coming and going at will. At least, he'd promised to take Ma Engle's funeral jewelry to Manny at the livery stable, letting her friend know she was okay and still on Copper's trail.

Without Crowdy as a fence separating her from Rafe, she had built a wall of her own as the sun slowly gave way to the moon. She adjusted her hat to keep the slanting rays off her face, thinking back to that morning.

Shortly after dawn, she and Rafe had turned east on the Fort Towson Road where it crossed the Boggy River. From there, they'd headed north on the old Military Trail that eventually led to Fort Smith, Arkansas. And Judge Parker. Not a happy thought and one she hoped hadn't entered Rafe's mind, but she figured he'd been stewing all day about confronting federal law officers there. She hoped he had better sense.

But that wasn't her main concern, not now. By the light of day, she'd realized she'd lost whatever sense she had the night before when she'd fallen into a frenzy for Rafe. Not smart. Lady Gone Bad made men want her. Not the other way around. She must stay cool and detached to achieve her goals. Still, she needed Rafe's help, and men could be touchy about rejection. If she explained her position, maybe he'd understand and not take it personally.

"I was in love once," she finally said.

"What?" Rafe glanced over at her, eyebrows raised in surprise.

"You must have been, too." She swallowed hard to moisten her throat, which had gone dry. "At our ages, couldn't help but have been."

"Only once?"

"Once was plenty."

"What happened?"

"I'm making a point."

"What point?" He turned Justice near her, and his black boot strafed her red boot.

"I discovered romantic love isn't real."

Rafe cleared his throat. "And other love?"

"For family."

"That's real?"

"Yes. And the love between me and my horses."

"How do you think husbands and wives get together?" he asked.

"Bargains. One herds cattle, farms. The other cooks, cleans, raises babies."

"Anything else bring them together?"

"Lust. You know. Like a mare in heat. Stallions can't resist."

Rafe chuckled, shaking his head as he glanced over at her. "You've got it all figured out, don't you?"

Lady darted a frown at him. "It's not funny."

"Let me get this straight. Men and women join forces for convenience. Is that right?"

"Seems so."

"You're right. It can happen that way. But not always. What about your parents?"

She hesitated, considering. "Devoted to each other."

"Love?"

"Yes."

"But not romantic?"

"The family kind of love." She thought back, remembering Da bringing Ma a bunch of flowers, a pail of blackberries, a shawl from town, and Ma's delight, reaching up to pat his cheek, give him a quick kiss on his lips. "But I don't think they count."

"How can they not count?"

"They're my Ma and Da." She felt a painful burning in her chest, remembering the loss of her parents. She just couldn't stand to ever go through that type of loss again.

"Want to talk about us?"

"No." Lady took a deep breath. "I mean, yes. There is no us. That last night? Too many emotions rolled into one. Won't happen again."

"Lady," he reached over, took hold of her hand, and squeezed.

She jerked away and turned Jipsey to force space between them.

"No, not Lady." He urged Justice toward her, boot scraping against boot again. "After last night, you're Sharlot."

Frowning, she looked over at him. "No. You mustn't use my name. You'll forget to call me Lady when we're at Robber's Cave. Besides—"

"No, I won't." He gave her an intense look. "What's your full name? You know mine."

"Rafe, it's not necessary—"

"If you don't tell me, I'll harass you all the way to Robber's Cave."

She sighed, shrugging her shoulders. "Sharlot Eachan."

He smiled, gray eyes lighting up. "Lovely. Suits you."

"My parents thought so."

"Is that Irish?"

"Da, yes. Ma . . . Sharlot's a Choctaw word."

"That's why you're here? Indians?"

"And the wonderful land."

"Eachan seems familiar. I wonder where I've heard it before?"

"No telling." Lady shook her head, thinking it best not to talk about her name or her parents any more. She wanted to make a point, but couldn't seem to get there.

Ahead she saw antlers nailed to a post oak with chattering birds clustered on top among the green leaves. As the horses approached, the birds grew silent, and then rose into the air with a flutter of wings and flew away. Yellow, orange, and blue wildflowers studded the tall green grass on either side of the road, their sweet and tangy scents swirling on the breeze flowing down from the northern mountains.

Lady wished she could feel as beautiful and serene as the landscape, but she felt too much turmoil inside for peace.

"There's the cutoff to Antlers Spring," she said, pointing at the antlers. "It'll make a good place to stop for the night."

"Rest the horses before we head up into the mountains."

Lady nodded, gazing into the far horizon where the land rose in green waves toward the north. They had some hard riding ahead of them, but unspoiled beauty to enjoy, too.

As she turned Jipsey down a narrow trail, she glanced at Rafe. "I was trying to tell you something."

"About being in love?"

"I was nineteen. He was twenty-three." She smiled wistfully in remembrance. "He showed up at the farm looking for work. He was good with horses. He said he wanted to stay, and marry me. That's what I wanted. What I needed. No son, so Da required a son-in-law to help with the horses. At nineteen, I was a romantic fool."

"You're not the only one," Rafe said, voice soft and gentle. "What happened?"

"Turned out he was a horse thief. That's why he knew animals so well. Stole two of Da's prized stock."

"Law catch him?"

"Da didn't want to make my pain any worse. He let it go."

"So you became the son and daughter all rolled into one?"

"No choice. I learned my lesson well. I couldn't let any of us be hurt like that again."

"What happened to the rustler?"

"Shot in the back by another horse thief in the Bend. Or so I heard."

"What's his name? Maybe I know about it."

"I don't want to talk about him. It's over and done with. Long time ago now."

"What about your parents?"

"No more. I just wanted to explain why we aren't going to roll around in any more springs."

"Sharlot, I'm not like your fiancé. I respect women. I

put horse thieves behind bars. And I make commitments I keep."

"I keep my vows, too." She glared at him. "But you're not one of them."

"Don't be so sure. Miles to go before we reach Robber's Cave." He grinned, giving her a naughty look. "I intend to take advantage of every one of them."

Chapter 28

"This isn't a medicine spring, is it?" Rafe asked as he rode Justice close to Antlers Spring. He eased up on the reins and sat still in the saddle as the gelding lowered his head and drank from the deep green pool of water.

"No." Lady let Jipsey guzzle beside Justice. "You can tell by the smell. It's just good water for travelers."

"Looks safe enough around here." He checked the area for danger, but saw nothing that might be trouble. Hackberry, blackjack, post oak trees. Grass, wildflowers, bugs. Somewhere nearby would be rabbits, possums, squirrels, and deer. Predators like coyotes and hawks wouldn't be far away, not with such rich pickings.

"Unless somebody joins us by sundown, we'll most likely have the place to ourselves tonight."

"Glad to hear it." Rafe had discovered at the Boggy Saloon that he didn't like sharing Lady . . . no, Sharlot. It'd take him a while to get used to saying her given name, but he'd get there, or use both. She'd managed to go from being Lady Gone Bad, notorious outlaw singer, to Sharlot Eachan, tough but tender partner, in a short enough time to make his head spin. One thing for sure, he had to keep her on the straight and narrow, no matter how much she wanted to stray. Course, that didn't mean him. She could stray as much as she wanted with him. And he'd be happy to help her along the way.

"Good place to fill our canteens," Lady said, "but we'll never be short of water in Choctaw Nation."

"Far as I know, we don't have to cross any big rivers up north."

"Nothing we can't handle."

"Let's build a campfire behind that rock away from the spring in case we get company. Fire will keep predators away," Rafe said.

"I'll make some cowboy coffee."

"Wouldn't pass it up." He tossed a quick smile her way. Even tired and disheveled, maybe a little blue about her dumb-as-a-post, horse thief fiancé, she still appeared as inviting as a cool drink of water on a hot day. He was ready for that drink right now, but he knew how to bide his time.

When he'd built a fire pit with rocks ringing sandy soil, he laid on dry wood varying in size from twigs to branches to a trunk that ought to burn down and last the night. He struck a match from a tin he kept in his saddlebags and got a blaze going. That task done, he helped her unsaddle Justice and Jipsey, and then hauled their paraphernalia over to the fire.

While he set both rifles within easy reach, she unrolled the blankets they carried behind their saddles and spread them out, side by side, in front of the fire. She sat down on her blanket, then unbuckled her gun belt and set her six-shooter aside. She closed her saddlebags.

When the dying sunlight played across her auburn hair, highlighting the red, he itched to set her hair free from its neat chignon and bury his face in the long, silky tresses. He clenched his fists to control the impulse, watching as she performed the simplest of tasks with the grace she brought to everything.

She spooned coffee grounds into two tin mugs blackened with use and filled them with spring water, and then set the mugs on the fire to boil. She rummaged around in her saddlebags, and pulled out cheese, crackers, and jerky that she set on a red and white check napkin.

Glancing up, she gestured with her hand toward the meal. "All ready for you, sir."

"Looks good," Rafe said. "I'm so hungry I could eat a horse."

"And chase the rider," Lady finished, chuckling at the old joke.

"Chase you more likely." Rafe sat down beside her, feeling heat from the fire, the day, and his desire gnawing away at him.

Lady ignored his remark, picked up some food, and started to eat.

He didn't know when he'd seen anything so delectable as Sharlot nibbling a piece of yellow cheese. Rosy lips, white teeth, pink tongue were all meant for something much, much better. He quickly lost his appetite for anything but her.

"Aren't you hungry, after all?" she asked, using another napkin to pick up both mugs and set them aside to cool. "Coffee's about ready."

He'd be a fool not to eat when he had the opportunity, so he picked up a cracker and a piece of cheese. They tasted like dust in his mouth, but he chewed anyway, gaze burning into her as the sun slowly sank and night wrapped them in a cozy cocoon. A coyote howled in the distance and was answered by another. Something rustled in the grass, and then grew still.

All his senses were on alert, heightened by her nearness. He picked up his mug to wash down the food and took a big drink of coffee. Scorched his mouth. He swallowed hard, shaking his head.

"Bet that burned." She held up her canteen. "Cool water will help."

He tossed back the water and felt quick relief. He wiped his mouth with the back of his hand, screwed on the lid, and held out the canteen. As she reached for it, their fingers touched, sending another fire burning through him.

She snatched the canteen away. "Feel better?"

"Thanks." He nodded in agreement, but nothing helped the blaze she'd ignited inside him. The coffee was cool in comparison.

"Finished eating?"

"Thanks." Words had pretty much left him as his body took over, his cock straining against his blue jeans at just being near her.

She tightly rewrapped what was left of the food, stored it in her saddlebags, and then got up to hang the bags over the branch of a tree. "That ought to keep out the raccoons."

He patted the blanket beside him. "Ought to make plans for when we get there." He tugged off one boot and sock, and then the other. He eased both feet into the cool spring water and felt a little relief. But nothing could help the ache he felt for Sharlot, except the lady herself.

Hesitating, she looked out into the night, and then sat down beside him, holding out her hands to the fire as if cold. "I don't know how much we can plan ahead of time. Try to get a lead on Copper and that deputy marshal."

"Lady . . . Sharlot," he said, reaching out and pulling pins out of her chignon so that her hair tumbled down her back.

She inhaled sharply, turning to glare at him. "I told you we weren't—"

"What if we made a bargain?"

"We already did that."

"Personal."

"What do you mean?"

He sighed, doing his best to look miserable. "Or you could take pity on me?"

"You're the least pitiable man I know."

"It's your fault."

"My fault?"

"How long do you think I can be around a woman like you without, well, having my needs met?"

Lady's mouth dropped open in astonishment. "I can't believe you said that."

"I'm desperate." He reached up slowly and twined a lock of her hair around a fingertip. "It's a long way to Robber's Cave."

"I suppose just any woman would do, so we'd better find a willing one." She jerked her hair away from him.

"You've been teasing and tormenting men for a long time."

"They deserve it."

"Payback for that fiancé?"

"You don't know anything about it."

"I think I do." He gently took hold of her hand and slowly, repeatedly stroked the palm with his thumb. "You can hurt me. I won't break. I'll take the fury you've wanted to unleash for so long."

She jerked her hand away and jumped to her feet. "I can't tell you anything."

"You can tell me everything." He slowly got up, so as not to spook her, and stood in front of her. "Want to slap me? Hit me?"

"No!" She spun around and presented her back to him.

"Want to kiss me?"

"No!" She was breathing hard, as if from running, maybe wanting to run away, but she stood still.

He placed both hands on her shoulders and gently massaged the way he would a spooked animal. "I need you.

You can tease and torment me, hurt me any way you want, but take mercy on me and, at least, let me kiss you."

She shrugged off his hands and turned around to face him. "Why won't you let me be? You came to the Bend to capture me. Is there no end to what you want of me?"

"No," he said on an exhale of breath. "You caught me first. Handcuffed me. Rescued me. Doesn't that make me yours?"

"You're not a horse! Yet you sound like you want to be broken to my saddle."

"Worse things I can think of."

"Rafe, stop it," she said, voice trembling. "Remember why we're together. This doesn't help achieve our ends."

"I told you, I want another bargain."

"Oh, what is it?" she snapped, turning from him and taking several steps away closer to the fire.

"You're not a cold woman."

She kept her back to him, picked up a stick, and poked at the fire.

"You're not a bad woman, no matter your song."

She poked the fire harder.

"But you're a needy woman."

She threw the stick in the fire and whirled around to face him.

"Need makes you weak. I know. I'm needy, too," he said, desperate to find the words to reach her.

"I'm not weak!"

"Vulnerable then."

"No!"

"Sharlot, we're sparking off each other all the time. Desperados will notice and use it against us. That makes us both weak."

She took a deep breath, inhaling sharply.

"We can take care of each other's needs. Nobody else has to know. Then we finish our other business."

"And go our separate ways?"

"If that's what you want."

"No love?"

"If that's what you want."

"You said a bargain."

"Right. We already have one. Why not another?"

She glanced back at the fire, body stiff, back straight. "I can't take a chance on—"

"No need." He kept his voice gentle, hardly able to believe she was actually listening to him, considering his offer. And yet, it was like her to get what she wanted on her terms, and he wouldn't have gone this far if he hadn't thought she wanted him as much as he wanted her. "I carry French caps."

"What?" She swiveled to face him.

"I'd never endanger a woman. Caps are made from the gut tube of a sheep."

"Oh!" She put both hands to her cheeks and stared at him in embarrassment, blushing a pretty shade of pink. "I see. Deputy U.S. Marshals are always prepared. Colt .45. Ammunition. French caps."

Rafe didn't say anything. Maybe he'd gone too far. She wasn't as knowledgeable as she'd led the world to believe. Maybe he wasn't handling the situation right at all. He'd thought she wouldn't want romantic. She'd said so. He thought she'd like making another bargain. She'd done it before. Now, he feared he'd lost his chance at wooing her.

She put her hands on her hips and looked him up and down. "You think you're man enough?"

Hope leaped in his chest, but he wouldn't get cocky, not with unpredictable Lady Gone Bad. "If you're woman enough."

"What kind of bargain did you have in mind?"

For a moment his mind went blank. Had he actually

talked her into it? His body caught on fire at the thought. "Equal. I take care of you. You take care of me."

"No strings attached. Either one of us can walk away from the deal whenever we want."

"Wait. We must complete our first bargain before either one of us can end this one. Fair?"

She hesitated, cocked her head to one side as if considering the bargain, and then held out her hand for an agreement shake.

He simply stared at her in amazement, unable to believe the moment. When reality hit him, he felt weak in the knees, but he quickly rallied. He gently shook her hand, and then lifted it to his lips and seared her palm with a kiss.

Chapter 29

Lady felt Rafe's whisper of a kiss go straight to her gut where it exploded like a stick of dynamite, flames licking out to singe every bit of her. Fever turned to chills, and she shivered as her mind raced along with her body.

She'd been a fool to think she could walk away from what Rafe made her feel. She'd tried to reject him. She'd known it was the smart thing to do. But when he'd told her that he needed her, he'd melted her right down to her toes.

He was so different from Derry Atwater, that long-gone, rotten-to-the-core fiancé. She desperately wanted to know if sex, forget romantic love, could always be as good as Rafe had revealed at Medicine Spring. Most likely she was making excuses for being in heat, which was nothing more than a physical reaction to an extremely desirable man, namely Rafe Morgan.

She'd been playing with fire so long, with low-cut satin gowns, emotional songs, the come-on teasing, that when she finally got burned she shouldn't have been surprised. And yet she had been. After Derry's betrayal and the death of her parents, she had iced down her emotions, pushing her anger and hurt deep inside, and believed she was beyond the needs other people felt. Maybe she had been, but not from the first moment she'd set eyes on one big, bad deputy marshal.

She'd intimately known only one man. Derry had been a slam, bam, thank you, ma'am sort of lover. She hadn't figured she was missing out on much till Rafe showed her different. Now that she'd made her bargain, she could only hope it was a good one.

So far she didn't have any complaints. Rafe continued to hold her hand, nibbling each finger in turn, creating a sensual result that another man probably needed total body contact to achieve. She was beginning to think Rafe knew a lot more than just how to be a lawman.

"Sharlot," he said, his voice vibrating low as he placed her hand over his heart and smiled down at her, firelight dancing in his smoky gray eyes. "Do you want to draw straws to see who gets their needs met first?"

"I don't want to even think about finding straws." She frowned at him. "No hay in sight and the grass is green." She could feel the rapid beat of his heart against her palm, and her heart matched his tempo.

"Twigs?"

"If you stop touching me, I'm gonna make you regret it."

He chuckled, pressing her hand harder against his chest. "Last thing I want is to annoy you."

"That's mostly what you've been doing since the moment we met."

"About time I changed that, isn't it?"

"I wouldn't disagree."

He smiled, a wolfish movement revealing white teeth. "What kind of thanks do I get in return?"

"The pleasure of Lady Gone Bad's company."

"Good. But not good enough." He slowly pulled her hand down his body, fingers catching against one button after another, until he stopped at the first metal button of his Levi's.

"I'm thinking you're not wantin' to wait," she said, her voice husky as she pushed lower to the bulge that was waiting for her, only her. She massaged in a slow circle. "You gonna bust out all the buttons of your jeans before we're said and done?"

He pushed long fingers into the loose hair on either side of her face. "Hope you're good with a needle and thread."

"Maybe I ought to sew your Levi's up for good."

"Then what would you do?" He tilted her face up, so he was looking down into her eyes.

"Guess it'd be a cryin' shame."

"I'd be doing the cryin'."

"Not alone."

He smiled again, predator to prey. "Darlin', I'm gonna strip you down to your birthday suit and ogle you by fire-light."

"Not if I strip you first."

He chuckled, pushing fingers deep into her hair, grasping her head for control as he lowered his face and pressed feather-light kisses across her forehead, the tip of her nose, then down her cheek to her ear where he toyed, hot, moist breath followed by a hotter tongue that delved into sensitive skin before blazing a path down her neck to her shoulder where he nibbled and licked and kissed until she felt her knees go weak.

She grabbed the front of his shirt and hung on for dear life, not sure if her own legs would hold her up any longer. When he worked his way back up her neck to her lips, teasing and tormenting with sharp nips followed by soothing kisses, she moaned and reached up to wrap her hands around his neck. His fingers dug into her hair as his kiss turned hard, insisting and demanding, so she opened her mouth to allow him entry, but he sucked her tongue into his mouth so that she was the aggressor. She was desperate for more, so much more of him, as she crushed his thick hair in her hands and pulled him against her, mouth to mouth, tongue to tongue, body to body. Fire lapped at her like water on a bank, and she wanted to drown in it . . . in him.

When he finally raised his head, she actually felt dizzy. She clutched the fabric of his shirt again, steadying herself as she looked up in wonder at him.

"Not annoying you now, am I?" he asked, looking pleased with his actions as he rubbed her shoulders with strong hands.

"Only if you keep your clothes on." She smiled, feeling pretty wolfish her own self.

"Didn't we agree you'd go first?"

"If we did, I changed my mind."

"Lady's prerogative."

"I want your shirt off."

"Take it."

Nostrils flaring in excitement, she inhaled sharply and caught his scent of sage and leather mingled with wildflowers and buffalo grass. Nature gone wild.

Wanting to savor every moment, she started with the cuffs of his shirt, slipping free each button before she reached up to the collar. From there she made a steady descent, button after button, pulled out the hem, more buttons till his shirt was nothing more than a husk ready to be shucked.

"Take it," he said again, voice vibrating low and urgent.

"Not so fast." She grasped the waistband of his Levi's. "More buttons. A lady's work is never done." She popped the top button, and then the next. "You're not wearing drawers!" she exclaimed in surprise.

"Wouldn't want to slow you down."

She glanced up at his face, saw the amused smile, and

then shrugged. He was giving her exactly what she wanted and making it easy, so no need for her to turn prim and proper. She was only two buttons away from revealing the heart of him, the hard heat of him, and her hands trembled in anticipation.

"Darlin', I'm waitin' for some help here," Rafe said, voice tight with suppressed tension.

She dropped to her knees, quickly undid the last buttons, jerked down his blue jeans, and came face to face with a whole lot more than she'd expected, or seen before except on a stallion. Thick. Long. Dark. "May I touch?"

He chuckled, an amused sound drawn from deep in his throat. "If you don't, I'm gonna be in trouble."

She put out a fingertip, gently touched the throbbing head, and then closed her hand around his shaft. Hard. Hot. Heavy. She felt a corresponding heat in her core, a searing knowledge that what she held belonged inside her. Only this long length of him could ease her burning ache.

"You gonna hang me out to dry, or you gonna give me some help?" Rafe asked, his voice husky.

"I don't know what to do." She knew she sounded embarrassed, and she felt that way, too.

"I'm happy to educate you."

Rafe wrapped both her hands around his cock, covered them with his own, and began a movement, rhythm, friction that had him groaning with increasing need. She felt her own excitement build when he dropped his hands and she continued what he'd taught her, feeling empowered in a way she'd never experienced before this moment. She felt him grow hotter and harder, if that was even possible, as she stroked his long length, gaining mastery over him as she gained more confidence with every single motion.

"Kiss me quick." He pulled away her hands and jutted forward, angling toward her mouth.

Uncertain, surprised, even shocked, she hesitated at his

next lesson. Yet she also felt emboldened and determined to learn how to please him. She gently kissed the pulsing tip, heard him groan, and then felt his hands on the back of her head, pulling her face toward him. When his shaft filled her mouth, he moved in and out, deeper, harder, quicker with growing urgency.

Now she understood the type of kiss he wanted. She gave to him what he'd given to her on the banks of Medicine Creek, reveling in the power and the pleasure. When ecstasy overcame him, he quickly pulled out, shuddering with release on the ground nearby.

He glanced at her, eyes like silver fire, a flame she had ignited, nurtured, and stoked to brilliance.

"I'll take that shirt now."

Chapter 30

"You look entirely too pleased with yourself," Rafe said, shucking off his shirt and tossing it toward her.

Lady caught the garment with both hands, and then rubbed her face against the soft fabric like a contented cat, smiling slightly.

"Now it's your turn," he said, drawing her attention back to him, real flesh and blood, not spun cotton.

She set aside his shirt, and then looked him up and down, letting her gaze linger here and there as if she was branding him.

Not a fanciful man, he still felt scalded, stroked, wound up for another round of passion. He didn't even know how he could respond so quickly. It had never happened before. Yet this was Lady Gone Bad, and she could inspire a whole mountain of men with the lift of one eyebrow. One man was a goner, for sure.

"About my birthday suit?" She put one hand on her hip and the other in her hair, striking a notorious erotic pose.

He felt his prick jerk in response. At this rate, she might have to bury him at Antlers Spring. But at least he'd die happy. "I'm ready for your show and you don't even need to sing."

"Singing is not part of our bargain anyway." She tossed

back her hair, highlights blazing crimson in the firelight. Agate eyes sparkled like precious jewels. When she touched the first button of her blouse, she hesitated, as if unsure.

"Don't stop now."

She backed up to a nearby tree and leaned against the rough bark. She plucked off one boot and sock, then the other, and lobbed them at him.

He caught the flying missiles, amused that she was testing his reflexes. He set them out of harm's way. He wanted to be comfortable for the coming show, so he sat down on his blanket near the campfire. Plus, this way he was near his Winchester and Colt .45 in case somebody tried to catch them by surprise, maybe a little too easy when they were so distracted with each other.

When he turned back, Sharlot stood in the light of the fire, all soft shadows and wanton curves.

"You ready?" she asked, her voice husky with repressed emotion.

"Ready since the first time I saw you in the Bend."

She tossed him a mischievous look. "You and all the other bad hombres."

"Yeah. But they lost out."

"And if they hadn't?"

"They'd be in jail."

Chuckling, she made quick work of the buttons on her blouse, and then unbuttoned the waistband of her split-skirt. She slowly eased the blouse off one shoulder, then the other, and tossed it to him.

He caught the blouse, crushed it in his hands, and was enveloped in the scent of lavender and lemon. Sweet and tart. Exactly like Lady Gone Bad.

When Sharlot slowly pushed the skirt lower and lower till it fell in a pool around her bare feet, he took a deep breath to keep from reaching out and grabbing her. She kicked the garment toward him, and he added it to the growing pile, never taking his gaze off her.

She stood completely still for a moment, letting him feast his eyes. She wore a white sleeveless, scoop neck chemise with matching drawers that brushed the top of her knees, but not much was left to the imagination since she didn't wear a corset. Full breasts. Long legs. Narrow hips.

"You bought that underwear in Paris, didn't you?" He didn't remember it, didn't care about it, but he knew women set store by what they bought. He wanted to please her, so she'd please him.

"Good eye. Fine muslin with lace on the bosom and hems of the drawers."

"Nice. But I prefer a bosom without lace or muslin."

She chuckled. "Are you sure you're up to bare flesh?"

"Good thing I'm not wearing my Levi's."

"You'd be busting out more buttons?"

"I'm that up to it."

Still smiling, she lowered her body to all fours on her blanket, and then slowly crawled toward him. A shoulder of the chemise slipped down one arm to reveal breasts like ripe melons tipped with cherries, just waiting to be plucked.

He broke out in a sweat, his entire body rigid with need. She wasn't going to make it easy on him. She was going to make him suffer. She might even make him beg. He no longer cared. Pride be damned.

Sitting on his haunches, legs spread, prick at attention, he clenched his fists at his sides as she moved inch by slow inch toward him. He could've run a mile by the time she leaned down, swiped the tip of his shaft with her tongue, and then gave him a quick, wet kiss on the lips.

"Help," she murmured.

She didn't need to say more. He pulled the chemise up over her head, tossed it aside, cupped her bare breasts with his hands, and then jerked her against his chest. He pushed his prick between her legs as he fell over backward with her straddling him.

He held his body still, felt her tremble, both of them breathing fast. A branch collapsed in the campfire, and sparks flew upward, bathing the night in a fiery glow. If she didn't need him to be tender, gentle, slow, he'd follow that explosion with his own fiery, molten eruption.

Instead, he cradled her head with his hands, pressing quick kisses to her lips, and then plunging inside to ravage, tasting and nibbling with increasing intensity. Body burning, he reached down and cupped her butt with both hands, squeezing and massaging while he pushed upward with his cock, sliding against fine muslin turned wet with her desire.

She set him on fire when she drew her mouth away from his lips and pressed hot kisses across his chest, nibbling and sucking as her hands pulled at his hair. She clenched her legs around his hips and rode him, and he pushed up in response, harder, faster, building toward a climax between her legs.

And then he stopped all motion, gritting his teeth. "No, Sharlot, not like this. I want to be inside you."

"Rafe, please, don't leave me this way."

"I won't. I promise." He lifted her and set her gently aside, sweat beading his forehead with the effort to stay in control.

"I need you." She reached out to him. "Our bargain."

He pressed a tender kiss to her lips, and then turned away. He jerked open his saddlebag, rummaged around, and found the French tips. Never had he wanted anything more than to be bathed in her hot juices, but he had promised to protect her, so he was going in clothed.

When he had the French tip in place, he turned back to her. Nothing was going to stop him now.

He pushed her back against the blanket, tugged down her drawers, tossed them aside, and then lowered his body between her spread legs.

"If you fail me now, Rafe, I'll never forgive you."

He grinned, teeth white and sharp in the firelight. "Did that horse thief of a fiancé fail you?"

She turned her head to the side, eyes downcast.

"Look at me."

She glanced back, and nodded.

"I'm gonna burn him right out of your mind. Your body."

She nodded again.

He put a hand on each side of her face and held her still, body to body, heat to heat, and pressed a gentle kiss to her lips. "When we're done, there's never been anybody before for either of us."

"Nobody but us," she echoed.

He gripped her, raised her hips, feeling the slick, wet heat invite him inside. He mustn't rush. He shuddered with the need for control. Easy. Gentle. Slow.

"Rafe! I can't wait." She lunged upward and rammed him home.

Nothing for it now. He couldn't stop or slow down, couldn't do anything but plunge away into her burning, secret depths, over and over, harder and harder, wiping out all that had gone before, imprinting himself so deep, so strong, so hot that she would never want any man but him, ever again.

When he heard her cry out his name, felt her clench and spasm around him, he finally let go, found his own release.

He fell back against the blanket still inside her, drawing

in quick breaths, satisfied for the first time since he'd seen her onstage at the Red River Saloon.

"Rafe," she murmured after a time, moving closer, moving her hips. "You ready to ride again?"

Chapter 31

"I want more!" Lady turned in her saddle, giving Rafe a look hot enough to set his clothes on fire.

He smiled. They'd already stopped twice along the road. "If you polish my knob any more, I'm not going to be able to wear Levi's for a month."

"Bargain's a bargain."

"We're almost at Robber's Cave."

"I'm thinking a quick stop."

"Outlaws'll be lurking. Want to put on a show?"

"Bet they'd pass the hat."

Rafe chuckled, tossing her a steamy glance. "And fill it."

"One way to make money."

"Better way. You sing. Nothing more."

She winked, then threw back her head and sent a peel of laughter across the trail to join the musical gurgle of nearby Fourche Maline Creek. Just as quickly, she turned serious and guided Jipsey close to Justice. "We're running out of time. We've got to get down to business and pick up leads here. No choice."

"With so many outlaws in one place, we stand the best chance we'll ever get."

"So many horses, too."

"Think some desperado will turn up with Copper?"

"Fingers crossed." She experienced a sinking sensation

in the pit of her stomach at the thought of not finding the stallion in time. If some desperado put a bullet in Copper's head because he limped, she'd never be able to forgive herself. But that wasn't going to happen. She felt as if all the long trails she'd followed led here, the heart of horse-thief country deep in the Sans Bois Mountains, a place Epona would surely roam.

If Lady's totems blessed her and gave her strength, she would save Copper and achieve justice. But Spider Grandmother and Epona worked in mysterious ways and in their own time. Lady had to count on herself, not await divine intervention, or she might lose everything.

"Surprising names out here. French trappers?" Rafe asked, glancing around. "That what happened to the Indian names?"

She shrugged. "Guess the French stuck. This was all Wichita and Caddo land, villages and farms in the valleys. Most likely Comanche and Osage hunted game here, too, before the American government forced much of Choctaw Nation to start over in this wilderness. Long before that, Indians who built earth mounds lived here."

"I heard Fourche Maline Creek translates roughly as Bad River."

Lady winked. "Want to be bad on Bad River?

He grinned. "What does Sans Bois mean?"

"Without Trees."

"I wonder what the first Indians named these creeks and mountains." He gestured at the high peaks rising in the distance.

"Something poetic?"

He glanced back at her, chuckling. "More like Pretty Sparkling Water instead of Cross at Your Own Peril?"

Lady laughed. "I hadn't thought about names giving warning."

"Fourche Maline Creek might look a lot more dangerous in a rain storm."

"True. But it's beautiful right now."

"Bet a lot of the outlaws who frequent Robber's Cave discovered it during the War. Guerrilla fighters from Missouri and Arkansas could've used a place like this after raids on Union forces and sympathizers."

"Sure. But after the War Between the States," she added, "amnesty was granted to Federal guerrillas, but not to those of the Confederacy."

"Mistake. Caused more trouble."

"True. Many of the Partisan Rangers kept fighting. They were condemned anyway, so they robbed banks and trains."

"You sound sympathetic."

"A number of outlaws steal only federal, still striking back at the Union."

"War's long over now, going on twenty years."

"Not long enough, not when you consider the wounds. One small example. U.S. General Ewing's Order Number Eleven. He decided that he could control his section of the country better if nobody lived there, so he burned and depopulated a vast area of western Missouri, mostly farm families. Wagon trains miles in length were seen heading west. Behind them dense columns of smoke rose in every direction. Hundreds of folks crowded the banks of the Missouri River. Steamboat captains saved them."

"A lot of depredations happened on both sides. Scars make a man, a nation, tougher."

Lady glanced at Rafe, wanting to see if he understood what she was trying to explain. He might be seeing things a little less black and white than when she'd first met him, but at heart, he was still a by-the-book lawman. "I'm saying some outlaws you hunt are bad men, American criminals hiding out in Indian Territory. You're right to arrest them. But others are Confederate heroes, or sons of heroes, still engaged in the conflict, taking back what the Union stole and giving it to the needy like they did during the War."

Rafe snorted. "Excuses! You wouldn't believe what I've heard in my time. No matter the past, if they break federal law, deputy marshals are coming after them."

Lady sighed. "There's a big difference, between, say, Zip and Crowdy, but you'd take in both."

"If they broke federal law, yes, I'd take them to Judge Parker." He gave her a hard stare. "Crowdy breaks Indian law, then lighthorsemen deal with him."

She frowned, eyebrows drawing together. "When there's a bad crime, like murder, lawmen are nowhere to be found."

"We do the best we can." He sounded regretful. "But we can't be everywhere."

Lady turned a cold shoulder to Rafe and urged Jipsey ahead, feeling tears sting her eyes. She blinked hard, not about to give in to her emotions. No lawman had helped hunt down her parents' murderers, nor solved the crime. And that included Rafe Morgan. She had to get her head on straight. He was just another no-good lawman, looking to make arrests the easy way so he could collect fees. When she'd seen Rafe's face on the wanted poster, she'd started thinking of him as being on her side. *Wrong.* Scratch him and he bled the law. She'd been a fool to let her body get in the way of her mind.

"Nobody can say for sure, but we figure Jesse and Frank James and Cole and Jim Younger used this area," Rafe continued, riding up beside her. "Belle and Sam Starr, too."

"Cole is in federal prison. Twenty-five years for robbery." Lady realized Rafe had no idea how upset their conversation had made her.

"Belle and Sam are there, too. Nine-month sentences."

"First time for them."

"That's why Judge Parker went easy on them."

"I believe there's a lot more fiction than fact about Belle Starr."

"She was foolish enough to marry Jim Reed. He rode with Quantrill's Raiders," Rafe said.

Lady kept her voice calm and even, her tone reasonable. "William Quantrill was a teacher before he formed a state guard unit of Partisan Rangers to protect people. They battled Union occupation armies and Kansas Jayhawkers. Missouri tried to stay neutral, like Cherokee Nation and Choctaw Nation, but was forced to take sides. Brave men like Quantrill helped save lives."

"But he took lives to do it."

He was getting her riled up. "If you invade a place, burn homes, steal food and livestock, murder people, you've got to expect folks to take offense and defend themselves. Belle Starr's family's home and businesses were burned out. The Youngers and others like them were childhood friends defending their homes and neighbors."

"Belle married into the Cherokee Starr family. They have a place north of here at Younger's Bend. Hear she entertains outlaws," Rafe said.

"Old friends," she corrected him tartly. "Deputy marshals don't like Belle Starr because she rides to Fort Smith and helps Indians win in Judge Parker's court."

"I don't dislike the so-called Bandit Queen. If she brings evidence that gets defendants off, I'm okay with it. But she's associated with outlaws her whole life."

"Think you can't love an outlaw? I don't believe you listened to a word I said. Anyway, Belle Starr has created a fascinating image that gives her power and prestige. And that's not easy for a woman."

Rafe glanced at her. "You didn't model yourself after Belle Starr, did you?"

"Could do worse."

"You ever met her?"

"No. But I'd like to. I heard she was raised a lady in Missouri and went to college at a female academy. She's smart. Her mother was a Hatfield related to the feuding Hatfields and McCoys. Her father did well in business. But the War ruined the life she might have led. Still, she hasn't let that stop her. I heard she had a piano hauled out to Younger's Bend. Books, too. She must love to read and play music. I saw a recent photograph of her. She has excellent taste in clothes. Horses, too."

"Good taste, huh? That alone makes her an upstanding citizen."

"Doesn't hurt."

"Maybe she's been smart enough never to get caught before. Or lucky."

"Smart and lucky doesn't always save you." Lady felt tears sting her eyes again, remembering her parents.

"Lady . . . Sharlot, did I say something to upset you?" Rafe reached out to squeeze her fingers.

She slapped his hand away.

"Look, I understand these people are your friends."

"Not all of them."

"Okay. Enough of them help you that you feel loyal. But some are mean as rattlesnakes and prey on the defenseless. My job is to help those who can't help themselves."

Lady took a deep breath to keep from turning on him in fury and demanding an answer as to why he hadn't helped her when her parents were murdered, their home and barn burned, horses stolen. She couldn't trust him. She must never forget that fact. "Right now, we're in this together. I was trying to give you a different outlook to help you fit in. Maybe I was wrong."

"No, you're right." He shook his head as if trying to clear it. "I needed to hear what you said."

"Remember, there are always two sides to a story," she emphasized, her voice cold, back straight. "People aren't black, white, or red. They're gray."

Lady urged Jipsey ahead, pushing Rafe as far from her mind as she could get him. She had to focus on the business at hand and stay alert for danger. And she had to remember he was her enemy, not her friend or lover.

They rode silently along Fourche Maline Creek, following a trail that wound through a narrow valley caught between outcroppings of sheer rock cliffs, sandy bluffs, and riotous green vegetation. She saw white tents pegged here and there on the narrow valley on the other side of the creek where small herds of horses contentedly chomped grass and basked in the sun. Time was limited. When the horses ate the grass down to its roots, the outlaws would have to move their herds to greener pastures.

She felt an easing of tension in her chest at the sight of so many beautiful animals in a wide range of colors. Buckskin, black, and shades of sorrel. She looked for some sign of Copper, but couldn't pick him out at a distance. Later, she'd get permission to ride among the herds to search in earnest.

Drinking in the soft air scented by sweet gum, willow, and maple trees along the creek bank, she noticed small caves and rocky trails in the surrounding hills. Hackberry, oak, hickory, and pine trees provided cool shade from the heat of the sun. A squirrel raced to the middle of the trail, stopped, chittered, and shook his tail in anger at the interlopers before scampering up a nearby tree. Lady chuckled, knowing just how the squirrel felt. Songbirds trilled in the treetops, a hunting hawk cried out, and a vulture silently and patiently crouched overhead.

She let nature seep into her soul, comforting and soothing. She hoped the carrion eater watching them from above wasn't a harbinger of their future, but she'd heard no warning cry in her head from Epona.

About that time, two sorrel horses carrying familiar barrel-chested figures leaped over the Fourche Maline and thundered down the trail.

"Lady!" Bob hollered, plucking his hat off his head and waving it around high in circles.

"Lady Gone Bad!" Burt rode beside his brother, a big grin splitting his face. "You made it! We didn't think you was comin' after that fight. And the fire."

"Dang Hayes Brothers," Rafe muttered in disgust. "Now we'll never get rid of them."

Lady chuckled, feeling her good humor restored at the thought of how much Rafe was going to hate sharing her with other men.

"Hey!" Lady took off her red hat and gave a friendly wave. "Got a good place to camp?"

Chapter 32

"Fast John," Burt called, riding up close. "Zip Rankin and his gang got in last night. You gonna fight again?"

"Is he looking for trouble?" Rafe asked.

"Set to hornswoggle the best horses, most like," Bob said, following his brother.

"Looking for us?" Rafe asked.

"After all that trouble at Boggy Saloon," Lady added.

The Hayes Brothers glanced at each other, sputtered, and then laughed so hard and loud all the horses shied, dancing across the dirt road as the riders struggled to get them back under control.

"Boggy was bodaciously burnt up—" Burt started to say, but gasped for breath as he heaved with more laughter.

"And tetotaciously exflunctocated so bad ever last b'hoy and g'hal in Indian Territory who wanted in on that fight got here fast for the next."

Rafe and Lady stared at them in amazement, but as realization dawned, they joined the laughter.

"What you mean," Rafe said, getting his breath back, "is we made Zip look good so he's not after our hides."

"Fight and fire at the Boggy is a legend that'll dang near outlast us all," Burt said, continuing to chuckle.

"Tale gets any taller, eagles'll be nesting in it," Bob added, shaking his head.

"One thing," Burt said. "Nobody, and I mean nobody, ain't never gonna try to make Lady Gone Bad sing when she ain't got a mind to."

"Caps the climax!" Bob hollered, grinning from ear to ear.

"So everybody's square?" Rafe asked, pushing for more information.

"Far as we know," Burt said, turning serious. "But Zip's not a man to cross."

"So we'd better be on our toes around him," Rafe said.

"Gotta keep an eye on a man that savagerous," Bob agreed.

"Far as I'm concerned, if he leaves us alone, we leave him alone," Lady said. "I'm here to sing and find a horse. Nothing more."

Burt and Bob chuckled, glanced at each other, and then laughed hard all over again, tears twinkling in their eyes.

"That's what you said the last time," Burt gasped, tipping his hat to her in respect. "And you know what ensued."

"Crowdy was tired of the Boggy anyway." She shrugged, still smiling, and looked up ahead. "You see him around?"

"No," Burt said, "but that Indian could be standing right next to you and you'd never know it."

"He's the beatingest," Bob agreed.

"Hope he shows up," Lady said. "We need to make camp. Guess I'll sing tonight since so many are already here."

Burt and Bob guffawed again, punching each other in the shoulder.

"Now what's funny?" Lady asked.

"Bob here bought a ten-gallon hat to pass," Burt said. "B'hoys'll feel guilty till they fill it, so you oughta make out like a bandit."

"Good thing you're riding with a fast gun so as to keep the money safe." Bob nodded in Rafe's direction.

"That hat," Lady said, winking, "is smart thinking. Thanks."

Bob ducked his head, skin turning pink at the compliment.

"Got you set up with a tent so you can change and all," Burt said, not to be outdone.

"Appreciate it." Lady nodded, smiling. "You two are making this easy for me."

"Nobody's gonna mess with you no more," Bob added.

"Lady's our big bug here and gets the best we got to offer," Burt agreed.

"Right friendly of you." Rafe was getting sick of the brothers' admiration. He wouldn't call his feeling jealousy, but it came damn close. He'd had Sharlot's full attention so far on their journey, and he didn't like losing it, or sharing her. And he hadn't even gotten past two men. Wait till she attracted hundreds. When his temper flared, and it was bound to, he'd have to rein it in.

He inhaled sharply, dragging in air to clear his mind. He had to get back on track. He was here to get a lead on Crystabelle and Lampkin. What Sharlot did or didn't do wasn't part of his plan. And he wasn't about to waste an opportunity to scout out Robber's Cave and memorize outlaw faces.

"The Viking's here, too." Bob jerked his head down the road.

"Who's he?" Rafe asked, surprised he hadn't heard of the outlaw.

"Story goes he's a rancher adopted by a Cherokee. He runs cattle and horses north of the Canadian River in Cherokee Nation." Lady shrugged. "He got that moniker cause he's big and blond."

"Brought Angel, he did." Burt took off his hat, and ran a hand through his hair. "Heard she's a looker."

"Hellcat, I heard." Bob grinned, eyes sparkling. "We'll finally get a gander at her and decide for ourselves."

"Who is she?" Lady asked in confusion, looking from brother to brother.

"Heard the Viking bought her with a herd of horses," Burt said.

"Bought her?" Lady asked in disbelief.

"Probably not true." Bob sounded disappointed, lowering his head with a hang-dog expression.

"But you could ask her." Burt brightened, appearing excited at the idea. "G'hal to g'hal."

"If I meet her I will." Lady glanced around the group. "And if she wants, we'll help her escape. Won't we?"

Burt and Bob grinned, pumped their fists in the air, and then twirled their horses in tight circles of celebration.

"Lady, I'll follow you anywhere," Burt said.

"You sure know how to liven things up," Bob added. "I'm all in."

"Let's don't get ahead of ourselves." Rafe didn't want to get involved in some sort of domestic squabble that could land them all in trouble. "We'll wait to see what the situation is, and then do what needs to be done."

"For now," Lady said, "night's coming on. I need to get to my tent."

"Let's go!" Burt hollered, raising his hat, turning, and thundering down the road, Bob hard on his heels.

"Lady's here," they hollered. "Lady Gone Bad is coming! See her sing tonight!"

Rafe glanced over at her. Neither moved as the Hayes Brothers disappeared around a bend, their voices echoing through the valley.

"Guess you're on stage from now on," he said.

"I'll give the Hayes a cut of the hat. Having a tent is a lifesaver."

"They're sure looking out for you."

"Rowdy boys, but good at heart."

"Bet you say that about all the outlaws."

She raised an eyebrow, giving him a long, smoldering look. "Just the lawmen gone bad."

"Better be only one and he better be present."

She pursed her lips, reached over, ran a hand down his shirt to his Levi's, and gave a quick squeeze.

Chapter 33

"Lookin' for trouble?" Rafe asked, voice a rough growl.

"Think I found it?" She pressed his growing erection, and felt an answering response in her own hot depths.

"What do you think?"

"Not sure." She looked mischievously into his smoky eyes. "More proof?"

"Always happy to oblige a lady." He leaned over and set his mouth to her lips, nibbling, licking, and then pushing deep inside.

She moaned as she returned his kiss with escalating fervor, massaging his rigid shaft while a fiery, moist ache built in her center.

When a crow gave a raucous cry overhead, both mounts stamped hooves, bridles jingled, and saddles creaked.

Spell broken, Lady pulled back to look at Rafe's angular face, all smooth, tanned skin with a slash of dark mustache. Gray eyes hot with desire. Full lips moist and puffy with kisses. Strong pulse rapid in his throat. She knew she looked much the same as he and felt shaky with unfulfilled passion.

"Much more and we'll be putting on a show for free." Rafe glanced around the area as if expecting to see an audience.

She looked, too, but for the moment they were alone aside from the uninterested wildlife.

"Might be the last time for a while." He turned back to her.

She nodded in agreement.

He rode Justice to the side of the trail, leaped down, dropped the reins in a ground-tie, and then walked back to her.

"You planning something special?" she asked, teasing him.

"Wouldn't want you to get out of practice." He held up his arms to help her dismount.

She hesitated, wanting him but wanting to be practical, too. She had to get ready for her show. The Hayes Brothers had made it clear that a big group, probably her largest audience yet, waited for her to perform.

She inhaled, caught his unique scent of sage and leather, and was completely lost to desire. Practical be damned. She needed and wanted him more than anything else. She hooked a leg over her saddle horn, and then slid down into his arms. He pulled her hard against him, body to body, letting their tension thrum in unison, building hotter and wilder.

"Make it quick," she whispered in his ear, hardly able to form words in her passionate haze.

"Any way you want it." He wrapped strong fingers around her hand. "Let's leave the horses here to graze."

She plucked off her red hat and hooked it over her saddle horn, ready to go.

He tugged her after him as he pushed through tall grass, around bushes, climbed up a rocky rise, and around a bend. He leaned her back against the thick trunk of an ancient pine tree and pressed hot kisses to her lips as he fumbled with the waistband of her split-skirt.

Dragging her hands from around his neck, she swatted away his slow, clumsy fingers, and quickly unbuttoned her skirt and drawers. Unable to wait a moment longer, she started on the buttons of his Levi's, but stopped cold. "French cap?"

"Hell and damnation!" He jerked away from her, reaching into his back pocket. "Just a minute."

She leaned back against the tree and closed her eyes, impatiently waiting for his touch, acutely feeling her desire burn hotter, intensely knowing only he could satisfy her.

"There!"

Putting large hands around her waist, he jerked down her skirt and drawers, kicked them aside, lifted her up to straddle his hips, and then drove home in one swift movement.

She cried out at the sudden invasion, the hot, hard length melding them together, and clung to him, arms around his shoulders, legs tight around his hips. He pumped like a rutting stallion while she gripped with her inner muscles like a mare in heat, giving him thrust for thrust, heat for heat, a slick, hot ride that drove her to the edge. And over.

He caught her moan in his mouth, thrusting with his tongue as he thrust below with his shaft. His own groan mingled with hers as they gripped each other in a final spasm of mutual ecstasy.

Rafe held her close a long moment, breathing hard, then gently set her down. She leaned back against the tree, so weak and limp she could hardly stand upright as her heart pounded fast in her chest.

"No other men." He gestured toward Robber's Cave. "No matter how many throw themselves at your feet."

She wondered how he could think she'd want or need anybody else except him. Not after that demonstration of his prowess. A cool breeze wafted across her naked skin and she shivered, feeling acutely vulnerable. She stepped into her drawers and skirt.

"Tell me what I want to hear." He pinned her with molten steel in his eyes as he buttoned up his blue jeans.

"We have a bargain. No men but you."

He nodded, a quick snap of his head, and pulled up her drawers and split-skirt as if to make certain no other man touched her.

While she tied and buttoned, she got her breath back under control. She felt satisfied and lazy, not wanting anything more than to snuggle with Rafe, sitting on soft pine needles under the tree. But now was not the time.

"We'd better go." She wanted to say more, but resisted the urge to let him know that she was coming to care too much for him.

He smiled, a sensual quirk of one corner of his mouth. He held out his hand.

She clasped his warm, strong fingers, and let him lead her back the way they'd come. As they moved toward their horses, hands joined, she felt something odd. Instead of closer now, she felt as if they were drifting apart. Bargain or no bargain.

"When I get you settled in your tent, I'm going to scout around. Get the lay of the land in case we run into trouble and need to make a fast escape."

Now she understood. He was turning back into a lawman. Hot anger turned passion cold. "Don't you dare cause trouble. You're here as Fast John, nothing more."

"I know—"

"If you go nosing around these outlaws and they get a whiff of lawman, we'll both end up six feet under. Maybe Burt and Bob, too."

"Give me a little credit for having some sense." He led her down the last bit of rough ground to the horses. He stopped and looked at her. "Remember, we're here to get leads. I'm hoping to find Lampkin. With enough proof, I can put him away."

She squared her shoulders. "I know why we're here, but I need to make money, too. When I put on that crimson gown, I'm Lady Gone Bad, and I'll do whatever I have to do."

"I will, too."

She put on her hat and tugged it low. She put a foot in Jipsey's stirrup, swung up into the saddle, and looked down at him. "Burt and Bob will help me now. You go ahead and see to your own business."

Without waiting for Rafe's response, she set heels to the chestnut's sides and thundered down the trail. Even as she put distance between them, she felt too much of her heart stayed behind with her lawman.

Chapter 34

Rafe let her go. No point in riling Sharlot any more. They both had jobs to do. Better get on with it. He ought to feel lucky. How many times in a man's life did he get a chance with a woman like Lady Gone Bad? Scarcer than hen's teeth. But instead of feeling lucky, he felt like he was losing her to a bigger world than he could ever offer her. He hated the feeling. But no point in dwelling on it. He had no chance to control Lady, but he had a chance to find Crystabelle and Lampkin. That's where he must focus now.

As he mounted Justice and headed down the trail, he already felt his body craving a woman he . . . well, liked, admired, lusted after. Anything but thinking he might be in love with Sharlot. She could just as easily ruin his life as save it. No, love didn't enter into it. They rode opposite sides of the fence. They had a bargain to help each other reach their goals and meet their needs. Nothing more.

With her firmly in place, at least in his mind if not his body, he kept watch for trouble. All seemed peaceful enough as he crossed the low water bridge on Forche Maline Creek and followed the trail that climbed sharply up toward the northeast. He heard voices, laughing, arguing, talking, as he wound his way through dense, green undergrowth.

When he came out on a wide, flat plateau, Robber's Cave clawed up into the sky like a gray top hat to tower over the entire valley. Sheer rock cliffs formed the sides of the mesa. Tall pine, oak, and other trees nestled around the sides, giving the appearance of bushy green whiskers.

No wonder outlaws used the place. From Lookout Point on top, a man could easily see for miles around in every direction. Nobody would catch him unawares. Plus, Robber's Cave was dang hard to reach, so that made it even more ideal. Not surprising lawmen had never caught a single desperado here.

In front of the mesa, grass and shrubs had been cleared to make a wide open space that was now filled with people. They were a rough-looking bunch, sporting six-shooters and hunting knives, fringed leather and rough cotton, cowboy hats and tough boots. Women in colorful clothes wound their way through the groups of men, offering food and whiskey, maybe more. Sitting on tree trunks and smoking tobacco, a number of men focused on poker games.

He glanced around for Lady's tent, but didn't see it. He figured the Hayes Brothers had found her some privacy. She was probably resting before she changed clothes for her performance. Burt and Bob had better not be playing lady's maids, or they'd get an earful at the least. He'd find her later. First he wanted to scout the area.

As he headed for the base of the mesa, he checked out every woman he passed, hoping she'd turn out to be Crystabelle. He didn't care how far his sister might have fallen since she had been kidnapped. One way or another, he'd get her back on her feet. He also kept an eye on the men, but he wondered if Lampkin would be so bold as to appear here, taking a chance on giving away his double life.

When he walked up to the base, he saw the infamous cave, wide mouth yawning dark in the shape of a triangle, point down. Only way to reach it was across a wide expanse of downward sloping flat rock slab. Dangerous. But once inside, an outlaw had a good hideout, a snug place out of the weather, and another defensible position. Even looked like the slab in front was concave enough to catch and hold rainwater. Man could hole up there for a good, long while. The cave looked deep, too, drilling back into the mesa. He'd like to explore, but he didn't have time.

Instead, he glanced up and saw Burt standing on Lookout Point. He waved to get attention.

Burt saw him, and then gestured down at the cliff face.

Rafe looked where Burt pointed and saw a crude set of stairs, mostly natural rock formation, leading to the top. He quickly started the climb, using rock indentations as handholds till he stepped up and over the edge.

He'd found Lady's tent. Set back in one corner, the small white tent couldn't be seen from below. It was a perfect location for her to change to fancy clothes and not tear or dirty them trying to climb up. He started toward the tent.

"Wait!" Burt said, holding up a hand in warning. "We're letting Lady rest before she changes. Nobody disturbs her."

"Not even me?"

"Fast John, for sure not you."

"See your point." Rafe nodded. "She's okay?"

"Right as rain." Burt gestured around him. "Bet you never saw nothing like this."

Rafe gazed out over a green panorama that turned hazy purple in the far distance. "Beautiful country."

"You bet." Burt stepped closer. "Lady's singing from up here."

"Is it safe?"

Burt appeared shocked, even offended. "Wouldn't let nothin' happen to her."

Rafe nodded, realizing she'd probably climbed up here plenty of times.

"Folks can ogle her. Hear her good, too. Natural anteater."

"Ant . . . amphitheater?"

"What she says." Burt smiled, white teeth flashing. "Go on down in back and take a gander. Stone corral sure do beat all."

"I'm heading there now."

"Hurry up. Lady'll want you front and center."

Rafe made his way across the top, watching his footing so he didn't stumble across loose rocks or fall into deep crevices. A few twisted evergreens clung to the surface and he used them for support. Taking one last look at the breathtaking scenery, he started down a slope that was more dirt than rock.

At the bottom, he faced broken boulders and a thick forest, so he took a narrow trail that wound around the base of the mesa toward the front. He dodged huge rocks jutting up from the ground and discovered a narrow entry into what had to be Stone Corral.

Sheer rock walls rose straight up into the sky and enclosed an area perfect for a horse corral. All an outlaw would need to do to pin animals inside was to close the open, narrow side, probably with timber or other rocks. He looked around, impressed by the solid walls and soft, sandy floor. When he noticed a natural cleft in the wall, he checked and saw stone steps leading out. He followed them around and down to the front of Robber's Cave.

He glanced back. If he hadn't seen Stone Corral for himself, he'd never have known the hidden area was there. But he'd remember. If he ever tracked a horse thief back here, he'd know exactly where to look.

With the sun descending in the west, casting long shadows across the mesa, Rafe knew Lady would be singing soon before the light was gone. He started to go wish her luck, but decided he ought to leave well enough alone.

Running out of time, he looked for Crystabelle, but he hadn't gone far when he heard somebody call his name. He glanced up and saw Bob motioning to him, so he walked over there.

"Looks like Lady's in good hands," Rafe said. "If I can be of any help—"

"Got it under control." Bob jerked his head to one side. "Over there. Viking and Angel. I'll take you to meet them. After that, I gotta run."

Rafe didn't want to bother, but he remembered the role he was playing, so he tried to look interested. "So, is she a looker or not?"

"Fast John," Bob said, grinning ear to ear. "Huckleberry above most all persimmons. Lady excluded."

"Got to see her then."

Bob zipped around and moved fast for such a big man. Rafe trailed in his wake, keeping an eye out for Crystabelle.

When Bob quickly stopped, Rafe almost ran into his back. He couldn't see anything around the broad shoulders.

"Viking and Angel, this here's Fast John."

Rafe had to peer around Bob to see the couple.

The Viking was seated on an upended slice of tree trunk, legs spread wide. Long hair, bleached almost white by the sun, hung about his broad shoulders, a feather tied Indian style at the crown. He turned blue eyes the color of the sky up at Rafe, saying nothing as he judged the newcomer. The Viking wore nothing but a leather fringed vest that showed off heavily muscled arms and shoulders with massive thighs outlined by leather trousers. He appeared more savage than any Indian Rafe had ever seen.

The woman known as Angel knelt at the Viking's feet,

her face buried against his knee, hands clinging to his leg. She wore a simple red skirt and a white blouse unbuttoned low enough to show cleavage. Long, wild hair about Rafe's own sorrel color flowed down her back and obscured her face. She looked a hell of a lot more devil than angel.

Bob stepped back. "Fast John's got good stories out of Tombstone."

"Not better than mine," Angel muttered, not looking up. "I got kidnapped and sold. Now I'm a slave to this big brute." She pinched the Viking's thigh.

He covered her fingers with a large hand. "She's a storyteller." His deep voice carried the lilting cadence of a Northman.

"Am not. Did you or did you not buy me?"

"Bought you. Freed you." The Viking shrugged, rolling his eyes at the men watching them. "Shouldn't feed a hungry dog. Follows you home and won't leave."

Angel slapped his shoulder with her free hand. "I'm not a dog!" She tossed back her hair and looked up at Bob. "Don't forget your promise to introduce me to Lady Gone Bad. She's my hero, along with Belle Starr."

"I will all to pieces." Bob winked at Rafe, and then hurried away.

Rafe stepped up into the space left by Bob and saw Angel's face for the first time. He froze in absolute shock and astonishment.

He'd found Crystabelle.

Chapter 35

On the summit of Robber's Cave, Lady gazed out across a wide expanse of brilliant green wilderness slashed by deep, dark gorges and up-flung boulders. Below her, men and women in colors ranging from dull black to vivid red moved here and there, jockeying for better viewing positions, looking up, growing silent in anticipation.

Lady appeared her best, and knew it. She wore the new Paris gown with a stylish fringed apron in front and a high bustle in back, all in eye-catching crimson. She even wore fancy underwear with a corset that lifted her breasts while allowing her to draw deep breaths. Red heels gave her extra height. She'd let her hair down, knowing men found long tresses desirable. She wished she had her guitar, but her voice would simply have to do.

She checked the front of the crowd for Rafe, but for some reason he'd abandoned her just when she needed his support. She guessed if he didn't have a bargain, he didn't show up. He was probably searching for Lampkin. Still, she felt hurt. But she couldn't let her feelings matter or stop her. She had the Hayes Brothers to help her. Bob was down below, holding the ten-gallon hat and keeping an eye on the crowd. Burt had placed a canteen of water and a shawl behind her. He planned to introduce her. Who would have ever thought the Hayes Brothers could turn out to be such good showmen? Maybe they were destined for a new line of work in the near future.

She looked for Rafe again, and then gave up. She glanced at Burt and nodded, ready to go.

He smiled in encouragement and stepped up beside her. "Ladies and gentlemen," he called, deep voice carrying across the plateau. "Take your places and get ready to hear . . ." He made a dramatic gesture toward Lady. "The one, the only, the bodaciously divine . . . *Lady Gone Bad*."

Cheers, catcalls, and foot-stomping rose up from below.

Lady felt chills tingle her spine and took a deep breath. She'd never been presented this way before, and she didn't know quite how to respond. Flutters in her stomach alerted her to the fact that she was not as calm as she would like to be. She was just so excited to be singing for such a large crowd.

"Did you hear me say *bodaciously divine*?" Burt called, motioning to the audience for confirmation.

Voices below called out even louder, chanting Lady's name.

"Lady Gone Bad is *your* huckleberry . . . today, tomorrow, and always." Burt held his arms out wide as if encompassing the entire crowd.

Lady could hardly believe Burt was generating all this excitement for her. She hoped she didn't disappoint after his amazing introduction.

"Ladies and gentlemen, I present to you," Burt hollered above the noise of the crowd, "the one, the only . . . your very own singing sensation . . . *Lady Gone Bad*." He made a final, elaborate gesture toward Lady, and then stepped back out of sight.

She stood alone. Hundreds of people looked up at her.

She knew she must project so her voice carried to them. And she wanted to connect emotionally with each and every one of them.

For a moment she froze, but she noticed a movement to her left and glanced over there. On the edge of Lookout Point, a white mare reared and pawed the air. Surprised, Lady wondered how the horse had gotten up there just as the mare disappeared into thin air. *Epona.* She felt comforted, not alone nor abandoned at this critical hour.

And Spider Grandmother must surely have spun a web that had drawn all these people to Robber's Cave. So many outlaws, plus their folks and friends, would normally never gather in one place out of concern about garnering too much attention and making themselves too vulnerable to the law. Justice must surely be within her grasp.

Peace settled over Lady. She smiled and held out her arms, as if embracing the audience below.

"Thank you so much for being here deep in Choctaw Nation. I know you have many favorite songs."

Cheers followed her words.

"First, I'd like to sing "Swing Low, Sweet Chariot," composed by Choctaw Freedman Wallace Willis while he was working at Spencer Academy, a Choctaw boarding school. He was inspired by the Red River that reminded him of the Jordan River. I know this song means a great deal to all of us."

I looked over Jordan, and what did I see
Coming for to carry me home?
A band of angels coming after me,
Coming for to carry me home.

Lady took a deep breath, thinking she'd never sung so well, so clearly, and with so much emotion. Her voice floated over the valley as if carried on the wings of angels, and she knew this time, this place, was meant to be.

Swing low, sweet chariot
Coming for to carry me home,
Swing low, sweet chariot,
Coming for to carry me home.

She felt as if she was finally coming home, letting go of the pain, the anger, the loss associated with her parents' terrible deaths. Justice would be done. She felt it deep in her bones. She would soon be able to let the past stay in the past and move on into the future.

Words and music flowed through her as she moved from one song to another, watching the crowd sway in time to the music. She had never soared so high, so long, or felt so able to enhance the well-being of others. A humbling experience. She would eventually need to come back to earth and deal with the difficulties of life again, but not just yet.

When the time finally came for the songs to end, she smiled at the audience, feeling loss as well as gain from the experience.

"I realize you all have much more planned for the evening, so as the sun goes down, I'd like to end with "The Ballad of Lady Gone Bad," one of my favorites and I hope one of yours, too."

Cheers, cat-calls, and foot-stamping rose up from below as the audience agreed with her.

They always curse to lose their horses.
They surely cry to hand over their gold.
But on Lady's trail at the wide Red River,
They better make sure not to ride alone.

She clapped her hands and beckoned to everyone. "Sing with me now!"

She's a wild woman, a renegade, a lady gone bad.

As the last note fell away, Lady felt relaxed and satisfied at a job well done. She looked again for Rafe. This time she found him. Shock caught in her throat, turning her mute. He was locked in the arms of a tall, slim woman with long sorrel hair. He'd broken their bargain already. She felt sick to her stomach. And furious!

She bowed her head, looked up and saw Bob passing the ten-gallon hat. "Thank you very much. Enjoy your evening."

Stepping back from the edge, she glanced at Burt.

He winked and moved in front of her. "Now, folks, give generously! Lady done sung her heart out for you. Bob is passing the hat. If he don't find you, you find him. We all want Lady to sing for us again, so be generous. Thank you."

He turned toward Lady, grasping her hands, squeezing, and then letting go. "You done good, real good. You're our huckleberry."

She smiled, although she felt hard, hot pain in her chest. "I want you and Bob to take fifteen percent of the hat."

"But Lady—"

"I mean it. You two made all the difference and deserve it."

Burt grinned. "Thanks. You trust us to count it?"

"You know I do." She reached up and patted his broad shoulder. "You ought to think about doing more with your showmanship. You're good."

He ducked his head, then looked back at her. "You think?"

"Yes, I do."

"Bob and me been talkin'. We're thinkin' we could get you lots more places to sing so you could rake in the money."

Lady smiled. "And you'd get a percentage?"

Burt nodded, looking hopeful. "Twenty, maybe?"

"Let's shake on it." Lady held out her hand.

"You mean it?" Burt appeared astonished, but thrust out his big hand.

After they shook, Lady realized she was already moving onward, letting the past go, stepping into her future. She'd find Copper soon. Somehow, some way. She just knew Epona would never allow him to be put down.

Burt tossed his hat into the air, and caught it when it tumbled back down. "Let's go tell Bob."

She smiled at his happiness, but she was burning mad inside. "Let me change clothes."

"Don't want you to ruin that fancy dress."

"I'll need it for the next performance, won't I?"

"You bet. There's gonna be plenty of 'em." Burt gestured toward the tent. "I'll wait right out here for you."

"Thanks, Burt, for everything."

She jerked open the tent flap, and stepped inside. She planned to dress for trouble. That meant her green split-skirt and blouse, cowboy boots, and most important of all, her six-shooter.

If Rafe Morgan thought he could toss their bargain aside so easily, he had another think coming. And he was going to get it right quick.

Chapter 36

Rafe felt a blaze of fury strike him from behind like a violent storm front. He whirled, right hand dropping to his Peacemaker. Sharlot bore down on him, scattering well-wishers who backed off as if escaping lightning strikes.

He didn't know what he'd done, but she must think it was pretty bad, certainly worth ignoring those of her audience who wanted to thank her for her performance. Light dawned on him. He hadn't been front and center. He hadn't whistled and clapped. He hadn't been there when she'd finished her spectacular performance. He *was* in deep trouble.

He glanced at Crystabelle, the reason why he'd ignored Lady. Caught between the two women in his life, he'd let one come out on the short end of the stick. Sharlot wasn't a woman to take that lightly, or at all.

Lady marched up to Rafe, stopped, raised a hand, and slapped him hard across his face, eyes blazing fire. "You low-down conniving polecat!"

"You know him!" Angel grabbed Lady's hand. "I'm your biggest admirer!"

Lady glared at the other woman and tried to tug her hand free, eyes blazing even hotter.

"Introduce us quick!" Angel hung on to Lady's hand.

Rafe's face stung, but the discomfort was mild compared to his situation. "Lady, this is Angel." He tried to smile. "You sounded good up there."

"Good?" Lady finally jerked her hand free and turned on him. "How could you tell when you were in the arms of this . . . this strumpet!"

"Oh!" Angel's eyes grew wide. "You *do* know him." She tossed Rafe an admiring glance.

He glared at her. "Be quiet!"

"Not a word." Angel grinned, teeth tugging at her lower lip. "I'm all ears."

"Lady, let me explain." He held out his hand, but she slapped it down, stinging his skin again.

"Is this . . . this hussy all our bargain means to you?" Lady asked.

"She's got nothing to do with our bargain."

"Nothing?" Lady's chin jutted forward as she put her hands on her hips. "Broken bargain means I can entertain plenty of offers around here."

"We're drawing attention," Rafe said, dropping his voice. "I didn't break any bargain."

"Then who the hell is this sorrel-haired, green-eyed, long-legged, scantily-clad strumpet who had her arms around you?" Lady gestured toward the other woman.

"Me!" Angel clapped her hands together in delight.

Lady and Rafe glared at her.

"Better own up." Angel grinned, raising an eyebrow at Rafe. "Or you're never getting out of hot water."

"Keep your voices down!" Rafe hissed, looking from one woman to the other.

"Don't tell me what to do," Lady and Angel yelled at the same time, and then looked at each other in surprise.

Rafe sighed. Nothing was going according to plan. Sharlot was getting a big head due to her performance and the Hayes Brothers kowtowing to her. And something had happened to Crystabelle. She wasn't the same soft-spoken, gentle schoolteacher he'd left in Bonham. That big, blond Viking had to be to blame. If he'd sullied Crystabelle's reputation as a lady, there'd be hell to pay.

When he realized both women were staring at him, silent, he knew he had to do something . . . anything, as long as it was fast and smart. But he couldn't let Sharlot know he was pleased about her jealousy.

"Lady, there's something I haven't told you."

She regarded him with skepticism. "Only one thing?"

"Oh bother," Angel said, flapping a hand toward Rafe. "Men are such babies. Don't know why he can't find the words to tell you I'm his sister."

Lady starred at her in shock. "You are?"

"All my life," Angel said, chuckling.

"I guess I owe you an apology." Lady gave the other woman a thorough once over, looking at her from head to toe. "You do favor him. And really, you look much more like a lady than a strumpet."

"I hope not!" Angel patted her hair. "I've been working on this look with you in mind." She winked, chuckling. "Angel gone bad."

Rafe gasped. "Don't even think such a thing."

"I'm not your little sister anymore." Angel turned serious as she focused on Lady. "What do you think? Could you write a song about me? I'd help!"

"You're a lady and a schoolteacher. You can't go around doing things like this," Rafe said, trying to reason with her. Yet he was beginning to fear the wildness of Indian Territory had somehow infected Crystabelle.

"Okay for me, but not for her?" Lady asked, giving him a hard stare.

"That's not what I mean."

"Have you been looking for your sister all this time?"

He was in trouble, bogging down deeper every moment. "Lampkin, too."

"And you didn't tell me?"

"Don't be mad at him," Angel said, patting Rafe's arm. "He's such a worrier. I imagine he's had all sorts of ideas about outlaw power plays and such."

Lady raised an eyebrow, questioning Rafe.

"Thought crossed my mind that my sister could be used against me and make it harder to rescue her."

"I'm right!" Angel tossed back her hair, and then pointed a finger at Rafe. "Look, enough of this chitchat. I've got to get right back to the Viking."

"Before he sends somebody after you?" Rafe hissed, frowning. "Crystabelle, are you truly okay? Has anybody hurt you? I've been out of my mind with worry."

"Truly, I'm fine."

"But you're not safe, not here. We'll walk away right now and hide you. I've got a lot of questions and you've got a lot of explaining to do."

"Brother dear, I don't have time for answers. I've got to keep an eye on the Viking, not the other way around."

"What do you mean?" Rafe felt more confused than ever. "I can buy you new clothes and get you back to Bonham."

"But you can't buy me the Viking."

"Why would you want him?" Rafe asked, a puzzled look on his face. "Didn't he buy you like a slave?"

"Silly! I'm in love with him." Crystabelle smiled blissfully, combing long fingers through her hair as she gazed longingly up at the sky. "He loves me, too. Not that he realizes it yet. But that's a small matter. I must stay with him long enough for him to understand that I'm his own true love."

"What!" Rafe blinked hard, looked in confusion at Sharlot, and then anger washed over him.

"Let's lower our voices," Lady warned. "We don't want to draw attention."

"Are you out of your mind?" Rafe grabbed Crystabelle's upper arms and shook her. "You are going with me right now. If you won't go back to Bonham, I'll take you to Fort Smith, lock you in a jail cell if I have to."

Angel jerked free. "Touch me again and I'll yell to high heaven that you're not Fast John. You're Deputy U.S Marshal—"

"Better not say it," Lady interrupted. "Too many ears around here."

"You wouldn't expose me, would you, not after I explained my position?" Rafe asked in astonishment, feeling hurt.

"Big brother, I'm a woman desperately in love. I won't leave my man."

"What about your job as a schoolteacher?"

"Too dull for words." She winked at Lady. "Plus, I have role models now. Lady Gone Bad. Belle Starr."

"But they're outlaws," Rafe protested, wondering how he could have lost his sister this way. "Lady, help me explain to her why—"

She smiled at Angel, holding out her hand. "My real name's Sharlot. What is yours?"

Angel grinned, shaking hands. "Crystabelle. But call me Angel. Nobody uses their real name in Indian Territory, so why should I? Even he's Fast John."

"Good reason for it," Rafe said. "Crystabelle, I've heard enough of this nonsense. You can stay in Lady's tent till we leave. We've got more business here."

"Yes. I'm looking for a horse," Lady said.

Crystabelle rolled her eyes. "More horses than people around here."

Lady chuckled, beginning to like Rafe's sister, especially now that she wasn't competition.

Rafe knew he had to get this situation under control, so he tried reason again. "Let's go up to Lady's tent and—"

Angel gave Rafe a quick hug. "I'll always love you, but I'm not going with you. The Viking is a once-in-a-lifetime man. I'm giving it everything I've got." She grinned. "I'll invite you to the wedding."

"Lady, please talk some sense into her," Rafe pleaded, feeling as if he was losing the battle.

"You're a lady and a schoolteacher," she said. "Are you sure this is the life for you?"

"It's good enough for you and Belle Starr, so it's good enough for me. I want to be famous, too."

"Will this Viking help you get there?" Lady asked.

"Right now, it's enough that he's the most gorgeous man I've ever seen. And he rescued me. He bought me with four horses. He said I fit in with the sorrels." She tossed back her long mane of hair that was the color of a sorrel horse's glossy coat.

"But I thought you were kidnapped," Rafe said.

"Not by the Viking. I wouldn't give up my reticule on the train when those outlaws were stealing everything. They got mad and kidnapped me along with my carpetbag."

Lady chuckled. "Gave them a hard time, did you?"

"They're disgusting brutes."

"They didn't hurt you, did they?" Rafe asked, fists clenched. She must have really made them mad, since he had rarely heard of outlaws kidnapping anybody.

"Made a mess of the clothes in my carpetbag looking for jewelry. Most exciting thing they found was my underwear." She rolled her eyes. "'Course, they liked that."

"Do you know who they are?" Rafe asked.

"Sure." Angel shrugged. "Zip Rankin and his gang."

"Did you say Zip?"

"Yes. They're mean. I can't tell you how glad I was to get away from them. If the Viking hadn't come along looking for horses to buy soon after I was taken, well, I don't want to think about it."

"You aren't the only one who has had a run in with Zip. He's a dangerous man." Rafe rubbed the bruise around his throat. "I owe the Viking a thank you."

"I'll thank him for you. The Viking rescued me and he'll marry me." Angel stepped back. "Got to go now."

"Wait a moment," Lady said. "You know how to reach Rafe at Fort Smith. If you're in Delaware Bend, look up Manny at his livery stable. He'll get me a message or he can be a friend."

"Thanks," Angel said, turning to leave. "Good to know."

"Not so fast," Rafe said. "I want to thank you for Justice. He's a great horse."

Angel smiled. "I knew he was perfect for you the moment I saw him. Got my friends to deliver him under the cover of darkness. Bet you were surprised to find him waiting for you at dawn."

"Shocked, more like it. But glad, too. First hint I'd had that you might still be alive." He reached out and squeezed her hand, realizing that she was all grown up with a mind of her own. "Wasn't the first time you've surprised me."

She laughed, clasping his hand with both of hers, then letting go. "Won't be the last time either."

Rafe shook his head. "I hope this is it. Come on with us. We have a lot to talk about. I want to know exactly what happened to you. I'd like to get names, if possible, for arrests. And we can discuss your future. If you don't want to teach school, you can—"

"Oh no!" Lady pointed toward Lookout Point in horror.

Rafe whirled around, smelling smoke. Lady's tent was on fire. Red and orange flames shot up into the sky along with billowing black smoke. Top of Robber's Cave looked like a dang inferno. And no water up there to douse the raging fire.

He grabbed Sharlot's hand, and then Crystabelle's fingers. He tugged both women with him as he ran toward the fire, trying to figure out a way to save Lady's belongings. He dodged the crowd that had started toward the blaze, too. He bumped into somebody, felt Crystabelle's hand slip away, and glanced back. She was lost in the crowd. He started to turn back for her, but Lady pulled hard at his hand.

"Look!" Lady pointed to the north side of the mesa. "Pecos Pete is running away from the fire."

"Means he set it. And that means Zip Rankin is set on revenge." Rafe glanced around. Everybody else was focused on the fire, so nobody noticed the outlaw scrambling down through trees, scrub, and rocks to get away.

"Can we put out the fire?" Lady cried. "My beautiful gown. All my—"

"Too late!" Rafe kept an eye on the outlaw. If they didn't move quick, he'd get away. He glanced back, hoping Crystabelle had caught up with them. No sign of her. He had to accept that she was a grown woman and knew her own mind. If she wouldn't listen to him, she wouldn't listen to him. Zip was a danger to them all, and they had to deal with him before things got worse.

"All that cost a pretty penny and I'm broke," she spit out with fury.

"Trust Burt and Bob to salvage what they can." He tugged her against the flow of people. "One thing for sure, your legend will be even bigger after this fire. They'll probably call you Blazing Lady Gone Bad, a woman so hot she sets the world on fire."

"That's not funny."

"But true."

"Let's go get that scoundrel Pecos Pete!"

Chapter 37

Lady led the way, frantic to cut a path through the crowd that was bunching up near the base of Robber's Cave. Several men climbed upward, carrying blankets and canteens to put out the fire. Burt and Bob stood tall on top, motioning left and right as they directed the firefighters. She really appreciated their help.

She'd been willing to let bygones be bygones, but if Zip and his gang wanted to push their luck, she was going to accommodate them. Their sins were piling up, what with insulting her at the Boggy Saloon, kidnapping Angel during a train robbery, and now setting fire to her tent. Rafe would never let all that go. She wouldn't either.

When she reached the base of Robber's Cave, she lost sight of Pecos Pete since he was headed down the side. At least they'd gotten past the crowd. She glanced up at Rafe. He squeezed her hand in encouragement.

They were running out of daylight. They had to get the outlaw before the woods turned dark or he'd be even harder to track.

"We'd better split up." Lady leaned close to him. "Cover more ground."

"Hate to leave you alone."

She patted her Colt .44. "Take more than that sidewinder to get me."

"We know where he's got to come down. Lots of rock and thick growth out there that'll slow him down."

"Us, too. But there's a trail back in the woods leading down to Fourche Maline Creek. If he gets on horseback and hits that trail, he's gone and nothing we can do about it."

"Get our horses?"

"Take too long." She glanced around to make sure Zip or Heck wasn't sneaking up on them. All looked clear. "Why don't you try to catch him on foot while I head over to the trail? If he sneaks past you, I'll get him there. You can join me."

"Sharlot, I don't want you in danger. Isn't there another way—"

"No time for anything else." She gave him a quick hug, and took off running. She stumbled over rocks, catching her falls on tree trunks, and finally slowed down to pick her way through growth too thick for a horse, almost too much for a woman. If she could've turned her body into a snake or a raccoon, she'd have been aces.

She kept trudging deeper into the shadow of the thick undergrowth and tall, ancient trees. The sharp scent of life and death hung in the air, rotting black vegetation warring with purple wood violets. She trampled all underfoot as her clothes snagged and tore on briars and thorn bushes. At this rate, she was going back to civilization in rags. Didn't matter.

By the time she hit the trail, she was breathing hard and her heart hammered in her chest. She leaned against a broad tree trunk, letting her head sag forward in exhaustion. She had to be steady and strong, particularly if Pecos Pete snuck past Rafe. Even if she got the drop on him, the outlaw might not stop at the sight of her six-shooter.

She heard Rafe shouting about the same time she heard a horse thundering down the trail. Pecos Pete was getting away. Blast his ornery hide. Good thing she'd remembered the trail, or he'd have been gone.

Odd thing. His horse must be hitting rocks, roots, or something since the pace sounded uneven. Maybe the outlaw hadn't made it clean into the saddle, hanging onto the side, trying to get his foot into the stirrup. That'd be good for her if he was off balance.

She drew her Colt .44 and stepped to the side of the trail, keeping under cover. She counted to ten, then stepped into the center. Clutching her pistol in two hands, she held it steady as the horse and rider, dark shadows in the shade of the trees, burst into light from a break overhead. For a moment, his sorrel looked familiar, but then they rode into shadow again.

"Halt!" she shouted above the drumming of horse hooves, that odd, uneven gait more apparent on what appeared to be a level trail. "I'm warning you!"

Pecos Pete didn't slow. He hit the horse from side to side with the ends of his reins, kicking at its ribs, urging the animal faster. He looked like he was going to try to run her down as he made his escape.

Lady kept her aim steady, and stepped back just as they came abreast of her. She pulled the trigger as Pecos Pete kicked out, the pointed toe of his boot connecting hard with her chest. Her bullet went high as she fell backward. He raced away down the trail.

Gasping, she was almost unable to breathe from the blow and the burning pain. Still, she couldn't let him escape. She rolled to her stomach, rose up on her elbows, steadied her hands, aimed, and then stopped in shock as she got a better look at the horse.

Forgetting her injury, she leaped to her feet. She could hardly believe she was looking at a sorrel stallion with white left fore stocking, right fore sock, white left hind stocking, and right hind sock.

Putting two fingers to her mouth, she whistled, one short, two long, and two shorts. Pain made her dizzy, so she took short, shallow breaths, focus never straying from the horse.

The sorrel slowed, hesitated, and then turned around. Joy filled Lady's heart, driving out the pain. She repeated the whistles. The horse neighed, and then leaped forward, racing toward her.

"Copper, come here, boy!" she called, tears filling her eyes and spilling down her cheeks in relief and joy. She'd finally found Da's prize stallion. She almost hadn't recognized him. He'd grown in size but was boney and skinny, obvious signs of mistreatment. Worst of all, nobody had dealt with his special horseshoe, so he now favored his back right hoof. She could only pray that Epona wouldn't let him go lame.

Anger at the way he'd been treated warred with the happiness she felt that she'd found him. She aimed her revolver at Pecos Pete as Copper came to a stop in front of her, lowered his head, butted her chest, and put his head over her shoulder in a strong hug.

"What in blazes are you doing to my horse?" Pecos Pete yelled as he leaped down, hand slapping leather.

"Better not," Lady said, stepping away.

Copper kicked out, knocking the six-shooter out of the outlaw's hand with one hoof and pawing down his face with the other. Pecos Pete fell backward and stayed still, blood running from the wounds on his face. Nostrils flaring, Copper sniffed the outlaw, put a hoof on his chest, and then looked to Lady for instructions.

"Good boy!" Lady picked up the outlaw's pistol and tucked it under her gun belt.

"You all right?" Rafe called as he ran up. He glanced down at Pecos Pete, then back at her. "Guess now I know why you went to so much trouble to get this horse back."

She grinned, tears misting her eyes. "He's the best."

Copper nickered and tossed his head.

Lady chuckled. "Keep talking like that and he'll get a big head." She walked over to the outlaw and kicked him in the side. "Wake up!"

Pecos Pete looked at the horse looming over him, the hoof ready to cave in his chest, and squeezed his eyes tight.

She kicked him harder. "You got some talking to do. You can do it easy, or you can do it hard. And if you lamed Copper riding him when he limped, you're gonna be lamed, too."

Pecos Pete groaned, not opening his eyes.

"Lady, can you prove this is your horse?" Rafe asked, looking over the sorrel.

"That's right. Prove it," Pecos Pete hissed.

"Check the left ear at the base, small triangular cut. Da wouldn't allow a branding iron near his animals."

"Don't prove nothin'." Pecos Pete coughed. "Get this worthless jackass off me. You can have him."

"Copper, let Fast John check your ear." Lady gently stroked down the blaze on the stallion's long face.

"It's here," Rafe said, touching the mark. "Pecos Pete, you're looking at horse theft. Destruction of property. Kidnapping."

"Think mighty highly of yourself, don't you?" Pecos Pete taunted.

"Whatever he thinks, I'm you're worst nightmare," Lady said, voice sharp as ice bullets.

Chapter 38

Rafe had never seen Lady so cold, so remorseless. He couldn't blame her. She had her horse back, but the animal wasn't in good shape. He'd found his sister, but she wasn't safe in Bonham. He'd survived the necktie party, but his face was on a wanted poster. All due to Zip Rankin and his gang playing fast and loose with other people's lives.

Zip, Pecos Pete, and Heck Humby deserved a visit to the Hangin' Judge, but Rafe couldn't take them in till he got his badge back. For that, he needed to catch Lampkin. So far, not an easy task, but he couldn't give up. His whole life was on the line.

And then there was Copper's notched ear. It was connected to two unsolved grisly murders. Horse breeders had been gunned down, burned out, horses stolen. No way to follow a cold trail. Zip Rankin's name had come up in connection with it. All the deputy marshals had been advised to watch for the unusual ear notch used instead of a brand, but nobody had figured they'd ever find one of the horses, not in Indian Territory. Yet here Rafe was with one.

Too many connections, coincidences, lines drawing together like the center of a spiderweb. Made him uneasy.

What the hell did Sharlot have to do with it all? He

knew enough about her now to know her parents had been horse breeders. If the family had been killed for their animals, why hadn't Lady been taken out, too? Had she set up the raid and never gotten her share? Or maybe they hadn't been her parents at all. She had a strained relationship with Zip, maybe dating back to his cutting her out of the horses. Outlaws didn't get along with each other any better than anybody else.

Still he couldn't see her as a stone-cold killer, but he might be listening to his heart and body, not his mind. He'd come to trust her, but now he'd better not. Where she was concerned, he'd have to think like a lawman, not a man.

He evaluated the scene before him. Sharlot had clenched fists on her hips and blood lust in her eyes. The horse was ready to kill at her command. At the very least, she and that animal had history, because no other way would a stallion be so ready to obey her.

"Pecos Pete, you've got five seconds to tell me who stole this horse, or I'll let Copper crush your chest like a rotten melon," she said, kneeling beside him.

"Got protection," Pecos Pete taunted. "Get that dad-blamed horse off me, or you're deep in snakes."

Rafe dropped his hand to his Peacemaker, glancing around. Was the fire a ruse to set them up, knowing they'd come running and follow Pecos Pete? Zip and Heck could gun them down, be gone, and nobody'd be the wiser. Hair stood up on the back of his neck. They had to get out of there.

"Lady, let's go. Could be a setup."

She glanced up at him, eyebrows drawn together. "No! He'll tell me—"

"Later." Rafe stepped toward her. "Let's get Pecos Pete up on the horse. You ride him out of here. I'll stay behind. Protect your back."

"I don't want to put any extra weight on Copper."

"No choice." Rafe jerked a length of rawhide off the stallion's saddle, and knelt beside her. "Call off your horse, so I can tie this man."

"Better leave me be!" Pecos Pete gave them a narrow-eyed stare.

She looked down the trail that led away from Robber's Cave toward the valley below. "Trap? Can't see far for the trees."

"Play it safe."

She stood, used a hand gesture, and Copper backed away.

Rafe flipped Pecos Pete over, tied his wrists tightly together behind his back, and jerked him upright. Blood dripped from his shredded face down the front of his shirt.

Picking up the smaller man, Rafe threw him facedown across the saddle. Copper shied, dancing sideways till Lady soothed him with one hand on his nose and the other on his reins

"Oh, no!" Lady hissed, putting a hand to her head as if hearing something. "You're right. Danger!"

"Help me!" Pecos Pete hollered. "They got me!"

Hoofbeats thundered, getting closer. Three riders came barreling up the trail. Six-shooters blazed away.

"Ride!" Rafe called, drawing his Peacemaker. "I'll hold them off."

"They'll cut you down!"

A shape melted out of the woods nearby, silent and quick, slipped the reins from Lady's hands, and leaped up behind the saddle.

"Crowdy!" Lady blinked at him in astonishment.

"Stone Corral." He turned the stallion, holding Pecos Pete down with one hand, clutching the reins with the other, and galloped away into the growing darkness.

Rafe pushed Sharlot behind him as he fired again and

again, laying down cover. They backed off the trail toward the brush line. Bullets zinged around them. When he ran out of ammunition, Lady handed over Pecos Pete's revolver. Rafe grasped it with one hand while he holstered his Peacemaker with the other. They crouched out of sight in the undergrowth.

Night would be settling in soon. Rafe figured it was the best luck they'd get since their rifles and extra ammunition were back with their horses. But as soon as they moved, they'd give away their position.

He watched the three outlaws. They stopped shooting, reloaded, and talked to each other in low voices. They were hanging back out of accurate six-shooter range, but they'd be pulling out rifles soon. Plenty of range and plenty of firepower. Rafe and Sharlot would be sitting ducks, even hidden in the thick foliage. He had to do something quick.

He peered between the bushes. He could make a run at the men and take out one, maybe two, before he was cut down. She'd have a chance to escape, get back to the Hayes Brothers, Crowdy, and her horse. Not the way he wanted to go out, but he saw no other option.

"Hell!" he whispered, peering at the three men. He recognized them now. "They can't let us live."

"You get a good look? Zip? Heck?"

"Yes." The third was the one man Rafe wanted above all. "And Lynch'em Lampkin."

"We know too much."

"They need us dead. Now I understand what happened back at the Bend. Lampkin is why Zip tried to get me strung up. He had to protect his tame marshal. I was sniffing around too close for their comfort."

"And they used me to get to you," Lady added, sounding disgusted.

"But we foxed them."

"Got to do it again." Lady sighted down her Colt .44. "If I move a little closer, I can get one."

"Rafe," Lampkin yelled, saddle leather creaking as he pulled out his rifle. "We can make a deal. No need to let this get out of hand. One deputy to another."

"Lampkin, I saw the ear notch on that horse Pecos Pete rode. I'm betting you were in on those murders with Zip and his gang."

Lady inhaled sharply and clutched his arm. "My parents!"

He ignored her, still not sure about her affiliations. "But we can let Judge Parker sort this out," he called.

Lampkin laughed, a sharp, grating sound. "Morgan, you're a damn, by-the-book fool. You'll be eating dirt by the time you're forty while I'm living like a king. Prime stock like the Eachan horses made us a pretty penny."

Hearing that, Sharlot screamed like a raging warrior and lunged out of the bushes, firing at the outlaws, catching them by surprise. She spooked their horses, causing them to rear and paw the air as she continued to scream and shoot.

Rafe cursed and leaped after her, laying down a cover of bullets till he reached her. Somehow, she'd managed to nick all of the outlaws, red blossoming on their clothes as they fought to get their mounts under control.

He grabbed her arm and tried to pull her back to safety. She fought him, kept clicking her empty revolver. He couldn't get a good grip, so he holstered his Peacemaker.

"You're all dead men!" she yelled, ramming her empty six-shooter into its holster.

Rafe grabbed her around the waist with both hands and dragged her backward. She struggled to get away, screaming and clawing the air as if trying to kill the outlaws by sheer anger alone.

As they reached the brush line, Lampkin got off a rifle

shot. Rafe heard it whiz by his ear. Felt it, too. He tossed Sharlot into the bushes. He fell on top and held her body down as more bullets hit leaves and limbs, knocking debris down on them. The scent of gunpowder filled the air.

"Lampkin, Zip!" he hollered. "We've got the horse. We've got Pecos Pete. You're next!"

He leaned down and whispered in Sharlot's ear. "We'll get them. But right now, we're crawling out on our bellies through thick brush where horses can't follow."

She nodded, taking deep breaths to get control. "Another bargain?"

He smiled, despite the situation. "Yes, bargain. Now let's get the hell out of here while we still can."

As she started out in front of him, bullets zinging around them, he knew one thing for dang sure. She'd had nothing to do with her parents' murders.

And if they could stay alive, he'd sure as hell see justice done.

Chapter 39

By the time they neared Robber's Cave, Lady felt as if she'd been on one of Quantrill's lightning raids. She was battered, bruised, scratched, but victorious. Tears of relief stung her eyes when she thought about Copper. She'd always hoped that she could find him, but a small part of her hadn't believed it. Now that she had him back, she could get justice for her parents and rebuild their dream. She even stood a chance at building a life of her own.

Spider Grandmother's web had caught Zip and his gang, but Lady must spring the final trap. She couldn't get ahead of herself. Zip, Heck, and Lampkin were powerful, deadly outlaws who stood to lose everything if they didn't win. They'd already proved they'd stop at nothing to defeat a lowly saloon singer and an ousted deputy marshal. Somehow she had to find a way to defeat them.

Night had fallen while they struggled under the canopy of trees. When they stepped out onto the open plateau, stars twinkled overhead like glittering jewels and moonlight bathed the area in silver.

Empty. Not a single person or horse remained where hundreds had been when they'd left. Only the acrid scent of smoke hung in the air.

"Where is everyone?" she asked, unease rippling through

her. She abruptly stepped back into the shadow of the trees. "Jipsey and Justice are gone, too!"

"Thought I'd see Crystabelle again." Rafe glanced around, and then walked back and forth, looking for sign on the ground. "Churned up. No way to follow a track, especially in this light."

She felt her chest tighten in concern. "Zip and his gang were on horseback. Do you think they beat us back here? What if they got Crowdy? Copper?" Fear clutched at her heart. She headed toward Stone Corral at a run.

"Wait!" Rafe went after her, quickly catching up. "Don't go in half-cocked." He grabbed her arm, spun her around, and pulled her tight against his chest. "They were bleeding. Maybe we took the fight out of them."

"Hope so." She shivered and wrapped her arms around him, seeking comfort and strength. "Please let Crowdy and Copper be okay."

"We go in armed for bear." He set her back. "You got ammunition left in your gun belt?"

"Yes."

"Let's load. I'll keep Pecos Pete's six-shooter."

Silence surrounded them except for the sound of bullets clicking home and then revolvers sliding back into leather holsters.

"Let's get moving." Rafe squeezed her hand.

Lady followed him, single-file. They stayed in the dark shadows near the tree line, moving quietly until they reached the base of the mesa. When he paused, she listened, but heard nothing except a few dull thuds that abruptly stopped. Most likely hunting animals. When he moved forward again, she hugged the stone face that rose up into the sky to skirt around the wide base. When she passed the jagged stairway that led above, she glanced upward and saw an owl take flight, hooting as its wings beat against the air.

When they neared their goal, she felt her heart beat faster in anticipation of trouble. Yet all remained quiet. Good or bad, no way to know.

Rafe stopped near the recessed area that hid the natural rock steps leading into Stone Corral. He raised a hand, indicating for her to remain still while he checked ahead. She didn't want to stay behind, but she didn't argue. Time was past for that kind of trouble. When he took a step, he kicked a rock that tumbled against other rocks. Noise ricocheted through the night.

The nearby cock of a rifle made Lady's blood run cold. Somebody was nearby, no way to tell if friend or foe. Rafe heard it, too. He silently stepped back to her. A bullet zinged close to them. She caught her breath, not daring to make any sound and give away their exact position.

"Another step and you're dead," a deep voice boomed out of the darkness along with another cock of a rifle.

A huge sense of relief surged through her. "Burt!"

"Lady?" Burt stepped out of the shadows, rifle held upright in one big hand. "You're alive?"

"Yes!" She threw herself against his broad chest, hugged him hard, and then stepped back, hoping she hadn't embarrassed him. "Did Crowdy and Copper make it here?"

He huffed, a sound of relief. "Yep. Crowdy told us 'bout your run-in. Did you settle their hash?"

"No. But I nicked them."

"Better'n nothin'. You got more lives than a cat, or an Indian."

"Got back here quick as we could," Rafe said.

"Bob's up on Lookout Point, rifle at the ready," Burt explained. "I'm keeping watch down here."

"What happened to everybody?" Lady pointed at the empty plateau.

Burt chuckled. "All that shootin' sent folks runnin' for cover."

"They left, just like that?"

"Seein' as how lawmen don't cotton to dodgy horse brands, they hightailed it out ahead of what could've been a posse."

Rafe shook his head. "I'd like to have seen it."

"Greased lightin'."

"What about our horses?"

"Got'm."

Lady let out her breath and sagged against Rafe, feeling his warm, hard body as the only stability in a constantly shifting world.

"Hey, Crowdy, she's here!" Burt called, and then motioned toward Stone Corral. "Go on back. I'll keep watch."

Lady hurried up, and then stepped onto the soft sand of the corral. Rafe came right behind her.

Surprised, she saw lots of horses. Six mares. Jipsey. Justice. And the Hayes Brothers' geldings. Pecos Pete, now gagged with a bandanna tied around his mouth, sat cross-legged with his hands behind his back in front of a huge boulder.

A kerosene lantern had been set in a niche in the rock wall to shed light on a stranger busy filing down Copper's hoof.

Lady glared at Pecos Pete, and then hurried over to rub the blaze on Copper's face as he nickered to her. "Is he going to be all right? Not lame?"

The stranger with sandy blond hair and full beard didn't look up. "Caught him in time, looks like. Somebody did a good job on that special shoe."

She pressed her face against Copper's blaze, hardly able to believe he was finally safe with her again.

Crowdy slipped up beside her. "Close call."

She turned and smiled at him. "Thanks. How did you find a blacksmith?"

"Horses here. Blacksmiths follow."

"I'm Rascal Reynolds." He glanced up and nodded before he went back to work. "Proud to do Lady Gone Bad a good turn. Sorry I can't forge you a new horseshoe, but I've got one that'll do till you get him home."

"That's wonderful. Thank you."

"He needs food and rest. That's all."

"Copper'll get it as soon as . . ." She trailed off, wondering what she was going to do with him. She glanced at Crowdy. "Fine looking mares."

He nodded. "I got mares. You got stallion. All set."

"You get your land yet?"

He nodded again.

"Where?"

"Takin' Copper home. Needs company."

She smiled, happy with his response. "Corrals. Fences. They're still usable. But the house, the barn—"

"Fix up or rebuild," he said, stroking between Copper's dark eyes. "It's the land that counts."

"You don't mind Ma and Da died there?"

"Medicine Doctor will clean out bad spirits."

She felt as if a great load had been taken off her back. "Da always said you'd make a good horseman someday. Once you set your mind to it."

"Day's here."

Rascal pounded the last nail into the horseshoe, lowered Copper's hoof, and stood up. "Okay. Checked all the horses. They're in good shape. I'm moseying out. Law could turn up. Don't want to be caught here."

"What do I owe you?" Lady asked.

"My pleasure." Rascal grinned. "Like to hear you sing again. Maybe out at your ranch some day."

"Any time when I'm there," Lady said. "And thanks."

Rascal picked up his tools and looked at Crowdy. "See

you at the ranch in a month or so." He stepped out of sight.

Burt came in right after the blacksmith. He held out a chamois bag with the drawstring pulled tight. "Lady, this is for you. Bob passed the hell out of that hat."

Lady took the bag. "It's heavy!" She pulled it open and peeked inside at a wide variety of coins. "Bob got all this?"

"More'n that. We took our twenty percent cut."

"Thought it was fifteen."

"Easier to split twenty." He grinned, white teeth gleaming in his black beard.

She smiled, too. "Best to start out as we're going on. At this rate, I can help Crowdy put my family's ranch back together faster."

"What ranch?" Burt asked, appearing surprised.

"Long story," Lady replied. "I'll tell you sometime. Right now, not much is left there, but it's important to me."

"Crowdy's a good man." Burt nodded. "Let him take care of the horses. We'll take care of the business. All you need to do is sing like an angel and look pretty as a picture."

"Guess I can try." Lady glanced down at her dirty, torn clothes. "But not tonight."

"Tonight," Rafe said, "we better stay on the lookout. If we didn't scare them off, Zip and his gang are gunning for us."

Burt nodded, clutching his rifle.

Lady glanced at Crowdy. "I'd feel better if you got the horses out of here tonight."

"Hide them in brush. Want me to come back?"

"No. Best thing you can do for me is head to the ranch. If anything happens to me, I'll know you're all safe."

"If they get you, I'll track down Jipsey and Justice."

"Good. I trust you to go forward with the ranch."

Crowdy nodded.

She looked around at Rafe and Burt. "That suit you? One less gun. Burt, you and Bob can take off, too. Rafe and I will hunt them down if they don't come after us first. But it's not your fight."

Burt looked hurt and shocked. "And miss out on another Lady Gone Bad legend?" He tucked his thumbs under his gun belt. "Figure we can make a pretty penny off your new ballad."

"What new ballad?"

"Lady Gone Bad's Shoot Out at Stone Corral."

Rafe threw back his head and laughed, startling the horses. "Burt, up to this point in life, you sure as hell missed your calling."

"Got inspiration now." He grinned. "Lady Gone Bad's Fire Fight at Boggy Saloon."

Rafe laughed even harder. "I don't want to miss any of this."

Lady shook her head. "You boys! We better get serious. If Zip's boots are filled with blood, he's mad as a hornet."

"And mean as a rattler," Burt added. "I'll go back out and watch with Bob. Nothin' ought to get by us."

After he left, Lady tucked the bag of coins in Jipsey's saddlebag. She had more than enough to buy new clothes, if she lived long enough to need them.

She walked over to Rafe who was checking the back side of the corral, where rocks and tree limbs had been piled chest high to close off the opening.

"Crowdy, help me remove enough of these rocks so you can get the horses out of here," Rafe said. "Sooner you're gone, sooner we can put it all back in place."

As Crowdy picked up a rock, he checked the area. "Better keep a guard back here."

"Hayes Brothers won't let anybody in close," Rafe said, picking up a huge rock and setting it aside.

"I'll help." Lady gave Pecos Pete a hard stare. "After Crowdy's gone, a certain outlaw has two choices. Answer my questions or meet his maker."

Chapter 40

Rafe walked past four saddled horses to the back of the corral and jerked down the bandanna gagging Pecos Pete. "You tell Lady exactly what she wants to know, or you get horsewhipped, maybe worse."

Lady stepped in front of the outlaw, planted her feet apart, and stood like an avenging angel, yellow light from the lantern illuminating her.

Pecos Pete rose to his knees, hands behind his back, and bowed his head. "I'm sorry . . . so, so sorry, Lady." He blinked back tears as he looked up.

"Sure been acting like it," Rafe said in disgust. He didn't figure sorry'd cut any slack with Sharlot.

"I'll tell you what you want to know. Just ask." Pecos Pete stared at Lady with awe, not fear, in his muddy blue eyes.

"Why did you call me those bad names at Boggy Saloon?"

"Had to do it to stay aces with Zip."

"Why did you set fire to my tent?"

"Followed Zip's orders."

"Why did you try to run me down with my own horse?"

"Didn't want to shoot you."

Lady sighed. "You got excuses for everything?"

"I'm real tore up. If I'd known that horse belonged to Lady Gone Bad, I'd have figured out some way to get him treated right."

"That brings me to the bigger question. Did you murder Ma and Da Eachan?"

He hung his head in shame. "Nasty business." He looked back up, unshed tears in his eyes. "I swear I didn't know Zip and Lampkin was gonna wreck havoc on that ranch."

"But did you do murder?"

"I swear on my mother's soul that I'm nothin' but a horse thief. Heck's a scout. We threw in with Zip and his gang for work. Not murder."

"My folks?"

"Zip and Lampkin filled your folks with lead. They fired the house, the barn. We were busy rounding up the horses."

"But why kill my parents?"

He looked down, as if into the past, and then focused on her again. "Made Zip mad. Lampkin, too. They both got short fuses."

"They got mad?" Lady's voice rose in anger, punching past her tight control. "But they were stealing the horses, not the other way around."

Pecos Pete sighed. "Your folks put up a fuss. Your pa threw down on Zip, winged him."

"Hope Zip hurt like hell."

"See . . . Zip, he don't allow nobody to mess with him. Your pa set him off."

"Da had every right, every reason to shoot. I just wished he'd killed the lot of you." Lady turned her back on Pecos Pete, shaking with fury.

"I'm so, so sorry," the outlaw mumbled, dropping his chin to his chest.

"Is he telling the truth?" she asked, reaching out to Rafe.

He took her hand, felt the coldness, and squeezed in comfort. He stared at the outlaw. He'd interviewed plenty, judging the truth of their words. From his own experience, Pecos Pete rang true. He doubted the outlaw was much of a liar, but he could be wrong.

"What about me?" Rafe asked, stepping in front of Lady to confront the poor excuse for a desperado.

Pecos Pete looked up. "You fooled Zip back at the Boggy. But not long. He knows his deputies."

"You were part of that lynch mob that tried to hang me back at the Bend," Rafe said, determined to get his own answers now.

"Zip thought you was putting two and two together. Lady was your excuse to be at the Red River Saloon. You was really there to catch Lampkin."

"I didn't know then," Rafe said quietly. "I recognized Lampkin riding with the necktie party at the Red River. Surprised the hell out of me."

Pecos Pete snorted, shaking his head. "Goes to show Zip ain't near as smart as he thinks."

"Neither is Lampkin," Rafe added.

"Who was that boy?" Pecos Pete asked. "If he hadn't helped out, you'd be six feet under and we wouldn't be here."

Rafe glanced at Lady, smiling.

"You don't mean—" Pecos Pete straightened his back. "Lady Gone Bad rescued you!"

She gave him a slow smile. "Fooled you, didn't I?"

"You're a huckleberry above a persimmon." Pecos Pete stared at Lady with admiration shining in his eyes. "Zip's been looking all over for that dang fool boy. Turns out it's a big joke."

"We're not laughing," Rafe said. "My face is on a wanted poster."

"Lampkin's idea. He thought it was a funny way of gettin' you out of the picture."

"How'd he do it?"

"Don't know. When you got away, we rode straight to Paris. He went to the courthouse. We went to the saloons."

Rafe nodded, thinking about the best way to handle the situation. "If we let you live, would you be willing to give all this information to Judge Parker in Fort Smith?"

"Yep! But I don't wanna hang. Can you put in a good word for me? Get me jail time?"

"I'll do my best to see you don't swing."

Pecos Pete rolled his neck, easing the strain on his shoulders. "I get outta prison? I'm goin' home to Texas and stay there. I'll even work the farm."

"Sounds like a good idea." Lady laid a hand on Rafe's arm. "As much as I want to get Zip and Lampkin, maybe we'd be smart to take Pecos Pete to Fort Smith first."

"Get my face off the wanted posters, pick up a few deputies, and come back with enough firepower to arrest Zip and his gang."

"Good plan." Lady glanced upward, sighing in relief.

Rafe followed her gaze, looking up at the twinkling stars in a velvety dark sky overhead. Moonlight turned spiky treetops silver. He wished he was alone with Sharlot and all the bandits were behind bars. But at least now they had enough information to set the past as right as possible.

"Quiet so far," Lady said. "I bet we sent them packing with their tails between their legs."

"Hope so. But we'll stay alert and skedaddle at dawn." He turned down the lantern. "I'll take first watch. Why don't you get some sleep?"

"Don't know if I can."

"You gonna untie me?" Pecos Pete asked hopefully.

"What do you think?" Rafe asked.

"Pecos Pete, just relax. Get some rest." Lady stood near him, glancing down with a slight smile.

Rafe thought she looked as good with twigs in her hair and rips in her clothes as she had when she wore a red dress and sang on Lookout Point. Guess he was prejudiced, but Sharlot sure did know how to catch and hold a man's attention. She'd probably charm Judge Parker, like she did every man, when she had to stand before him, explain her actions, and decry her life of crime. At least, that's what he hoped would happen.

"Trouble!" she cried out, putting a hand to her head as she glanced around in alarm.

Rafe looked for trouble, too, but saw nothing. Still, he reached for his Peacemaker as he put his back to the wall. He focused on their one weak point at the open end of the corral. Huge shapes materialized out of the darkness.

Yelling at the top of their lungs, Zip, Heck, and Lampkin leaped their mounts over the barricade and landed in Stone Corral, six-shooters blazing.

Chapter 41

Lady heard Epona's cry of warning in time to drop down beside the stone boulder where Pecos Pete crouched in front of the huge slab. Rafe had nowhere to go. He stood defiantly, legs spread, a Colt .45 in each hand as he returned fire.

Horses neighed in protest at the sudden entry of three massive animals into their space, dancing, rearing, and shoving against each other. In all the confusion and dim light, the outlaws' shots went wild, cracks and pops ricocheting off rock walls as the white smoke of spent gunpowder drifted into all corners of Stone Corral.

Lady focused on Zip Rankin, ignoring everything else as she drew her Colt .44. On horseback, he towered over them, owning the most powerful position. His face was set in a grim expression of savage glee. She bet he'd looked the same when he'd gunned down her parents.

"Untie me!" Pecos Pete hissed, struggling to get loose. "I'll help fix their flint."

"No time. Stay down!"

She fired at Zip, missed, fired again and again. Every time she had him in her sights, he shot at her, causing her to jerk back, or his horse pivoted at the last second. She knew Bob was above, rifle trained down on them, but she also knew he couldn't shoot for fear of hitting her, Rafe, or a horse that could fall on one of them.

Three against two. She wondered why Burt hadn't slipped in the narrow entry and turned the tide. Then she was back in the battle and fired at Zip again. She finally nicked him across one shoulder and felt a savage pleasure all her own. But in the next instant she saw Rafe get hit by one of Lampkin's bullets. He crumpled, dropping his pistols.

Fury made her see red. She aimed at Lampkin and pulled the trigger. The hammer clicked on empty. Out of ammunition. She quickly started to reload, looked up, saw Zip take aim. She got one bullet loaded and snapped the cylinder shut. Too late.

Zip fired. Pecos Pete leaped in front of her and took the bullet. He slumped back, bleeding.

She locked gazes with Zip. He looked surprised. Hesitated. She had her moment. She fired the one bullet she'd had time to load straight into Zip's chest. Blood blossomed across his shirtfront. He grunted in shock as his Colt .45 fell from his limp hand. He followed his pistol to the ground.

Lady quickly loaded another bullet and aimed her revolver at Zip. She felt sure he would rise again, shoot again, kill someone else she loved. He lay prone, motionless. Hardly seemed real. Justice! Finally. And she'd used Da's Colt .44 to get it.

She looked at Rafe. Was he still breathing? In her head, she heard a warning cry from Epona. She glanced up and saw Lampkin sighting down on her. She'd run out of luck.

Something moved to her right. Rafe! Alive. He fired at Lampkin. But the outlaw deputy fired, too. She felt an impact on her chest. She went down, sure she was dead.

Lampkin slumped in his saddle, and slowly slid to the ground.

Heck wheeled his horse around, jumped over the barricade, and rode off into the darkness.

"Lady," Pecos Pete whispered from where he'd thrown himself at her, knocking her out of harm's way a second time.

She set aside her pistol and gently eased him across her lap. "Save your strength. We'll get you help."

"Gut shot." His voice sounded sad, losing strength. "No tomorrow."

"Hang on."

"Pa rode with Quantrill." Blood trickled from his lips. "Like father, like son. Lived and died . . . for our womenfolk."

"Don't die." Tears burned Lady's eyes. There'd been too much death and destruction. She didn't know if she could stand any more.

"Put us in a song?" He attempted to smile, but instead winced with pain.

She eased him closer, smelled death on him, but clung to hope. "Yes. I'll sing about you both in a ballad."

"I'm Peter Hawkins. Ma's got a farm . . . near Bonham." He paused to draw a ragged breath. "See she knows—"

"I'll tell her myself that you're a hero. You saved Lady Gone Bad."

A smile touched his bloody lips.

Lady watched as the light slowly faded from his blue eyes and his ragged breath grew still. Yet happiness remained in the stare he'd locked on her.

Tears slipped down her cheeks. She raised a hand and slowly closed his eyes. "Sometimes good men lose their way. But Pecos Pete . . . Peter, you showed your true heart at the end."

Two rifle shots rang out in the distance. Jerking up her head, she stared past the barricade, but saw nothing move. Hopefully, Burt or Bob had kept Heck from getting away, but she wished no more death on anybody.

"Rafe?" she called out.

He lay slumped over, eyes closed, revolvers near his limp hands. Horrified, she eased Pete aside, holstered her six-shooter, and crawled over to him. She put a hand on his chest, felt a slow heartbeat, and rocked back on her heels. She took a deep breath. He lived, but he was weak.

She eased him onto his back to check for wounds. She found a graze on one shoulder that didn't worry her, but a bullet had gone through his side. Blood was pumping from the wound. She had to staunch the bleeding fast.

"Rafe." She fought back fresh tears. "Don't you dare die on me."

He slowly opened his eyes, clear gray turned cloudy with pain. "Sweet . . . heart."

"Please don't joke."

"You stole my heart . . . first time I ever laid eyes on you, sweetheart."

Lady froze, realizing he was declaring his love for her. Of all the damn times. Just like a man. Maybe he thought he was going to die, or he'd never have told her. But he wasn't. She'd see to that. "You've got that sweet heart. It's all yours. Just live."

He smiled, a slight twist to one corner of his mouth. "Better patch me up." And closed his eyes.

For the first time in so very long, she actually felt light-hearted. Rafe Morgan might be more trouble than he was worth, but he was *her* trouble and she'd make sure he lived to cause her a whole lot more.

She stood up, raced to Jipsey, fumbling for clean clothing in her saddlebags. A petticoat! She turned back to Rafe.

Three huge, dark shapes cleared the barricade and landed in the corral. The horses snorted, tossing their heads. Lady reached for her revolver to find it wasn't at her side. Her Colt .44 was on the ground beside Rafe. She dove to the ground, rolled for the gun, turned fast, ready to shoot the single bullet she had in the chamber.

But this time she was looking at the Hayes Brothers. Heck lay limp across the saddle of the third horse.

"You okay?" Burt asked, dismounting.

"Looks like Fast John's in trouble." Bob got down and bent over Rafe.

"I'm fine," Lady said, "but he was shot in the side. I don't think anything vital was hit, but I've got to stop the bleeding."

"How'd Pecos Pete bite it?" Burt asked, looking down at the outlaw.

"Saved my life. Threw himself in front of the bullet."

"Didn't know he had it in him." Burt knelt, pulled a knife from inside his boot, and cut free Pecos Pete's wrists. He stuffed the rawhide in a front pocket. "Man gives his life like that. Deserves respect."

"That's good," Lady said, jamming the folded petticoat against Rafe's wound, holding it down hard, feeling the fabric soak up blood. "Where were you? Bob had to stay on top. Watch for outlaws. Couldn't shoot down into this mess."

Burt lowered his head, looking sheepish. "Heck snuck up and cold-cocked me. Took me a while to wake up. Got myself a heck of a goose egg. I'm considerable sorry."

"Heck didn't get away. Burt brought him down," Bob explained.

Lady smiled at them, and then pulled up Rafe's shirt to examine the wound in his side. She didn't like the look of so much blood and torn flesh. "He needs a doctor."

"Won't find one around here." Bob shook his head in consternation.

"Fort Smith," Burt said. "Two or three days' ride. Will Fast John make it?"

"He's got to." She pressed a hand to Rafe's forehead, checking for fever even thought she knew infection couldn't have set in so soon. "You'll go with us?" She glanced up at the brothers, feeling a great sense of anxiety at the thought of getting Rafe help alone.

Burt blinked in astonishment. "We wouldn't let you go off by your own self with an injured man. That's rough country between here and there."

"I appreciate it." She felt blessed with so many people helping her. Almost like family. She bound Rafe's wounds, relieved the blood flow had slowed.

"Let's mount up," Burt said.

"We'll take it slow," Bob added.

The brothers quickly got the horses ready. They lifted Rafe to his saddle on Justice. She mounted behind to hold him steady.

"One thing," Burt said. "What'd you and Fast John do to set a bee in Zip's bonnet?"

Lady looked at him in surprise. She remembered the brothers had been on the outside looking in. "You two good at keeping secrets?"

Burt grinned, punched Bob in the shoulder, and mounted his horse.

"It's a long story."

"We've got a long road to go," Bob said, settling into his saddle.

Lady checked Rafe's bandages and was relieved to see no more blood loss. She draped a blanket around her shoulders and across his body to keep him warm. She put a hand protectively over his chest and felt the slow beat of his heart. *Her heart. Her sweetheart.*

Chapter 42

Rafe was lucky to be alive. And knew it. He woke with the dawn and Sharlot's arms wrapped around him. He managed to stay on his horse till they reached Fort Smith. Sharlot and the Hayes Brothers tried to get him to see a doctor first. He insisted on going straight to Marshal Boles with the four dead outlaws slung across the saddles of the horses Burt and Bob were leading.

Turned out, Boles already suspected Lampkin. Too much hadn't added up for too long. Zip Rankin and his gang had cut a wide, dangerous swathe through Indian Territory for years. Boles commended Rafe for bringing all four men to justice, and then reinstated him as a deputy marshal.

After that, life became a haze of doctors, stitches, baths, ointments, food, and sleep. Sharlot's face swam in the center of it all, but he couldn't remember much more than that. Not until three days later.

He awoke that morning with a clear head, if a weak body. He put on new clothes, a charcoal single-breasted sack suit and a white percale shirt. Sharlot's choice, paid for with her singing money. He didn't know when he'd dressed so fine, and he wasn't entirely comfortable. Soon he'd get his own money, pay her back, and buy something more suited to his life.

Now that he was up and about, he had one more problem to solve. Sharlot Eachan, the renowned Lady Gone Bad. When they'd laid all their cards on the table, she was all hat and no cattle. Mostly no cattle anyway. She might have spread a little information here and there among outlaws, but she'd never stolen or robbed anybody. He needed to get her name cleared with Judge Parker and Marshal Boles. Time was ripe to do it.

The Hayes Brothers rented a buggy and drove them to the Western District of Arkansas courthouse, barracks, and jail. The brothers insisted they wanted to make the trip from the hotel easier on Rafe. He suspected they really wanted an excuse to get a better look at the jail, because of the way they peeked in through the outside windows.

Prisoners had been known to languish in the damp, smelly confines of the basement jail for weeks or months before they reached court and a jury decided their sentence.

To one side rose the infamous white gallows with slanted roof. There was room for twelve to swing together. Thousands had been known to watch. Despite his moniker, the Hangin' Judge preferred rehabilitation to punishment, dignity to entertainment, so he'd had a high fence constructed around the gallows to keep out the crowds.

With Sharlot at his side, Rafe walked up the steps of the two-story redbrick building that housed the court. As he reached for the door, it crashed open and a young woman swept outside, almost knocking them over.

"Crystabelle!" he cried, grabbing her elbow.

She jerked back, glaring at him. "What are you doing here?"

"Me? I work from here."

Astonished, he looked her over. She'd completely transformed herself from the disheveled, sultry Angel to a prim and proper teacher. She wore a severe brown suit with a white blouse and a hat to match. Brown gloves covered her hands and basic brown shoes were on her feet. She'd pulled her hair back in a tight chignon.

"What are you looking at?" she hissed, brows drawing together in a frown.

"Crystabelle?" Lady asked in amazement. "That you?"

"Yes!" she snapped.

"Where's the Viking?" Rafe half expected to see the big blond man follow her outside.

Crystabelle smirked, curling her upper lip in derision. "I have no idea."

"I thought you were going to—" Lady stopped, cutting off her words.

"Are you planning to teach again?" Rafe asked, cautiously treading the choppy water.

"Yes! I'm going back to Bonham and putting my recent unfortunate experience behind me."

"If you'll wait," Rafe said, "we'll get done here and we can all go to dinner."

"No time. I have tickets for the stage to McAlester. From there, I'm taking the train to Bonham and civilization."

"Won't the Viking be upset?" Lady asked.

Crystabelle bit her lower lip. "If you must know, he kicked me out. Told me I'd be better off with my own kind." She raised her chin. "Well, I fixed *his* wagon. He'll get to spend plenty of time with *his* own kind."

"Crystabelle, what did you do?" Rafe felt more concerned all the time. She wasn't acting like herself at all.

"I'm not a woman to be scorned." She started down the stairs.

"Wait!" Rafe hastened after her. "You're done with him?"

"Can't you hear? I'm going back to Bonham. That's all over."

Lady followed hard on their heels. "We'd like to spend time with you. Please change your plans and stay over."

"No. A new semester starts soon. I must be there." She touched Rafe's cheek with a single finger. "Brother, I'm fine."

"Introduce us!" Burt called, long legs eating up the ground as Bob kept up with him. The brothers had transformed their appearances as much as Crystabelle. Wild black hair tamed and cut short. Clean-shaven with neat mustaches. Blue seersucker plaid sack suits with rounded corners. Derby hats.

"This is my sister, Crystabelle," Rafe began introductions.

"We're the Hayes Brothers. I'm Burt. This is Bob."

Crystabelle blinked, looked them over, and then laughed. "I do believe we've already met. You know me as Angel."

Burt's eyes grew round in surprise.

"Ain't that the beatingest," Bob said.

"I'm getting back to my real life." Crystabelle demurely clasped her hands together.

Burt glanced from Crystabelle to Rafe to Sharlot. "You've *all* been working undercover?"

"Sure glad I'm a showman, not an outlaw," Bob said. "I'd be catawamptiously chawed up."

"Nice seeing all of you again," Crystabelle said. "I'll trust you to be discreet regarding my sojourn in Indian Territory. I'm a teacher, after all. We're required to set a high moral standard."

"I'll come see you. We're due for a talk," Rafe said. "Glad you're going to teach again." He wished he could persuade her to stay longer, but she was hardheaded as a mule. Once she got her mind set, he'd never been able to change it, not since she was a kid. If he tried, matters only got worse. For now, he'd let her go, but they'd be talking real soon.

"Probably for the rest of my extremely boring life," Crystabelle said. "Now I have a stage to catch."

"Wait!" Bob held up a big hand. "We'll drive you."

"A gently bred lady like you shouldn't walk," Burt agreed, extending an elbow for her.

"How kind," Crystabelle said.

Rafe watched in astonishment as his sister walked away between the two tall brothers, each small hand tucked around a muscular arm.

Burt glanced back. "We'll return!"

"Do you think she's all right with them?" Rafe asked.

Lady chuckled. "They're probably trying to figure a way to put a teacher onstage."

"I wouldn't put anything past them."

"She's in good hands. Let's get this over with." Lady walked up the stairs and pulled open the door.

Chapter 43

When Lady stepped with Rafe inside the courtroom, she took a deep breath to steel her nerves. She wore a dark green stylish walking suit with a bustle in back, a hat with feathers over her neat chignon, and white gloves. She intentionally looked every inch the respectable lady. She'd sung for hundreds atop Lookout Point. She'd survived a shoot-out with Zip Rankin. Two powerful men weren't about to intimidate her.

She was surprised to find the area empty except for Judge Issac Parker and Marshal Thomas Boles. Judge Parker wore a dark suit, tie, and white shirt. He had a full head of hair cut short, with a mustache and long goatee, all turning white. Marshal Boles was a nondescript man wearing a dark gray suit. Both carried a sense of power and determination.

A waist-high dark wood fence blocked off the court from the entry. On the other side, two round wooden pillars rose up to the high ceiling. The walls were painted white with wood trim around doors and windows. The judge sat elevated behind a wide dark wood dais under a wrought iron chandelier with six round globes. Two rectangular tables with matching chairs filled the area directly in front of the judge's dais.

Marshal Boles rose from a table and motioned them forward. Rafe pulled open the swinging gate, and she preceded him inside.

"Welcome," Judge Parker said, stepping down. "Please join us."

Lady sat down with Rafe across from Judge Parker and Marshal Boles. While she remained physically still, her mind whirled with possibilities. The idea of losing her freedom, of being locked up, of being sent away from all she held dear, made her sick to her stomach. Yet she was determined to do whatever it took to clear her name. If she had to pay with jail time for achieving justice, she'd do it. But she figured Zip Rankin and his gang were at fault. Not her.

"Young lady," Judge Parker said, tapping a forefinger on a wanted poster that lay on the table. "Is this you?"

She felt her heart sink. No way around it. That was Lady Gone Bad's face on the poster with a long list of misdeeds. "Yes. But none of it's true. Didn't Rafe explain?"

"Yes, he did," Marshal Boles said. "Hard to believe a little lady like you accomplished so much on her own."

"Rafe . . . Deputy Morgan helped at the end." They were going to put her in jail, she just knew it. She felt trapped, cornered with no way out.

"Still, your actions are impressive. If true," Judge Parker said, watching her. "What were your intentions?"

"Justice. As a lady, most doors were closed to me. I found a way to kick them open and find the murderers of my parents. Please understand. If deputies had done their job, I wouldn't have been obliged to seek justice on my own." She glanced at Rafe for support, fearing more than anything being separated from him. Her heart might break at the loss.

"Sharlot did what none of us could do. I respect her

dedication." Rafe squeezed her fingers under the table. "She deserves leniency for taking the law into her own hands."

"She deserves more than that," Judge Parker said, breaking into a smile. "Miss Eachan, the court is impressed with your motivations and your actions. Not that we normally condone vigilantes. But in this case, you brought to justice four hardened criminals when deputies couldn't. You deserve our thanks."

Caught by surprise, she felt her anxiety step down a notch. "Does this mean I'm free?"

"That's right," Marshal Boles said. "Judge Parker and I discussed the situation. We see no need for action against you, despite your reputation."

"I'm so pleased." She felt like dancing in the court, but remained still, back ramrod straight. She wasn't out of the woods yet.

Judge Parker nodded. "With limited resources, we can only do so much in Indian Territory."

"However, you have shown us a way that we can do more," Marshal Boles added. "With that in mind, we have a proposition for you."

"What?" Lady asked, raising her eyebrows in surprise.

"I recently commissioned Ada Carnutt to arrest forgers," Marshal Boles said. "She's the first woman to wear a Deputy U.S. Marshal badge from the Western District of Arkansas."

"Yes?" Lady tried to figure out what that had to do with her.

"You created the perfect persona to infiltrate outlaw gangs, or draw them to you," Marshal Boles said.

Understanding dawned. Lady nodded in agreement.

"What do you think about continuing as Lady Gone Bad, but working for us as a special agent on certain assignments?" Marshal Boles asked.

Lady glanced from one man to the other in astonishment.

"You would receive payment for each job," Judge Parker said.

"She wouldn't be a deputy marshal?" Rafe asked.

"No," Marshal Boles said. "She would work directly for me. And if needed, she would work with a deputy."

"That deputy better be me," Rafe growled.

Both men looked at him, and then smiled in understanding.

"Miss Eachan, is that the way the wind blows?" Marshal Boles asked.

"Yes. Rafe and I work well together." She tried to wrap her mind around the offer, but it hardly seemed real.

"Do you accept?" Judge Parker asked.

Lady looked at Rafe. "I like the idea. What do you think?"

"You're going to keep singing, aren't you?"

She nodded, seeing the advantages of the concept. She faced the judge and the marshal. "I'm flattered you asked me. I don't see how I can say no. I want to help others achieve justice, too."

"Add to your agreement that the only deputy you work with is me." Rafe squeezed her hand.

"My answer is yes, but I work only with Rafe Morgan."

"And I'll make sure she stays out of trouble."

Lady tossed a smile at the judge and marshal. "Not to worry. I'll protect him."

"Excellent." Judge Parker stood, smiling. "I'll let you settle the details with the Marshal."

"You both need time to recuperate." Marshal Boles got up, too. "Let's discuss this matter further at a later time."

"Thank you for your confidence in me," Lady said quietly, thoughtfully.

Rafe rose and pulled out her chair. After she stood, they quickly left the courtroom.

Outside, he clasped her hand, grinning down at her. "I had no idea they would suggest something like that."

Lady chuckled, squeezing his fingers, feeling almost giddy. "Now you aren't the only one working for the Western District of Arkansas. I'm so excited! Think how much good I can do for other people."

"I'm proud of you."

"Thanks." She glanced around, looking for the Hayes Brothers. "What's so great about this is that I'll still have plenty of time to sing, write new ballads, and entertain folks."

"And you wouldn't want to disappoint Burt and Bob. They're building a whole new business around you."

"Those two! By now, they're probably putting together an entire Wild West show. Does your sister play piano?" She chuckled, putting a hand on her hip in mock outrage. "No telling if they'll remember to come back for us. They were so besotted with the lovely Crystabelle, they may be driving her all the way to McAlester."

Rafe laughed. "Better set out on our own, hadn't we?"

She slanted a sultry glance at him, raising an eyebrow. "I wonder if I get my very own handcuffs?"

"If you do, what's the first thing you're gonna do with them?"

"Bet you'd like to find out." She tossed him a look full of mischief.

Chapter 44

Rafe leaned back against the rails of a white wrought iron headboard, hands cushioning his head, long legs stretched out on top of colorful quilts. Life looked pretty good from his second story window of the Riverside Hotel at the confluence of the Arkansas and Poteau rivers. Across the sparkling blue water lay the vibrant green of Indian Territory with Cherokee Nation to the north and Choctaw Nation to the south.

Fort Smith loomed large as a U.S. military and district court center, but also as a gateway to the West. For decades, Americans had come by horse and wagon, by boat from the Mississippi River to the Arkansas River, and more recently by railway trains. Times were changing, speeding up from horse to locomotive. In thirty years, he wondered if he'd recognize the place. He pondered if he'd still be around to make a difference. Shoot-outs like Stone Corral made a man think about his future, about what was important.

He glanced around the room, not fancy but homey. Tall armoire. Marble-topped table with washbowl and pitcher. Rocking chair. Clean, too. He'd stayed there plenty of times, but this time he thought Sharlot deserved better. A woman like her made a man see life different.

Businesses were shifting from the riverfront to Garrison Avenue. A swanky lodging palace was being built by H.T. Main. One hundred and twenty-five rooms, elevators, electric lights, billiard hall, offices, and parlors. Not to mention tiled floors and marble columns.

He could see Sharlot at the Main, enjoying that luxury. He glanced toward the lacquered screen painted in some fancy French scene. He heard the rustle of her changing clothes behind it. She'd said she wanted to slip into something comfortable and surprise him. He had a surprise for her, too. He'd clamped his handcuffs on a rung of the headboard, but left one half dangling.

Life was changing for him. Gone from black and white to gray. Just like Sharlot had told him early on. He rubbed the bandage covering the wound on his side. He'd been damn lucky. But it still hurt, reminding him of his mortality and the shortness of life.

Sharlot's face might be off a wanted poster, but she was still wanted. Maybe more than ever. The Hayes Brothers were promoting her singing career. The Western District of Arkansas was giving her special assignments. Deputy U.S. Marshal and his sweetheart. One thing for sure, he'd be damned if he was third in line for her favors.

Sharlot stepped from behind the screen in a sheer lilac wrapper, and put a hand on one hip. "Rafe! You're frowning. Are you in pain?"

Under that little bit of nothing, she wore only a white corset that pushed her breasts up into tantalizing mounds while pointing down to the apex of her thighs covered by lacy muslin drawers.

"First, Burt and Bob. Now Parker and Boles are eatin' out of your hands. Is no man safe around you?" He sounded cranky and he knew it, but didn't care.

"Are you jealous?" She walked to the bed, a teasing smile on her lips.

"I'm ready to knock heads together if any one of them gets out of line."

"You *are* jealous."

"Just letting you know how things stand."

She slipped out of her long wrapper, spread her legs, and sat down on him, wiggling her hips to get positioned just right. "Sweetheart, you're first in my life. Always and forever."

"Got you where I want you."

"Think again, Deputy." She gave him a wicked smile, then reached up and snapped a handcuff on his right wrist. "You're at my mercy."

He grinned. "Gonna show me how much you love me?"

Looking him over, she slowly licked her lower lip. "Where to start?" She jerked open his jacket, then ripped open his shirt, scattering buttons everywhere.

He groaned, felt his cock come alive and strain against his trousers. He raised his left hand to pull her close, but his stitches pulled, hurting.

She held his hand, toyed with each finger, kissing, sucking, nibbling, then pressed it back to the bed. "Don't even think about straining your stitches. I'll do everything."

"Sweetheart—"

She stilled him with a fingertip to his lips. She pulled the pins out of her chignon, letting her long hair fall loose around her shoulders like a cloud of spun chocolate. She leaned forward, pressing kisses and nibbles across his chest, teasing his nipples with her fingertips, letting her hair tickle him.

Hard as a rock, he growled, reaching for her again. "Get that corset off."

She pushed his hand back to the bed. "Mustn't hurt the doctor's good work." She ran a fingertip down his chest and teased his belly button. "I had in mind your trousers. They're in my way."

"Take 'em. Take me. Take anything you want."

"Yes, I'll take you."

She jerked off his boots and socks, pulled off his trousers and drawers. Then she stopped and simply feasted her eyes on him.

Made him hot, hard, and hungry, knowing he was giving her a show. "Let me loose and I'll prove how much I love you."

"Me first." She slipped off her drawers and slung them aside, leaving only the corset that pinched her waist, giving her an hourglass figure that begged to be touched, stroked.

"Come here," he growled, desperate to get his one loose hand on her. His bullet wound hadn't hurt as much as he was hurting for her now. He hesitated, remembering. "French tips?"

"Not this time."

She put a knee to either side of his hips, so that his prick just touched her hot wetness. She wiggled slightly, sliding him into her cleft. He put a hand on her hip and tried to push her down so he could sheath himself deep inside. She tugged his hand away, continuing to slide back and forth, growing slicker and slicker, teasing and tormenting.

"When I handcuffed you in the Red River Saloon, did you think about this? Wonder what it'd be like with me?" she asked, a mischievous glint in her agate-colored eyes.

"Yes!" He groaned. "But I wanted *you* handcuffed to my bed."

She leaned down and pressed a hot kiss to his lips, nibbled, and thrust into his mouth. He caught her tongue, sucked hard, letting her know how much he desired her. She shivered in response.

Raising her head, she looked into his eyes. "Are you ready to love me?"

He grabbed her bare butt with one hand, to hell with

pain or stitches, and rammed his cock home, sliding into her heated depths. She rode him hard as he thrust upward, moaning and groaning and writhing until they leaped as one over the edge into glorious ecstasy.

"I guess that'd be yes," she finally said, catching her breath.

He grinned. "Forever."

She pressed a soft kiss to his forehead, got up, picked up his trousers, found the key to his handcuffs, and came back to bed. "You might need two hands next time around." She clicked open the lock and set him free.

Rafe sat up in bed, rubbing his wrist, watching her.

She pulled the key out of the lock, and cocked her head. "What's this?" She slipped a gold ring off the handcuff.

"Thought you might like to make an honest man of me."

She tossed the handcuffs on the bed. "You're asking me to marry you?"

"If you don't say yes, I've got other means of persuasion."

"Like what?" She raised an eyebrow as she held the ring on an outstretched palm.

He jingled the handcuffs.

She chuckled. "In that case, I couldn't possibly say no." She slipped the ring on the third finger of her left hand.

He snapped a handcuff on her wrist and snapped the other on a rung of the headboard. "Show me how good a lady gone bad can be."

AUTHOR'S NOTE

Most of the locations in *Lady Gone Bad* are real places. I enjoyed visiting and researching these wonderful historic sites.

Today the former outlaw hideout, Robber's Cave, is an Oklahoma State Park. You can explore the cave, climb to the top of Lookout Point, walk through Stone Corral, and walk or ride horses along the old horse-thief trail.

Step back in time at Fort Smith National Historic Site in Arkansas to view Judge Isaac Parker's federal courtroom, the basement jail, and the re-created gallows. See museum exhibits for details about outlaws and Deputy U.S. Marshals.

Once known as one of the three toughest towns in the West, Delaware Bend is now at the bottom of Lake Texoma. The Bend was named for a Delaware Nation village on a bend of the Red River. Today, you can visit Dexter, a nearby town.

After devastating fires, Paris, Texas, rebuilt with a fascinating variety of architecture. You can view the 1868 Victorian Italianate Sam Bell Maxey House, the 1889 Wise House decorated with ornate Queen Anne scrollwork, the redbrick Santa Fe Station, or the replica of the Eiffel Tower topped with a red cowboy hat.

Antlers Spring continues to flow and is listed on the National Register as a notable historic site. In 1887, a few years after the events in *Lady Gone Bad,* the St. Louis and San Francisco Railway (the Frisco) established Antlers as a station on the Fort Smith to Paris line. At Antlers Frisco Depot, built in 1913-1914, you can tour the train station and the Pushmataha County Historical Society Museum.

I hope you'll fall in love with the Red River Borderland of Texas, the majestic splendor of Southeast Oklahoma, and the Indian Nations like I have while writing *Lady Gone Bad*.

Read on for a taste of *Angel Gone Bad* by Sabine Starr, available from E-Kensington next March.

Chapter 1

1884, Dennison, Texas

> "Harmony swooned into the muscular arms of the virile stranger with blazing blue eyes. 'My hero!' "

Angel paused and glanced up. Were the words she read from *Sweet Rescue in the Indian Territory,* her first dime novel, creating the desired effect?

Fresh-faced ingénues in flowery dresses and stout matrons in Sunday-go-to-meeting-hats sat absolutely still in rapt attention, eyes open wide, hands clasped to bosoms, faces pink with excitement.

Yep, she had 'em. Angel breathed a silent sigh of relief. Short lived, of course. She was in the last place she wanted to be, daring fate to smash her flat. At the Bonham Female Academy, reading, much less writing, dime novels was definitely *not* part of the curricula and could cause her to lose her position.

To protect her identity, she used a pen name, dressed flamboyantly in rich colors, and wore a blond wig to cover her sorrel tresses. She would never, ever read in Bonham or nearby communities. Angelica and Crystabelle Morgan must always be kept in separate worlds. Even with so much caution, she lived in fear somebody would recognize her.

But the Red River Book Club grew restless, corsets creaked, throats cleared, feet shifted. They weren't in the most comfortable of surroundings. Wolfpath Mercantile, named for the original community at Dennison, provided a location while the ladies squeezed into chairs from home. Wolfpath catered to a hardworking population, selling a wide variety of items, plus dime novels. A pickle barrel, bolts of cloth, sacks of flour and sugar, farm implements, jars of candy, and tins of tobacco cast a dizzying array of scents into the air. A checkerboard table had been moved aside to make room for the ladies, who sat facing the author with their backs to the front door.

Angel couldn't let personal worries intrude. She wanted to do her best and please these ladies who had taken time out of their busy lives to be here and support her. She raised her voice as she returned to Harmony's torrid adventures in the Wild, Wild West.

Wolfpath's front door was flung open. Boot heels rang out against the wood floor. Spurs jingled an angry tune.

Angel stopped in shock, looking up from her book and over the heads of her audience.

A sea of hats swiveled as the ladies turned to see who had the nerve to interrupt the quiet Sunday afternoon. Gasps of surprise filled the store.

"You may call yourself Angelica, but you're sure as hell no angel," the stranger said in a deep voice with the lilting cadence of a Norseman.

Heads turned from the intruder back toward the author. Embarrassed titters filled the room as the ladies pressed white handkerchiefs to their lips as if to hold in their excitement.

Angel felt her breath catch in her throat. Her greatest fear had just stepped through the doorway. She'd never expected to see Rune Wulfsson again, not after what she'd done to him. If he was here, he'd been released and was hunting her down for one reason and one reason only. *Re-venge.*

She felt her blood run cold. He was a formidable opponent. He knew too much. He hated her too much. She must be smart, think fast, and save the explosive situation. From schoolmarm to dance-hall slattern was not her idea of a successful future.

"Right on time." She pasted on a smile, although her jaw ached with the effort. "Ladies, may I present the Viking."

Hats whipped back around as the women took a better gander at the tall-as-a-tree Swede with blue eyes the color of a storm-tossed sky. Mad. Angry. Furious. None was a strong enough word for the blaze in his eyes or the clench of his fists.

Angel plunged onward, hoping to avert the next words out of his mouth. "I asked him to join us so you could see an example of how authors draw from real life to write their books."

The ladies oohed and took the opportunity, maybe a once in a lifetime event, to ogle a surefire, handsome hero.

Belatedly, obviously remembering his manners, the Viking whipped off his white, six-gallon hat, revealing close-cropped sandy hair, and gave a slight bow. Good manners didn't extend to his scowl, straight brows meeting over hooded eyes. One long-fingered hand dropped near the pearl-handled Colt .44 he wore in a fancy tooled gun belt that emphasized narrow hips and muscular thighs clad in form-fitting Levi's. A blue plaid shirt strained across his broad chest.

Angel sighed. Last time she'd seen him, he'd worn a fringed leather vest, tight leather trousers, and an eagle feather in long hair bleached almost white by the sun.

Cowboy gear suited him just as well. Even if he appeared thinner and a little pale, he couldn't have looked more delectable if he'd tried.

And that was exactly what had gotten her into trouble in the first place.

Las Vegas-Clark County
LIBRARY
DISTRICT
www.lvccld.org
Books, Movies
& More